W9-BIH-070

10/2021

**PALM BEACH COUNTY
LIBRARY SYSTEM**
3650 Summit Boulevard
West Palm Beach, FL   33406-4198

Praise for *These Nameless Things*

"Those who enjoy Jolina Petersheim, Carrie Stuart Parks, and Tosca Lee and who appreciate mind- and genre-bending fiction will want to add this to a reading list."

Library Journal

"In *These Nameless Things*, the edges of an earthly world bleed into the next. Trauma and guilt fold into an immersive fantasy that's eerie and precise in its world building."

Foreword Reviews

"In the tradition of C. S. Lewis, George MacDonald, and Neil Gaiman, yet with a style all his own, Shawn Smucker has invited us yet again into a magical story. Powerful, startling, and with a good dollop of heart, *These Nameless Things* will stick with readers long after they've read the final page. This book is a wonder."

Susie Finkbeiner, author of *Stories That Bind Us* and *All Manner of Things*

"*These Nameless Things* is an imaginative, dark, morally complex (and therefore realistic) exploration of the distorting effects of sin, guilt, hatred, and revenge on the human spirit. With a setting seemingly just outside Dante's hell, Smucker's novel is something of a blending of the *Divine Comedy* and *The Pilgrim's Progress*, indebted to both but carving out its own path."

Daniel Taylor, author of the Jon Mote Mystery series

"A poetic, heartfelt meditation on guilt, grief, grace, and forgiveness, reminiscent of both Dante's *Inferno* and *Lost*."

Anne Bogel, creator of *Modern Mrs. Darcy* and the *What Should I Read Next?* podcast

Praise for *Light from Distant Stars*

"A compelling tale of family and faith with a paranormal twist. . . . A tense novel exploring the breadth and limitations of loyalty, forgiveness, and faith. *Light from Distant Stars* is a memorable dive into the human psyche."

Foreword Reviews

"Smucker takes readers on a man's faith journey, reconciling his past with his present and reckoning with his views on God in the midst of life's hurdles. Told with elements of magical realism, Smucker's take on visionary fiction is an immersive reading experience."

ECPA

THE
WEIGHT
OF
MEMORY

Books by Shawn Smucker

The Day the Angels Fell
The Edge of Over There
Light from Distant Stars
These Nameless Things
The Weight of Memory

Once We Were Strangers

THE WEIGHT OF MEMORY

SHAWN SMUCKER

Revell

a division of Baker Publishing Group
Grand Rapids, Michigan

© 2021 by Shawn Smucker

Published by Revell
a division of Baker Publishing Group
PO Box 6287, Grand Rapids, MI 49516-6287
www.revellbooks.com

Printed in the United States of America

All rights reserved. No part of this publication may be reproduced, stored in a re-
trieval system, or transmitted in any form or by any means—for example, electronic,
photocopy, recording—without the prior written permission of the publisher. The
only exception is brief quotations in printed reviews.

Library of Congress Cataloging-in-Publication Data
Names: Smucker, Shawn, author.
Title: The weight of memory / Shawn Smucker.
Description: Grand Rapids, MI : Revell, a division of Baker Publishing Group,
    [2021]
Identifiers: LCCN 2020052938 | ISBN 9780800735319 (paperback) | ISBN
    9780800739980 (casebound)
Subjects: LCSH: Brain—Tumors—Patients—Fiction. | Cancer—Patients—Family
    relationships—Fiction. | Families—Fiction. | Grandparent and child—Fiction.
    | Christian fiction.
Classification: LCC PS3619.M83 W45 2021 | DDC 813/.6—dc23
LC record available at https://lccn.loc.gov/2020052938

This book is a work of fiction. Names, characters, places, and incidents are the prod-
uct of the author's imagination or are used fictitiously. Any resemblance to actual
events, locales, or persons, living or dead, is coincidental.

Extracts are taken from George MacDonald, *The Light Princess* (Lit2Go, 1864), ac-
cessed December 28, 2020, https:/etc.usf.edu/lit2go/28/the-light-princess.

21 22 23 24 25 26 27   7 6 5 4 3 2 1

To Maile

Is there a single person on whom I can press belief? No sir.
All I can do is say, Here's how it went. Here's what I saw.
I've been there and am going back.
Make of it what you will.

LEIF ENGER, *Peace Like a River*

Death alone from death can save.
Love is death, and so is brave.
Love can fill the deepest grave.
Love loves on beneath the wave.

GEORGE MACDONALD,
The Light Princess

And, so, there is
the weight of memory

LI-YOUNG LEE,
"The Weight of Sweetness"

Anytime to Three Months

er words hover in the air, hummingbirds, and I hold my breath, glance up at the clock above the door, and watch the red second hand twitch its way through a minute. I pinch my bottom lip in between my teeth. There is a small piece of paper under her chair, the tiniest corner torn off, left from the previous examination. What news did that patient receive? What diagnosis?

What will I leave behind?

"I'm sorry, Dr. Cortez," I say. "Can you repeat that?" Each of my blinks is like the shutter on an old camera, holding for an extra moment so that I see the negative of her on the inside of my eyelids. I reach up and rub my eyes. Why do I not feel a deep sadness?

I think it would be appropriate for me to feel a deep sadness.

"Mr. Elias," she begins again, and her words have a lullaby quality to them, as if she's explaining a monster to a child, the darkness sleeping under the bed, the movement subtly shifting in the corner of the room after the light turns off.

My mind wanders, this time to you, to the happiness on your face when you see me waiting outside of the school, or how heavy your eyes are when you're trying not to fall asleep. I think of all the made-up tales you have told me, all the imaginary friends, all the whispering voices. I realize in that moment that I can never tell you this news, because it's a monster far too scary, a story far too dark for an eleven-almost-twelve-year-old. There is relief with the realization that I do not have to tell you. That I will not tell you. So I look over at Dr. Cortez, finally ready to listen.

"Mr. Elias," she says, "do you understand what I'm telling you?"

I wonder how doctors can possibly appear to be so young. Like high school students. Dr. Cortez's hair is held together in a bright pink scrunchie, and she has no wrinkles at the corners of her eyes. We have become friends through the last months, closer as the news has become increasingly worse. She has always tried to soften the blows.

The thought hums through my mind that this is a practical joke, one of those television shows where they play pranks on unsuspecting chumps. I smile to myself, eager for this to be true. I actually check the room for a hidden camera. Perhaps in the light switch, or in that pointy wall mount behind the glass jar of cotton swabs? Or in the tiny pendant that sways, barely visible inside the neck of her blue blouse where the top button sags, undone?

But there is the knot on my head behind my left temple. That is no practical joke. And there are waves of nausea, moments when I nearly black out. Those are not practical jokes. And Dr. Cortez wouldn't lie to me. Maybe it's God. Maybe God is the prankster here.

My face must be suitably blank, because she tells me once again, for the third time.

"Mr. Elias? There is no treatment available," she says. too far along. I'm very sorry." The buds of tears forn the corners of her eyes, those eyes that have no wrinkl and the left side of her mouth twitches in a sad dance. Sh stands and turns away and pretends to rearrange the various pamphlets on the counter. I shift ever so slightly on the examination table, and the paper underneath me crackles like electricity.

She turns, holding out one of the pamphlets, and I take it from her smooth hands. She is a child. The words on the pamphlet read, "Hospice Care and You."

I take another deep breath. I am full to bursting with air. I let it out in a long sigh.

"Are you still blacking out?" Her voice is probing, gentle.

I shrug, nod.

"Are your pain levels okay?"

I nod again.

When I think I'll never find words again, five of them disturb the surface. "How long do I have?"

She clears her throat. "Mr. Elias, I don't normally . . ." Her voice collapses in on itself.

"Dr. Cortez, I've been trying to get you to call me Paul for over a year now." I try to chuckle, but no sound comes out.

"Mr. Elias . . . Paul . . ." she says.

"I understand," I say, and my composure seems to catch her off guard. I shrug and give her a small but heavy smile. "I'm fifty-eight years old. I've had many good years. But I have a granddaughter in my care. She depends on me. She has no one else, and I'll need to find someone to take her in." My voice cracks. I clear it. My words come out all breath. "It would help, I'm sure you understand, if I had some idea."

I have never felt so much like I'm underwater. I think of Mary. What was the last thing she thought, going under? Was she afraid? Was she thinking of me? Could she see the light from the midmorning sun, glimmering too far above her?

The doctor shakes her head. "I don't normally . . . It's a guessing game. You could live much longer."

My mouth tightens into a smile. "I understand," I say again, trying to nudge her with a kind glance. "Your best guess."

She breathes quietly, a bird quivering in the brush. She licks her lips. Her head tilts, and her hand moves instinctively to the unbuttoned collar of her blouse, hiding the triangle of tender skin. She can't make eye contact with me as she says the words, and this fills me with an immense amount of affection for her. It's all I can do not to move across the small room and hug her.

"The soonest? Anytime, really." She seems to be holding her breath. She doesn't know where to look.

Anytime.

"And the longest? Perhaps two or three months."

Three months.

Her chest quivers in what seems to be a stifled sob. It strikes me as both completely unprofessional and deeply human.

Between anytime and three months.

I feel a subtle relief. There it is. The finish line.

I think of you, and the relief turns sour. How can I leave you behind? Who will take care of you?

The idea comes to me as I sit in Dr. Cortez's office. I will take you back to my hometown, back to where I grew up.

Back to Nysa. I will show you the home I was born in, the creeks I fished, the small town where my friends and I caused trouble. To me it feels like the last safe place in the world, and if I have to leave you, that seems the best place to do it. I don't know who will take you in, but the idea of driving with you through these early autumn days feels so good that I decide we will leave today. This afternoon.

Or tomorrow. Yes, tomorrow morning at the latest.

I stand and take a deep breath, as if everything is finally beginning. I approach the door, and Dr. Cortez doesn't stand. I know she is very new at this—her face is in her hands. I reach down and my fingertips graze her small shoulder, and I squeeze her collarbone reassuringly. I'm surprised at how fragile it feels, like an eggshell.

"Thank you, Sarah," I whisper. "You have always been forthright with me. I know you've tried many things. And I appreciate that. This will get easier. Telling people. Don't worry."

She reaches up to squeeze my hand, but her reach stops somewhere short of her shoulder, short of my fingers. I walk away, breathing, each step a deliberate effort to keep going.

Outside, the late September air is soft and warmer than it should be.

I'm Afraid Not

During my walk home through the city, I reassure myself once again that I don't have to tell you about the diagnosis. The asphalt smells hot, and there is a distant beeping, perhaps from the road crew paving the next road over. The lunch hour has passed, and office workers have returned to their desks. The schoolchildren have not yet been released. The rest of us run our errands. Groceries. Post office. Doctors' appointments. It strikes me as strange that, besides the doctor, I am the only person in the entire world who knows what I know, that my end is near.

Anytime to three months.

I imagine traveling back to my hometown, entering that strange little peninsula of Nysa from the west, the dank smell of the river as we cross the bridge before driving Cat Tail Road through the woods, passing the Steward farm on the left, driving through all those cornfields. It's nearly fall now, but some of the corn will still be standing, lining the roads like high walls, and some of it will be cut down to dry stubble, leaving behind lines like a labyrinth. All the way to town. Maybe I'll even take you to the cabin on the shore of the lake. How much will I tell you about what happened there forty years ago? How much will I leave out?

How much do I even know for sure?

Anytime to three months.

I glance at my watch. My house is there on the left, and it observes my approach. I know that somehow the house knows about my anytime to three months. The morning paper leans against the front stoop—I was so distracted by the knot on the side of my head and the doctor's appointment that I was knocked out of my normal routine, forgetting to collect and read the paper after I walked you to school this morning. I pass the house, our house, and I turn left at the next alley and walk the five long blocks down to your elementary school.

That's when the first shadow of doubt creeps into my mind. I'm not sure I can keep this news from you. You are very perceptive for eleven-almost-twelve.

Not long ago, I thought I had received a phone call from your father, and when it turned out not to be him, what felt like a near miss almost crushed me. When I walked up to you at school that day, you reached out, took my arm in a gentle hold with one of your small hands, and gave a sad smile.

"It's okay, Grampy," you told me. "We'll be okay, the two of us."

How do you know these things?

It is still thirty minutes until your day ends, and the parking lot is full of teachers' cars, but there are no parents, not yet. I sit on the swing and the chains protest. The thin rubber seat pulls in tight against my hips as I sag down in the middle. I push myself gently, feet not leaving the ground. I close my eyes and remember that swaying, that freedom, forward and back, forward and back. The breeze kisses the sweat on my forehead, and I wonder if I'm sweating because of this thing inside of me that's making me die or if I'm sweating simply because it's hot for September.

I reach up and touch the marble-sized lump above my ear. It's a little larger than a marble now, and my stomach drops at this new realization. Evidence of the culprit. The root. The knot, always growing.

This unusual autumn day has gone from warm to hot, but the heat is comforting. It is weight, like a gravity blanket. I remember where I was the day Mary left me, how hot it was on the lake, how the water felt too warm to swim in. John, your father, only days old, had fallen asleep on my bare chest where I lay on the stale, golden sofa in the cabin. The top of his head was covered in night-black hair, fine baby hair, and he smelled like powder and sour milk and sweet drool. His eyes were small black embers rarely revealed in those early days, his yawning mouth somehow both tiny and gaping. I looked up over that fine black hair, through the glass doors that led out to the deck. Beyond it all, beyond his hair and his smell and the heat waving up off the deck, I could see the lake, and out on the lake I could see Tom and Shirley coming, each in their own kayak. Only them. And I thought, *Where on earth is Mary? And why are they coming so quickly?*

I hear the thunk of the heavy metal door.

"Mr. Elias?" It is Ms. Howard, your principal.

If Mary left me forty years ago next week, that means John's birthday is . . . today? Tomorrow? Did I miss his birthday?

"Yes?" I say without opening my eyes. I know today is Friday and that there's no school on Monday, and I imagine my

16

doctor going home and telling her husband, if she is married, about the old man she had to talk to today, the old man who is only fifty-eight and has anytime to three months left to live. Did I seem old to her? I imagine him drawing her close and the two of them not saying it but thinking it, how sad it would be to only have anytime to three months to live. We are all comforted by the misguided confidence that we have certain decades ahead of us.

"Mr. Elias," Ms. Howard begins again.

I jump, opening my eyes, because there she is, right in front of me. I don't stand up though. I sway there awkwardly in the swing, and she's not much taller than me, even though she's standing.

"It's about Pearl."

"Pearl?"

She nods.

"I hope she's not misbehaving."

"Oh, nothing like that. Nothing at all like that! She's doing very well. That's what I wanted to talk to you about."

I raise my eyebrows and wait. I am good at waiting for other people to speak. I have somehow developed a patience that almost enjoys the awkward silence.

Ms. Howard clears her throat nervously. I watch a gust of warm wind animate a few loose hairs on her head. "There's . . . it's . . . Pearl has been selected by her teachers to attend a weekend camp for high achievers. Not this weekend but next."

"Yes," I say. "No school on Monday?"

"That's right. The retreat isn't this weekend—it's next weekend," she repeats, as if talking to one of her students. "They'll go to a camp north of here, play games, go through leadership exercises. It's a wonderful opportunity for only a handful of children."

I think of Dr. Cortez sitting on her stool as I left the examination room, the tiny birdlike feeling of her clavicle as I squeezed her shoulder. I think of how one side of her mouth twitched. I think of her words.

Anytime to three months.

"No, I'm afraid not," I say vacantly.

"Oh, you can take some time to think—"

"No, not Pearl. I'm afraid not."

She stares at me with something like confusion. I can tell she is not someone who is used to hearing the word no.

"It would really be a wonderful opportunity for—"

"Not Pearl," I say, each word a dead weight. "I'm afraid not."

She purses her lips. I close my eyes and lean back in the swing, begin that soft front-and-back movement. Even with my eyes closed I can feel her disdain cling to me like humidity. I know what she is thinking—I am causing my grandchild to miss out. I am too old, perhaps, to recognize the opportunity for what it is. I'm not a fit parent.

I can hear the light scuffing of her footsteps back to the school. I hear the heavy sound of the metal door opening.

"Ms. Howard!" I suddenly say, untangling myself awkwardly from the swing.

"Yes?" she asks, pausing, cautiously hopeful.

I walk across the playground, limping. My right foot has fallen asleep. "What's the date?"

"The date? Of the camp?"

"No, today," I say.

"Today?"

"Yes, today's date."

She stares up into the hot sky, the ash-colored sky, hovering as it is above us, perhaps threatening a thunderstorm later. Her gaze pierces the humidity and finds the sun even there, even while it is hidden. She shakes her head and wrinkles her brow. "The 22nd?"

"September 22nd?" I ask.

"September 22nd," she says, flitting inside, the door crashing scornfully behind her.

I wave at her absently, return across the expanse, and sit back in the swing. And for the first time since the doctor's words—*anytime to three months*—I feel quiet tears forming behind my eyes and my throat aches, because today is John's birthday, and I have not seen him for four years. You have not seen your father since you were seven-almost-eight, and in a week it will be forty years since Mary left me. It is a tornado of memory, and I glance up, certain I will find the sky in a boiling state of Armageddon. But there is no approaching lightning, no funnel cloud. The gray actually appears to dissolve like melting cotton candy, and the blue seeps through.

A bell rings from the bowels of the school, and a few of the doors unlatch. The parking lot has filled with parents, and all the children spill into the heat, their feet sliding like sandpaper on the pavement. As my rough hands try to dry my face and stop up any more tears that might think about leaking out, your wispy voice calls out to me, and it's like you're in some faraway place, calling to me from a land I will never find.

The White-Haired Woman

Grampy! Why are you swinging? I want to swing!"

"Go on." I stand, taking your backpack, but the first thing you do is hug me, and I hold you there in the heat. You move quickly to the swing, and I watch you. As you glide, your long, dark hair moves in a rhythm, trailing out behind you like a comet, then clutching tight against your back, then flying again. Your eyes remind me of your father's—dark as coal, glittering.

The sun brightens, and I notice people around me shading their eyes, still watching for their children to come out. A man who left his house wearing a flannel in the autumn heat takes it off and ties the arms around his waist. A woman steps smoothly out of her shoes and stands on the warm pavement in her bare feet, arms crossed.

"You know," you say in your innocent voice, "we had a helper in our class today."

"Like a teacher's aide?"

You nod and giggle. "The swing gets my stomach."

I smile. "You're good at swinging. Much better than I was. I always needed a push."

Emphasizing your independence, you strain against the chains, stretch your legs, flying higher. "She had very white hair, or silver, like moonlight." You seem disconcerted by the color. "She helped me draw a map."

"Is that right? A map? Of what?"

"Of the place where you grew up. There was a long bridge that goes over a river, and a lake on the other side, and a cabin on the shore."

Chills flash through my body, along with a hint of nausea I think might be the result of this sickness.

I have never told you about where I grew up.

I have never told you about the town or the cabin or what happened at the lake. If all was well, I wouldn't tell you about it for another five or six years, when you're older. But all is not well, at least not with me. *Anytime to three months.* Time is running short. I am left wondering what things to tell you and what things I will take with me, what things you will never know.

"The silver-haired woman said she needs my help to find something, something that means a lot to her. It's somewhere in the town where you grew up. When are we going?"

My chest feels hollow. It has been a while since you've made things up like this, but the ring of truth laced through your tales unsettles me. In kindergarten you told a lot of stories, but you were little, and the squeakiness of your voice gave you a pass, comforted your father and me, because of course a tiny little girl would have imaginary friends to take tea with. Of course a six-year-old's bear told her fairy tales and guarded her bed at night. Of course.

But at some point, it started feeling a bit odd. And now that you're eleven-almost-twelve, it feels like a kind of willful misbehaving. The silliness is gone. At eleven, your eyes bear the light of seriousness, and you are often taken aback when I don't entirely believe your stories.

"Where I grew up?" I clear my throat, and my next words fade. "Is that right."

I watch you swing. Maybe you did have an aide in class. Maybe it was a simple exercise, a coincidence. Is it so unlikely that a child would draw a map with a cabin or a lake? I am suddenly relieved, talked back to earth by the quiet sound of the breeze and the dimming of the world as a cloud swallows the sun. I look for your teacher, and I see her standing by the school.

"Ms. Pena?" I call out. "One second, Pearl. You can keep swinging."

I can't tell if you hear me or not—your eyes are closed, your face pure childish ecstasy as you glide through the air. I lay your backpack down beside the swing and drift in the direction of your teacher, my hands in my pockets.

"Mr. Elias, you're looking well." Ms. Pena says this with a flirtatious grin, though I am at least ten years her senior. I don't know if she does this to be funny or to make me blush. When she sees that I'm embarrassed, she grins, mission accomplished. She adjusts the straps on a little girl's backpack before sending her off with her parent.

"Yes, well, thank you," I say, reaching up and nervously touching the marble-sized tumor above my ear, hidden among the weeds of my hair. Still there.

It is always still there, no matter how many times I check. And it always seems the tiniest bit bigger, although that's not possible. Is it? That it would grow by the hour? By the minute?

"Pearl was telling me about her day." I try to keep my words light, but Ms. Pena can tell something is off.

"You're such a wonderful guardian," she says, again in a playful voice, trying to lighten things up. "I wish I had a guardian like you. Someone handsome to watch out for me." She seems almost embarrassed by her own boldness, like a small chipmunk darting out into the open before spinning around and vanishing into the shadows.

I don't know what to say to that—she has been fishing for a date ever since Pearl showed up in elementary school four years ago. I clear my throat and swallow hard. The day feels much, much warmer. When I don't reply, she takes a more serious tone.

"Mr. Elias, is everything okay?"

"Oh, fine, fine," I say.

I clear my throat again. Is this a side effect of my impending demise, or is it only from the fall pollen? Or is it because of Ms. Pena with her red lipstick, her shining smile, her fitted blouse?

"Pearl was telling me about the teacher's aide in class today," I begin, scanning Ms. Pena's face. She doesn't blink. She doesn't say anything. I continue. "She told me the aide was a woman with white hair who helped her draw a map. A map of where I grew up?"

The confusion finally sets in. "I'm sorry, Mr. Elias," she says, shaking her head. "We didn't have a teacher's aide."

"Did you draw maps?"

"Pearl may have drawn a map during art class."

"Was there a substitute or an aide in art class?"

She shakes her head. "Not that I know of."

With that short sentence the dread rises in me, and a dim

version of the chills I felt earlier. *Oh, Pearl. Let's not do this again.*

"Thank you, Ms. Pena. Thank you for your time."

Ms. Pena gathers herself, enough at least to regain her playful tone. "My time is your time, Mr. Elias. Remember that! My time is always your time!" She giggles, blushes, and turns to help another student. She peeks at me over her shoulder, but I turn, pretending not to notice.

An active imagination is one thing. Outright lies are another thing completely. I do not mind you pretending or drawing fantastical things, but this feels like an unnecessary deception, some deliberate crossing.

But the image of the white-haired woman is not one unfamiliar to me. I remember the stories Mary used to tell, and another chill spreads through my body, and a lightness, and I wonder again how long I have.

My mind is so distracted that at first I don't see that the swings are empty, both of them. They hang in that still day, barely swaying. And your backpack is no longer leaning against the swing.

You are gone.

The Emptiness

Oh, Pearl, I think—a common refrain.

When I see the emptiness of the swings without you, I feel the emptiness of the lake, the waiting for Mary to come around the corner in her kayak. Tom arrived first, leaving his kayak in the water and running past the cabin. Shirley arrived next, pulling both her and Tom's kayaks up onto the pier one at a time, then jogging to the cabin, hugging me, telling me what happened in words that didn't make sense.

Accident. Fell in. Tom's going for help.

Shirley paced, frantic, shrugging off my questions, saying over and over, "I don't know, Paul! I don't know!"

The sound of rocks from the driveway clattered off the bottom of Tom's car as he drove at a ridiculous speed away from the cabin. I handed the baby who was your father to Shirley and ran for my kayak, her shouting after me. I hear the sound of my feet slapping the wooden dock, the emptiness of the lake, how impossibly calm the water remained while inside of me a panic was rising.

Looking for You

I glance from the doors of the elementary school to the chain-link fence to the large gate at the opposite end of the playground. It's a security gate, wide enough for cars to pass through, and at the end of the day all the children leave that way. I walk quickly to the gate and look for you, hoping to see you wandering up the alley. When I don't see you, I turn and face the playground, the school. I check the windows, hoping to catch a glimpse of you.

Pearl, I think again. *Why?*

I watch the other parents and children shuffle out, some driving, most walking, winding their way up the alley or down the street. The children are jumpy, their voices squealing with pent-up energy, while their parents walk beside them, most of them with shoulders hunched from working first shift or third shift, or from not working, or from days spent waiting. I search for you among the forest of backpacks and blue jeans. Soon the expanse of pavement stretches empty except for a few teachers standing in a huddle by one of the doors, chatting at the end of another day.

Ms. Howard comes around the building. She always does

one last sweep of the schoolyard before going back inside. I have seen her do this a few times. She might be a bit of a nag, but she's a meticulous nag. Very thorough.

"Ms. Howard?" I say with relief, and she turns, sees it is me, and gives me a flat smile. I wish you would not have made me ask Ms. Howard for help. "Have you seen Pearl?"

Her head cocks to the side as if I'm speaking another language. "I'm sorry?"

"Pearl came out. I spoke with Ms. Pena. When I turned around, Pearl was gone."

"Oh no," she says.

Part of me feels that she says it ironically. She's not surprised at all that I have lost you again. Misplaced you. But I try to give her the benefit of the doubt. Maybe her "Oh no" was genuine.

"Is she running again?" she asks.

Ms. Howard is referring to a time period a few winters ago when you used to run away from me. At first your escapes filled me with worry, which soon became anger and eventually only embarrassment. When I realized that I couldn't make you stop leaving, I fastened a bracelet around your wrist that you couldn't take off, one that had our address and phone number on it. People all over our small city called or brought you home to me.

"No," I say. "It's not like that." But I wonder. Are you running again? Did the woman you saw in your classroom, the mysterious teacher's aide with silver-white hair, have anything to do with this?

Ms. Howard sighs. "If you allowed Pearl to take part in the camp, Mr. Elias, it might give you a nice break from the child."

A break. I know I am old to be raising a child. I do not need a break.

"Do you mind if I take a look back through the school one last time before I go home?" I ask, weary.

Ms. Howard doesn't say anything, only turns and leads me toward the metal door.

I reach up absently and rub the knot again. I can't help sizing the knot up. I used to be very good at convincing myself it was shrinking. It's amazing how successful we can be at fooling ourselves, but that was wishful thinking. I was so successful at talking myself into that illusion that by the time I went to the doctor, it was too late. Now I lay my index finger alongside the knot, like pointing a play gun into the middle of my head, and note that the knot reaches all the way out to the joint.

Inside the school, it is cool, almost cold. I suppose the sunlight streaming through all the classroom windows must have triggered the air-conditioning. The sweat on my forehead and the back of my neck now feels icy cold.

Ms. Howard hugs herself, rubs her arms briskly, and leads me through a set of double doors into the main hallway. "Pearl is a curious child," she remarks, and I don't know if I'm supposed to reply to that, or even if she meant to say it out loud.

I wait. The school is empty and quiet, and our footsteps sound rushed, out of place.

"There is much to be said in favor of children who have an imagination," she continues, seeming to conduct a back-and-forth conversation with herself. *Pearl is curious. Yes, but that is good.*

"Is there?" I can't help asking.

Ms. Howard glances over her shoulder as we turn a corner. "Of course," she says, clearly confused that I would even question such a premise. "Curious children, those with real imagination, shape the world."

Just as I am about to ask another question, this one about when, in her estimation, the world lost its shape, Ms. Davis comes out of the art room and nearly runs into us. "Oh! Ms. Howard, I'm sorry, excuse me."

Ms. Davis is long and narrow in every way, built like a sapling. Her face is a thin oval shape, her eyes are long and wide, and her hair reaches down to the middle of her back. She is at least six inches taller than me, and that's without the heels she is currently wearing. She crosses her thin arms. Everyone seems cold. There are shadows everywhere now that the school day is over—many classrooms are empty and some of the hall lights are off.

"I'm sorry," she continues. Apologizing seems to be her way of interacting with the world. Others say hello. Ms. Davis apologizes. "I didn't expect to see you without Pearl."

"Without Pearl?" I say.

"Yes, she was here only a few minutes ago." Ms. Davis peers around us, as if expecting to see Pearl fading away down the hall.

"She was?"

"She came back in from the playground and took the map she was working on today, and I gave her a few supplies. She said she needed it all for the trip."

"The trip?" I ask. I don't think I told Pearl we were going anywhere.

"I'm sorry. She said you're going back to the place where you grew up?"

Again, the strange sense that I'm in the middle of a dream. "Yes." I don't know what else to say. "Yes."

"Mr. Elias, if Pearl is going to be out of school for more than three days, you'll need to fill out an excused absence form. Otherwise the absences will be unlawful," Ms. Howard says, eyeing me suspiciously.

"Yes, yes. Of course. I'll take care of the form," I say, with no intention of filling out any form.

"Did she say where she was going?" Ms. Howard asks Ms. Davis. "We didn't see her on the playground."

"We could have missed her," I say. "Maybe she left as we were coming in. She could be outside waiting for me. Thank you, Ms. Davis."

She nods, a sad smile on her face. Why is everyone giving me sad smiles today? Has the doctor already called the school? Is social services on the way? Hospice? Can I not be given one day to hold this news to myself?

We turn to walk away, but then I remember something. "Ms. Davis, did you have a teacher's aide in class today, a white-haired woman?"

She looks confused. "No. We didn't."

Beyond her, the room is empty. "No visitors to class? No other parents?"

"I'm sorry, no," she says. "Why do you ask?"

"That's okay. Just curious." I turn to walk outside, even though I know you will not be there. You have never been one for waiting.

We walk the halls, Ms. Howard and I. We exit the building through the heavy door, and it smashes closed behind us, like an ending. We stand there scanning the playground.

"I can go check the other side of the building," Ms. Howard says, moving to do just that, but I stop her.

"No, she's not there."

"But I—"

"No, that's okay. She doesn't wait."

Ms. Howard stares at me. "Should I ask some of the teachers to help?"

I sigh. Shake my head. "I'm sure she went home. I'm sure she . . ."

I know, more certainly than I know anything else, that you did not go home. Where you went, I have no idea. But after so many of your disappearances and so many of your undramatic returns, I am feeling more annoyed than worried.

"Thanks," I say.

I walk away. Nothing in the world feels emptier than a vacant playground. A line of gray clouds drifts in front of the sun. I walk out through the wide gate at the far side of the schoolyard. When I look back, I see Ms. Howard still standing by the door, watching me walk away. She waves, and something like affection for her stirs deep inside of me. Aren't most of us doing our best with the path we've been given? She cares for Pearl—I know that. Couldn't that be enough?

The alley stretches ahead of me, long and narrow and mostly uphill for the five blocks between me and our house. I pass the empty lot, peering into the tall autumn weeds to see if you've nestled there like some runaway bunny, but you are not there. I cross the street, and when I think of you crossing streets, the anxiety I've been able to keep at bay begins to rise. I hope you check both ways. I know you will come home if you can.

But what if something happens to you, and you can't?

You remind me so much of your father at your age. He used to run away too when I put my foot down. He would shout something boisterous, something meant to hurt me, like, "But you'll never be as good as a mother!" and he'd slip out the door. He always came home after dark, listless and wordlessly apologetic. We were missing so many things back then, living with so many gaping wounds that had never been dressed. We had no idea how to tenderly care for each other's injuries. Silently walking around our transgressions seemed to be the kindest thing to do, and for many years I thought his wounds had healed. But some had festered. I know this now, much too late.

Yet in all of the wordlessness that existed between John and me, there was also quiet affection. He would move to my side of the couch as we watched baseball. Or come slide under the covers in my bed late at night, when the darkness took on a physical presence in the house. I could feel his eyes searching my face when he thought I was sleeping. You do similar things now, holding my hand and examining the lines, the veins, the patterns in my skin. And we usually do not talk about your running away or the strange things you say. We keep moving forward.

I move farther along the narrow alley, closer to home, still looking for you. I cross another street, and I enter that section of alleyway with tall brick buildings on both sides. The one on the left is the solid back of a building dotted with metal doors that lead to offices and a day care and a corner store. But the one on the right is derelict, vacant. The power lines above me droop, heavy. The windows— and this is the first time I notice this—have been closed in with cinder blocks, gray squares that form a kind of pattern along the three stories of brick. It is early afternoon, but in the alley it feels closer to dusk, it's cooler, and the shadows are thick and alive. There are wide metal vents, rusty and bent, that lead into the empty building, but I don't hear any air coming through. An aching sense of emptiness exudes from the building—it smells like dust and overheated rubber and something burning in the distance.

I come to the middle of the block where there is an old back door locked with a heavy chain. But the chain has slipped, and I see it's not actually locked and the door is open a crack. The chain hangs limp, and I imagine the bottom link is still swaying from someone recently passing through the door.

You wouldn't go in there, I think. *Would you, Pearl?*

Closer Than They Might Appear

I peek in through the narrow darkness and listen. The wind picks up and the door opens another inch, but the unlocked chain holds it in place. I check the alley. I lift the chain and pull it through the handle so that it makes a rhythmic clinking. I twist it into a loop and lay it on the crumbling alley. I look around again, nudge the door open another few inches, and poke my head inside.

"Pearl?" I call out in a quiet voice, too afraid to shout into the shadows. There is a sense of sleeping things that don't want to wake. "Pearl?"

I should walk home. You're probably there, resting in the armchair by the front window reading a book, or sitting at the large dining room table working on the map. You're probably fine. But the thought of even the possibility of you in this building, hiding alone, makes it impossible for me to leave until I have at least checked inside.

I push the door open, wide open this time to let in as much light as possible. The floor is covered in debris, dust, old boards, and plaster that has fallen from the walls and ceiling. It is an abandoned construction site—interior walls have been demolished, and new wires poke out of outlet cases, never reconnected. There is more light than I expected, and while the windows facing the alley have been filled in with concrete blocks, the windows facing south are still glass panes coated in a decade of grime.

"Pearl?" I say again, this time louder. My voice comes back to me after wandering the building and finding nothing. Another open door gapes by the far wall, revealing a stairwell going down, the beginning of broken stairs, and a thin handrail.

If you came in here, you will be down there. I know you well enough to know this.

"Pearl," I mutter, because while I don't entirely believe in ghosts, I don't not believe in them. And even more pressing, I am not completely naive about the types of characters who might be lurking in a building like this, in our city, at the end of a lukewarm fall day.

I go over to the steps and put my hand on the rail. It wobbles back and forth, barely attached to the wall.

"Pearl?" I shout down the steps.

Walking into the basement of that old warehouse is like descending into pitch-black water. I hold my breath. Something like old glass crumbles under my feet, and the air carries a strange combination of stale dust, moisture, and the smell of cats. Each step lets out a weary groan that shoots right up my spine alongside the fear. When I stop, when I am silent, I can hear something dripping in the basement, some liquid falling into a pool.

Drip.

Drip.

Drip.

Is there a lonelier sound?

At the bottom, I find myself standing in what feels to be a completely empty room, a never-ending stretch of smooth concrete under my feet, and an almost silky darkness that drips down the steps and fills the space like liquid rising. I close my eyes. I do not like the feel of the place. Across the way, the dim light glares off a thin sheet of standing water, completely still.

I hear a distant whistling.

"Pearl?" I call out.

The whistling stops.

"Pearl? Honey? Please talk to me. It's dark. I can't see anything."

"Grampy?" Your tiny voice scuttles along the edges of the walls and under the steps and flits along the ceiling.

"Pearl." I'm not sure what else to say.

"I'm sorry, Grampy."

"Honey, you're not in trouble. Come out. Please?"

"Maybe you should come in here. I'm under these boards."

My eyes adjust, and in the dim light, I can see a pile of wooden pallets that has partially fallen over, and a small crawl space in among them.

"Pearl." I sigh and get as low as I can. I inch my way back into that narrow opening, feeling the grit under my hands and knees, and you are there, in the darkness.

A light appears like a single eye, first skimming the floor, then lifting of its own accord and bouncing lightly through the void.

"Do you keep that flashlight in your backpack?"

36

"Isn't this place kind of like the old cave where the giants live?"

"I'm afraid it's too small for giants," I reply, trying to find a comfortable position.

"You only think that because you're one of the giants," you say.

"Oh, is that right?" I smirk, but you remain serious.

"This is the cave of the giants, the ones that eat little boys and little girls."

"Are you a giant, or are you a little girl about to be eaten?"

"A little girl, of course!" you protest.

"If I eat you, can we leave?"

"Grampy!"

"Okay. I'm sorry. Go ahead."

"There are many of us little children trapped here in the mean, ugly giant's nasty cave, but only I have found the important map."

"A map of where?" I ask.

You start to talk but clamp your mouth shut.

"You can tell me, Pearl. I'm not really a giant."

"I know, Grampy," you say, your voice quiet and unsure of itself. "It's a map of Nysa, where you grew up."

Again, a soft chill puts goose bumps on my arms.

You stand as well as you can inside the tiny space and move to the opening. "C'mon, Grampy. Let's go."

You don't want to talk about the map. That's fine, because I don't either. I follow you out between the boards, out into the building's basement, which now seems much less dark than it did before, especially after being under the pallets.

"I'm sorry, Grampy," you say.

"C'mon. You're right. Let's get out of here."

That's when I hear the metal door upstairs slam shut. My heart skips a beat. I reach down and take your small hand. It's dry, and I can feel the fine dust from the concrete on it, like chalk powder. You follow me up the stairs, across the room to the door. It's closed.

"The wind must have blown it shut." I push the bar, expecting it to be locked and us to be trapped. But it pops open, and we are bombarded by the fresh autumn air, now much cooler than it was only minutes before, and the slate-gray sky above us. The wind is like breath.

I drop your hand and wrap the chain back around the door handle. When I finish, you reach up and grab my hand again, and we drift up the alley. Your hand feels even lonelier and smaller than it did in the dark, the alley feels lonely and narrow, and the sky, even as the clouds break up, seems lonely and tired. We pause at each street between the school and our house, look both ways, and walk across, my steps long and ponderous, yours short and sometimes turning into skips to keep up.

"Why did you go in there?" I ask you. "Places like that aren't safe here in the city."

You smile. "The woman from class. She was helping me with the map. And she gave me this." You hand me a quarter. "See the year?" you ask, pride in your voice.

I hold the quarter up closer to my face, rubbing it to wipe away some of the grime.

1979. Forty years ago. The same year your father was born. The same year your grandmother left me. Dread seeps into my neck, my eyes, my hands. It's a tightening, a filling up, a kind of heat. I've had this feeling before, this hollow sense of low-grade dread, and I realize it was that day forty years ago when I was lying on the sofa, John on my chest, and our friends came back across the water without your grandmother.

Without Mary.

On that morning, I stood holding John in my arms, pressing his body to my chest with one hand while cupping his head in the other. I navigated the sliding door with my elbow without putting him down and walked out onto the deck.

I keep seeing it now, over and over again. Shirley bent at the waist, crying and gasping for breath.

"Where is Tom going?"

"He's going for help."

"Mary?" I asked, not able to say anything else.

She shook her head. "There was an accident."

"Grampy?" you ask me.

We are standing at the crosswalk. Two cars have stopped to let us walk, but I am lost, far away.

"Should we cross?"

I give a half wave to each car, and we pass between them. One of them roars behind us, formally registering the driver's impatience.

"Almost there," I whisper to you. I think again of the imaginary woman you have been talking about. "Pearl." I pause. "Tell me again. Why were you in that building? You have to be careful. Sometimes abandoned buildings have people in them who might hurt you."

You smile again as we turn onto our street, and your smile is so innocent, so bright, so seemingly unaware of the weight of the world. "The kind white-haired woman took me in there. She wanted to show me that quarter. And she wanted to help me a little more with my map."

"Who is this woman, Pearl?"

"You passed her on the way in. You must have seen her. Besides, I already told you: she needs my help. She's lost something that means a lot to her."

I don't know what to say to you, whether to warn or threaten or keep questioning. I often feel too old to navigate this parenting role again, with the first failed attempt so near in the side-view mirror of my life, where the objects are closer than they might appear.

"Pearl, be careful," I end up saying, not sure what that's supposed to mean. I want to ask you if this is somehow related to your father, if this woman knows him, but I hesitate to bring him up because the topic always makes you so sad.

You smile and squeeze my hand.

"Can I see the map? When we get home?"

"Not till it's finished," you say with a mischievous smile.

The First Drowning

We walk up onto the porch, I unlock the front door, and we are home. I can breathe again. I think of the tumor, the diagnosis, and I reach up and feel the lump under my skin. Still there. I think you might have seen me feeling it, so I try to turn the motion into a pushing back of my hair, a scratch of my ear. I smile down at you.

"Tea party?" you ask. I nod. And my mind spins back to Nysa.

I'm not sure why I was invited to Justin Thomas's Halloween party during my junior year of high school—I have a feeling he wanted to have a large party, one he could brag about on Monday, so he invited everyone. I didn't know Justin well, although I watched him from a distance. He was one of the chosen ones, one of those high school kids whose life seemed so easy, so enviable, with his path already cleared for him. All he had to do was take long, easy strides all the way to the top.

If I can't recall why I was invited, I'm even less sure about why I went. I didn't fit in back in those days. I found my own skin difficult to live in, as if my soul had been given the wrong size outer garment. It's hard to explain. That discomfort led me to avoid people, more or less, but my parents were always trying to prod me into situations where I might make friends.

I wore an old sheet with holes cut all through it—a nod to Charlie Brown and his ghost costume. But my parents had not wanted to sacrifice any of their white sheets, so mine was an old sheet from the linen closet with small pink and blue flowers on it. When Mrs. Thomas answered the door, she took me in with a wry look on her face, more wince than smile, and motioned to the basement door. I nodded, the sheet shifting up and down, and walked to the stairs, holding on to the rail through the sheet. I was sure I would trip and fall the length of the stairway, breaking my neck, and the thought was a relief. Death was preferable. As soon as I walked into that house I wanted to leave.

There were only five or six kids there when I descended into the dark and shrank into one of the corners. Although I knew everyone at the party by name, I did not have what is commonly known as "friends" during those late high school years. I had a nervous habit of pushing the hair out of my eyes so that I could keep reading whatever it was I was reading. Books were my friends. Who needed people?

The basement was not pleasant. The ceiling was nothing more than naked floor joists and wires running alongside pipes, although it was difficult to see. The only light came down the steps from the upstairs hallway. The air was musty, even in the cool of autumn, and hovering all around was a sort of dampness mixed in with the more pleasant scents of hot apple cider and pumpkin pie.

The only thing about the party that I enjoyed was being

hidden in my sheet. It was marvelous being among the kids I was always with and them not knowing it was me. I wedged myself into the corner and sank down in the darkness. I thought I had managed to disappear.

That's when I heard whispers about the drowning. Gillian Hudson, who we all knew through the years mostly for her dedication to saying the Pledge of Allegiance with particular vigor, had drowned in the lake only that morning. I hadn't heard about it. I didn't know Gillian well, but it was a strange and mysterious thing to think that one of my classmates, someone who had been among us earlier that day, was suddenly most decidedly not among us anymore. I sat in the darkness and thought about death, about what had happened to Gillian when she sank to the bottom. Had she blinked and found herself on streets of gold, or had everything she'd ever known, even the universe she'd been born into, winked out like a light turned off?

Upstairs, the knocking began. The constant clang of the doorbell. The pounding of feet down the stairs and the squealing of girls and the back-pounding of boys. Soon there were so many teenagers that I couldn't see through their legs. I was still sitting, and I imagined that I was staring into a moving forest.

Someone turned on a strobe light, and the basement boomed with music. The sounds and the lights were hypnotic. I planned on biding my time until the end and, once it was reasonably appropriate, going outside to wait for my parents. If they took too long to come back, I even considered walking the five lonely miles back to my house, although that would take some working up to, since it was a dark road lined mostly by cornfields full of high, dried-out, whispering stalks.

A loud shout came from the other side of the basement, followed by cheering, and the whole crowd moved back. Someone nearly sat on me, then cursed. I started to panic, breathing hard. What if I couldn't get up? No one would hear me. What if someone else had already fallen on the ground and was in the process of being trampled? I peered down at the dark floor to see if someone needed help but saw only the strange, gangly legs of monsters and witches.

The crowd started chanting, "Pete . . . Pete . . . Pete," starting slowly at first but building into a crescendo. Pete was the name of the kid who had invited me, or whose parents had told my parents I should come over. Peter Singleton. Pete must have done whatever the crowd required of him, because there was another loud cheer, another pulsating movement. The group felt less like a gathering of individuals than a morphing, hungry mob, a single organism whose momentum could not be slowed. Panic rose in me again.

I couldn't take it anymore. I pushed my way through the shoulders and arms and annoyance. I smelled alcohol, a strange and foreign smell, and it seemed we were too young for all this, though we were juniors and I knew that juniors all over the country were drinking at parties and getting into trouble. Sowing their wild oats. It felt to me like we had all been swept up in something we wouldn't do on our own, something the mob was making us do. I don't know—maybe to them it was simply fun. I fled the basement and the pulsing, shadowy crowd, squinted against the hall light, and tripped through the foyer until I found my way outside, into the crisp October air.

The front stoop was bathed in light, and people were still arriving, so I made my way around to the dark side of the house, finally breathing, relief flooding me. I was alone. I stared out into the country and wished I had my license, wished there was a way to fly away from there, soar over the quiet fields and narrow groves of trees. But for some reason I had never gotten around to taking my driver's test. I resolved to get my license. That would free me from these things.

But simply being outside gave me what I had wanted. My only regret was that I didn't have a book and a flashlight so that I could while away the next two hours before my parents came back to get me.

"Watch it, Charlie Brown," a voice said as I tripped over something soft. I had to put my hands down onto the cold grass to keep from planting my face in the earth. But I didn't take off my sheet. It was kind of nice, the anonymity.

"Sorry," I mumbled. "Sorry." I turned to go.

"Wait a minute," a different voice called out, a girl's voice. How many of them were there, sitting up against the hedgerow in the dark? "Is that Paul? Are you trying to escape the party?"

"Maybe." I shrugged, glancing over my shoulder. A flashlight lit up and blinded me. "Who's asking?"

"Another escapee!" the original, deeper voice said exultantly. There were a few chirps of quiet laughter. "Sit down, good man."

"Well, I can't see a thing." My eyes were dazzled, but there was something in his voice that felt kind and welcoming.

"What's your name?"

I thought this was a third voice, another girl, but I couldn't be sure. Meanwhile, my eyes recovered. The flashlight beam dropped, but its glow illuminated the three who sat there.

One of them had a kind of werewolf mask perched on the top of his head. The girl beside him, the middle one of the three, wore a quaint blue dress and ruby-red shoes and had her hair up in pigtails. She was cute. The girl on the end was far enough away from the flashlight that I couldn't get a good look at her. She wore some kind of a cloak with its large hood down, resting on her shoulders.

"I'm Paul," I said nervously.

"I knew it! I'm Shirley," said the first girl, and I recognized her from third-period art class. Not that we had ever really talked.

"Hi, Dorothy," I said.

"Hey, Paul, pal," the guy said in a radio announcer's nasally drawn-out voice, and the girls laughed again. "I'm Tom. Lucky for you it's not a full moon."

"And I'm Mary," the second girl said. "I'm the Grim Reaper." Her voice and the way she carried herself couldn't have been any less threatening. She seemed to be drowning in her costume, and her voice lilted like silk rolling in the breeze.

I almost burst out laughing at the contrast between her kind voice and her foreboding costume. Her tiny hand came up out of the deep sleeve of her cloak, and the feel of her skin was a revelation. Her hands were ice-cold but soft. I didn't want to let go. For the rest of the night after touching her hand, I was in another realm. I was floating. I'm not sure how I managed to form words, much less express actual ideas.

I fell to a sitting position among them, not knowing that what I had actually tripped into were not strangers who had also escaped the party but the best two years of my life.

"Well," the boy named Tom said, "the real question is, now what?"

The Tea Party

I am standing by the front door, remembering that first time I met Mary. I haven't thought about that for a long time.

You have gone inside to hunt down the plastic cups and saucers your dad bought you when you were five. The house smells like pinewood floor cleaner. I am, if nothing else, organized, and I keep a clean house. There seems to be something crucial in keeping a clean house for you, a tidy place for you to grow up. Or, I should say, seemed. Past tense. The doctor's diagnosis makes me question everything: what we are doing, what I have done. Should I have found a younger family to raise you a long time ago so that I would not be all you have? Is that what was at the root of Ms. Howard's judgmental glance—scorn at the idea that someone as old as me could be trusted to live long enough to raise someone as young as you?

There is the light sound of toys clinking together, and your fairy voice calling from the living room. "Grampy! Teatime!"

I walk through the house, and it feels like the first time.

The entrance hall feels dingy—the baseboards in need of a fresh coat, the scuffs on the wall, the ceiling light with one bulb out. I really should paint the walls, but it all seems so pointless now, repairing, tidying up, fixing things. For what? For who? In six months, I will be gone. Maybe three. Maybe next week. Somehow, during our walk home, during my search for you, the weight of the diagnosis had lifted, but now it circles, eyes up the terrain, and settles.

"Grampy!" you call again, and I turn the corner.

There are three place settings. Three tiny plastic cups on three tiny plastic saucers.

"Pearl," I ask in a quiet voice, "are you expecting a visitor?"

"I invited the silver-haired woman," you say, not even bothering to look up, so busy arranging and running back and forth to the kitchen.

I sigh. "Does she have white hair or silver hair? You can't seem to make up your mind."

You shrug off my inquisition. "It shimmers and shines. It depends on the light."

"It depends on the light," I repeat, raising my eyebrows skeptically. You giggle.

We sit there on the floor for quite some time, my back against the sofa. I notice your eyes occasionally flitting up to the side of my head, where the now slightly-larger-than-marble-sized knot juts out into the world. And my eyes are drawn over and over again to the third place setting. I can't help it—I keep checking the front windows, looking over my shoulder, waiting for the woman to walk into the room. But she does not.

"I have something I need to tell you, Pearl," I say.

You take me in with your big, dark eyes. I clear my throat.

It's aching now, the knot. I rub my jaw and squint, staring over at the bookshelves that hold all of our favorites.

"We're going to go away for a bit."

"Back to where you grew up?" you ask, but there is no excitement in your voice. Only wariness. Perhaps a little skepticism.

"Pearl," I begin, nearly losing my patience. "Yes. Back to where I grew up."

"Where my daddy grew up?"

"Your daddy grew up here, in this house. We're going back to where he was born."

"Do you think we'll find him there?"

"I don't think so."

"Is that why we're going?"

"No."

"Then why?"

"I need to go back. I need to see if my friends still live there. I'd like to show you around."

"Are we coming back here after we see where you grew up?"

I can tell it's a hard question for you to ask. "I'd like it to be your town too."

"So, we're not coming back?"

"I don't know. Not yet."

A silence falls around us. You lift up your plastic teacup, raise it to your lips, close your eyes, and drink a long and deep draft of the pretend tea. "So good," you whisper. When you open your eyes, you suddenly seem too old for tea parties. Why have I not recognized it before?

"Pearl," I say hesitantly, "aren't you getting a little old for all of this . . . pretending?"

"Grampy, drink your tea before it gets cold."

I lift the empty cup.

"What's it like?" you ask.

"Where I grew up?"

"No, the tea," you say, giggling.

I smile. "The tea is fabulous. A little too hot, actually. I might let it cool."

You laugh quietly again, then sit up straight as if corrected by someone to watch your posture. "What's it like where you grew up?"

"I haven't been there for forty years. I don't know what it's like anymore."

"What was it like?"

"Nysa was kind of like an island. I guess technically it's a peninsula. The lake surrounds it on three sides. The river lines the western side. So we were always surrounded by water. We called ourselves an island even though we weren't, not really."

You take another sip from your teacup.

"I always thought it would become more popular, like one of those beach towns where everyone goes for vacation. The lake was enormous. I've always imagined that rich people bought up the waterfront property and built their mansions there after I left. I hope not, but who knows. The truth is, I really don't know what it's like. I've never been back, and I've never checked up on it."

"Did you like it?"

"I liked it very much. We knew almost everyone on the island. There was a small town, one main street, but I grew up out in the country. Most of the island is farmland. Or it was when I was a kid."

"Did you have a lot of friends?"

I think of the Halloween party. "No, not many, but I was happy."

"Did you like your house?" you ask, stirring your tea with a tiny spoon. When you ask questions in that serious, absentminded tone, you could be twenty years old instead of eleven.

"My house? It was okay. There were places in Nysa that I loved, but my house wasn't one of them. My parents were kind but a bit absent. I'm sure they loved me. In those days children ran free."

"Like me." You smile.

"You're a throwback," I say, smirking.

"What about the field between your house and the road?"

The room feels colder.

"The field," you say again. "Between your house and the road. The one along the woods."

I don't know how you know this. Your voice is very matter-of-fact.

"What about it?"

"It's on the map I'm drawing."

Yes. The field.

"There were fields everywhere," I say, trying to steer the conversation away from these things you should not know.

"Not just any field," you say. "I mean the field where Grandma saw the woman for the first time. The woman with the silver hair. She told me all about it."

The Field

The four of us walked through the field late that night: a werewolf with his mask off; Dorothy, carrying her ruby slippers; Mary, dressed like death, in her dark cloak with the hood resting powerlessly on her shoulders; and me, no longer Charlie Brown, carrying my cut-up sheet under one arm. My house was the closest, and I think they were intrigued by me, the new guy, so we left Justin's place and started walking to my house. Our feet made lonely sounds on the smooth back roads. The air moved in fits and starts, now breezy, now still. It was dark in the way only a back-country road on a chilly fall night can be.

What happened on our way home could be easily explained by the fact that it was Halloween, we were sharing spooky stories, and we were all a little jumpy. We were bound to see things that weren't there.

"How far'd you say?" Tom asked me. It wasn't a complaint. I think we were all enjoying the walk.

"About five miles or so, give or take."

"Your parents won't mind?" Mary asked, shaking her head

back and forth to free her hair from the cloak. She had a very concerned voice, a very kind voice.

"To be honest, they won't even notice."

"Sounds like my folks," Tom said, and there was an ounce of bitterness around the edge of his words. "They couldn't care less about me coming or going. As long as I close the door and turn off the lights."

"Close the door, Tom!" Shirley shouted, laughing. "Turn off the lights!" Her voice softened. "My parents think I'm spending the night at Mary's."

"And my mom thinks I'm at Shirley's," Mary admitted. Even though Shirley and Tom both thought this was hysterical, Mary's voice made me think she wasn't happy about the deception. Or maybe it was something else.

"How'd you all become friends?" I asked. Tom and Shirley were familiar to me—our school wasn't that big. But I couldn't place Mary.

"Mary and me, we've known each other all our lives," Shirley gushed. "Our parents knew each other from something or other. Some nearby town. Something our moms did together. I can't remember. But Mary only moved to Nysa last year."

"What about you?" I asked Tom.

He smirked. "I'm tagging along."

Shirley smacked his arm playfully. I couldn't tell if the two of them were together. They obviously liked each other. I glanced over at Mary. It was hard to see her face in the dark, but her soft voice made her sound pretty. Her hair blended in with the shadows.

I wish you could have seen her as I first saw her on that night. The fact that she was practically invisible in the dark didn't make her less beautiful—it made her more so. It blurred the lines between her physical body and the world around us, so that Mary became part of the night, part of the fields, part of the air. Her physical form was only the center—the rest of her stretched out into everything else.

I guess that sounds strange. Someday you'll understand what I'm saying.

Honestly? Sometimes I feel that way about you, when I go up and check on you at night and you're sleeping, and the darkness is all around. I can hear you breathing, and I can see the shadows around your eyes, the waves of your hair on top of the blanket, but everything that is the essence of you sometimes seems to fill the room. You are much more than what lies in that little body.

The field. Yes, the field is what you asked me about.

The four of us came to a particular place where the corn was high in one field but had been harvested on the other side of the road. That side was actually a gradual hill, and I could see at the top of that narrow ridge the distant lights of my own house: the front porch light, which my parents left on whenever I wasn't home, and the kitchen light, shining through the one window.

I stopped. The other three stopped too.

"What's up?" Tom asked.

"Well," I said, "we can keep taking the road. It goes up that way." I pointed into the night. "Or we can cut through the field."

"It's not muddy, right?" Shirley asked.

"Nah," I said, shaking my head. It had been a dry fall. The cornstalks in the field beside us rustled loud and raspy.

"What do you think?" Tom asked. "It's your house."

I shrugged. "It's a lot quicker cutting through. A little dirtier. There's a narrow stream we'll have to hop. Besides that, easy as pie."

I glanced around. It was hard to read everyone's expressions in the dark. Shirley laughed. She was almost always laughing at something. But this laugh sounded nervous.

"Onward," Tom said, making a large sweeping motion with his arms, beckoning me to lead the way through the field.

So I did. We left the road.

What if we hadn't?

My Own Flesh and Blood

Grampy! Your tea is getting cold again."

I raise the small, empty plastic cup to my lips and take a long drink. "That is delicious," I say with a smile.

You look at me with sincere eyes. Those eyes. They're so expressive, so open to the world and eager for whatever it might have for you. I worry for the one thousandth time about you, about what will happen with no one here to care for you. No one here to find you when you run away, no one here to drink your tea or hear your stories or read your maps.

That is why we're going back. That is why I have to take you there. There must be someone where I grew up who can watch over you. My parents are gone. My friends, the few I had, are as old as me. But there has to be someone.

For a brief moment, I think about your father. My little boy. Where is he?

How he has failed you. The depth and width and breadth of that failure are a weight on me. It would be so much easier for me to leave if he had not fallen apart, if he had not left you with me. I think of him a million times a day. I think if he had died, I would know, wouldn't I? Wouldn't I feel it in my bones? My own flesh and blood couldn't pass away without me knowing it any more than I could lose a finger or chop off a toe without noticing. Right?

"Will you take me to the stream when we're back in Nysa?" you ask. "Will you show me the stream where you used to play, the one in the field?"

"How do you know these things?" I ask. For some reason I feel so, so sad.

"What?"

"The stream. The field."

You smile patiently. "Grampy, you're so forgetful. I told you. That woman is helping me with my map."

"Ah, yes," I say. "The woman with the silver hair."

Crossing Over

You're right. There was a stream, and we came to it in the dead of night. I knew we needed to hurry so that we would get home before my parents left to pick me up at the party they didn't know I had already left. They wouldn't mind if I brought friends home; in fact, they would probably be pleased. They didn't think I had any friends. I mean, I guess they were right. I didn't. Until that night.

There was something there with Mary and Tom and Shirley, something I hadn't felt before. They seemed to actually like being with me. They were happy welcoming me into their group. I fit. There was something about fitting that felt very nice. And it happened so quickly, without any effort. As I consider how we came together, something about it feels predestined, as if it couldn't have happened any other way. I don't know what to think about that.

"Jump over?" Tom asked. The four of us were standing there staring at the stream.

"It is kind of a big jump," I admitted.

Surprisingly, Mary was the one to insist we cross. I would have expected it if it came from Tom—brash and assertive Tom. Or even Shirley—she could have pressed us to do it in her laughing way. But Mary?

I shrugged. "Don't fall in."

The water swept away from us. It was five or six feet wide and murky in the night.

Tom, full of nervous energy, shouted, scaring us, and suddenly took a quick run up to the stream and jumped. He sailed over, his foot landing at the edge of the water on the far side, and he stumbled forward.

"Whoo!" he shouted. "That's how it's done!"

I could feel the girls' nervousness coming off of them in waves.

"I don't mind walking you around," I said. "I really don't."

Mary pushed a wisp of hair behind her ear. "It's okay. I can do it."

"Let me go first, please?" Shirley begged.

I laughed. "Go for it."

Unlike Tom, she backed away from the stream quite a ways in order to get a running start.

"Get a good jump in, Shirls!" Tom shouted, and even I could hear the nervousness in his voice. But to her credit, she was fast. That was something I'd learn about Shirley in the coming years—she could run when she had to.

She flew right up to us, running barefoot and clutching her ruby slippers, one in each hand. Her last step splashed at the edge of our side of the stream, and she launched herself across. She landed in the water on the far side and started to slip backwards, but Tom reached out and grabbed her, lifted her to safety.

"Yes!" I shouted. "Nice one, Shirley!"

The two of them were close in the dark. They stood there, him holding on to her for an extra second.

"Get a room!" Mary shouted, laughing.

They glanced over at us, each taking a half step away from the other.

"Very funny," Tom said. "Very funny."

Mary whispered, "Do you mind walking me around? I don't think I want to try after all."

"Are you sure?" I asked. "Shirley made it."

"Barely! But I mean, if you don't want to . . ."

"No, no," I said. "I don't mind. I'll walk you."

"I don't think I want to jump," she said to Tom and Shirley. I expected them to protest, but they didn't.

"It's okay," Tom said.

"We'll wait here," Shirley added.

"Actually," I said, "do you mind going on up to my house? It's the only house up there, with the lights. Tell my parents I'll be home in a minute. I don't want them driving all the way over to the party to get me."

"Okay," Tom said, and he and Shirley turned and started walking up the hill through the brittle stubble of harvested cornstalks. My house felt like a long way off from there. The front light was a lonely star.

"You sure?" I asked Mary again.

She nodded, and the two of us turned and walked along the stream, toward the road and the bridge. The space between us felt charged by something, like there was an invisible force there, pulling us together, pushing us apart.

"What's your story?" I asked her. The night seemed less dark as I walked there beside Mary.

She smiled at me bashfully. "What's that supposed to mean?"

"I don't know. Tell me something about you." I felt brave, unabashed. This was not my normal, intimidated self. In the darkness I found a kind of courage.

"It's my mom and dad and me. Mom works at the Nysa Diner, usually from around four in the afternoon until late, two or three in the morning. Dad works night shift at the warehouse over by the highway."

"That's far," I said.

She nodded. "I spend a lot of evenings at home on my own."

"Really?"

"It's okay. I like it. I like the quiet. Why do you think I chose to walk this way? It's a chance for some quiet." She smiled.

"I'm sorry. I'm asking too many questions. Messing up your quiet time."

"That's not what I meant."

We didn't say anything for a few minutes. The bridge was up ahead of us, and far off I could see the headlights of a car on a different road. The stars still shone. The dark profiles of the surrounding tree-covered hills rose around us like massive waves in the middle of the ocean.

"Have you lived out here for long?" she asked me.

"My whole life."

"In the same house?" She sounded incredulous.

"Yep. Same house. Same parents. Same everything."

She laughed, and it was light in the dark.

"How haven't I seen you before?" I asked.

She shrugged. "I've only lived here for a year."

"Still. Strange I've never seen you around."

We got to my road and walked up the hill, crossing the tiny bridge that spanned the stream. In the part of the field that lined the road, ten or twelve rows of corn still stood unharvested—the edge of the field the farmer hadn't yet worked—and they ran along the road all the way up to my house. They seemed to move even when the wind wasn't blowing, their voices dry and raspy.

Nysa was a beautiful place in the daytime, all rolling hills and patches of forest and that never-ending, crystal lake. But when the sun wasn't shining, the whole island turned dark and gave off this aura of something asleep in the deep places of the earth. It's hard to explain, but even with Mary that night, even feeling the approach of something like love, Nysa still gave me the chills.

Our feet were quiet on the road now that it was only the two of us. We barely made a sound. The night was somehow brighter each moment, illuminated by the stars, and our shadows stretched out in front of us.

"Shirley was fast," I said, chuckling nervously.

Mary smiled. "She's quick."

We both laughed.

She stopped.

I walked past her, turned. "What?"

She reached out and grabbed my arm, pulled me back. I could barely breathe. She held me close and huddled against my body. I thought she was going to kiss me.

"Who's that?" she whispered.

"Where?" I took a step back, pulling her with me. I didn't see anything.

"Right . . . there. That person in the shadows." She pointed up the road, into the darkness that rustled alongside the rows of corn.

Mary screamed.

I felt a pulse of energy, and my heart pounded so hard I thought I might have a heart attack. I wanted to run. Mary folded, put her hands over her face.

"Mary, I still don't see anything," I hissed.

"She's gone," she whispered. "She's gone."

We stood there completely still, terrified. Had this person Mary saw circled around behind us? Was she still waiting in the dark rows ahead? Could it have been one of my parents walking down the long lane?

"Who was that?" Mary hissed.

I had no idea.

The high rows of dry corn beside us exploded in movement, and three or four stalks fell down, bending out onto the road.

Mary screamed again.

It was Tom, followed by Shirley.

"What happened?" Tom asked, bending over, breathing hard. Shirley gasped for air beside him. "We heard you scream. Is everything okay?"

"There was a person standing in the road," Mary said, her voice hollow. I could tell she was still thinking about it, imagining it.

"A man?" Tom asked, concern in his voice. He spun around, took a few steps up the road. I admired his courage.

"A woman. She pointed at me," Mary whispered.

"What?" Tom asked.

"She pointed at me," she said, but this time she stared at me. "She pointed. She had the whitest hair, like moonlight."

Headlights wound down the road. It was one of my parents, on their way to pick me up at the party. I ran a hand through my hair.

Tom laughed nervously. "It was probably just some lost trick-or-treater."

"Are you okay, Mary?" I asked. Her screams had shaken me. My heart still pounded.

She didn't say anything. Shirley walked over and hugged her. Tom put his hands on his hips and stared up at the stars.

As my parents' car came closer, it baptized us in light. I stepped slowly out into the road and waved both of my arms over my head, relieved when the car eased to a stop.

My dad wound down his window and poked his head out. "Well, well, well," he said, grinning. "And who do we have here?"

I saw Mary clearly for the first time. Her hands were shaking, her eyes were wide, and when she glanced up at Shirley I thought I saw her jaw tremble.

And she was beautiful.

A Place in This World

hat does the woman look like?" I ask you.

"Drink your tea, Grampy. It's getting cold."

I lift the cup, take a long sip, and put it down. "Why won't you tell me more about her?"

"I already told you, she's very kind. She's tall. She helped me with the map. She wanted to see you in that old building, but you walked right past her." You shrug. "She said she needs my help. She's lost something very important to her. That's all."

You remind me of your grandmother, with your dark hair and your dark eyes.

"We're going to leave for Nysa in the morning. Are you okay to pack a bag?"

"How many days should I pack for?"

"Bring a week's worth of clothes," I say, offering a resigned smile. "We'll go from there."

Later, after you're in bed and asleep and I've seen your breath raising and lowering your tiny rib cage, I sit at the edge of my own bed. I take a wooden ruler and thin shoelace from my bedside table and wrap the shoelace around the circumference of the knot on the side of my head, marking the circle's endpoint with my thumb and forefinger. I stretch out the shoestring along the ruler to get the length of the circumference of my knot, my tumor, my anytime-to-three-months lump.

It's quite a bit bigger than it was the day before, although I admit my method is not exact. I stare at the shoelace, consider measuring again, think better of it, and stash both tools back in my drawer. I turn out the light and lie down on top of the covers, hovering there in the darkness.

I think about going home. Is Nysa home? I find it strange that I still think of it that way. Even now. It is a good idea, I know that much. It would be a safe place for you, I think, not like the city. The country would let you air out a bit, spread your wings, have some freedom. A nice family could raise you in a nice house with nice trips to the shore and vacations and all the trappings of a small-town school with football games and new No. 2 pencils. I hope Nysa hasn't become too snooty in the years since I was there, that there's still a farming element, a hardworking blue-collar section.

I have to find you a place, Pearl. I have to find you a place in this world, before I leave it.

Leaving

Morning breaks. I spend forty-five minutes on the phone with the lawyer who recently helped me write up my will, filling him in on my plans, giving him added instructions on what to do with the house if I don't return. It's a strange conversation. I feel like I'm talking about someone else's impending demise, someone else's house, someone else's granddaughter. When he asks about your guardianship, I tell him I'm working on it.

"You're working on it?" he asks.

"That's what I said. I'll straighten it out and be in touch." I hang up without saying goodbye.

You and I drive out of the city, and it's a strange thing to think I may never return. Never come home to the house I have lived in for so long. Never walk the alley to your school to pick you up. Never sit on the front porch, taking in the street, waiting for John to come back. Never sit on the floor in your room beside your bed until you fall asleep. I arrived in this town with your father when he was only a few months old. Now I am leaving with you. Sometimes the sadness and beauty of life are unfathomable.

You roll your window down, and the crisp autumn air floods in, whipping around us, holding little of the summer heat of yesterday. I feel one of those moments of true melancholy mixed with happiness—that aching combination of thankfulness and sadness and a sharp sense of being—right there in the moment.

The morning air is chilly.

"Pearl, keep your window up," I say, finding myself growing emotional in that moment of leaving. I try to cover up the emotion in a voice with hard lines and sharp turns, but I don't like the sound of it now that it is out, swirling in the air around us.

You start to put your window up, but I reach over and touch your shoulder.

"It's okay," I say. "Don't worry. The air is nice."

You smile that entire-face smile of yours, your hair is dancing around like wild black thread, and you turn to the window and put one hand out, wrestling with the wind. You reach across your body and take my hand resting on the center console.

"Feel how cold," you say, your eyes wide.

Cold. Is that what death will be like? Is that what waits for me on the other side—a long sleep? A never-ending dream? Or something else, something better? Or nothing? I have thought about this often since the diagnosis. What, if anything, waits for me on the other side? I feel like a kid on his first roller-coaster ride when it begins click-clacking its way toward the top of the initial hill. What will greet me on the ride down?

"Will I go to school when we get to your hometown?" you ask.

I reach up and touch the tumor on my head. It's on the left side, facing out my window and away from you. It feels tough, like a tree knot. I can feel it against my skull, and I imagine that I can feel it growing into me, lodging its roots, like an acorn pushing into the earth. I wonder when it first began, when that first cell appeared that would send everything else into blooming chaos. Was it there fifty-eight years ago when I was born? Forty years ago when your father was born? Eleven years ago when you were born? What strange things we carry unknown inside of us.

"Can I be honest with you, Pearl?" I ask.

You roll up your window so you can hear me better. The quiet that rushes in is almost too much, almost enough to make me ask you to put the window back down again so I can drown my senses in that peaceful roar.

"You're in love with Ms. Pena," you say in a very solemn voice.

"What?"

"You're in love with Ms. Pena. It's okay. I'm okay with it."

I am caught completely off guard. That was the last thing I expected you to say. "Well, for one, no, I'm not in love with Ms. Pena. And two, if I was, why would we be leaving?"

Your face twists in thought, so determined to connect the dots. "I've been thinking about this."

"I can tell."

"I think, well, first of all, you *are* in love with Ms. Pena, and everyone can tell. You're worse than Stevie in my class who likes Monica. It's so obvious, Grampy. But maybe you're leaving because you're still in love with Grandma, or you're afraid Ms. Pena won't love you back, or you don't think I like Ms. Pena—even though I do—and so we're leaving because you can't bear to be around her when you're so in love."

I blink once, twice, three times. I stare at the road in front of us. I start laughing and can't stop. The laughter comes up out of me like an eruption. Soon I'm laughing so hard I'm crying, gasping for breath, struggling to drive. You sit there smiling at me like the Cheshire cat. Finally, a full minute later, I catch my breath. That felt good, invigorating.

I smile and sigh and glance over at you. "You've clearly put a lot of thought into this."

"Why else would we leave so soon?" you ask, and I see what I have done to you with this knee-jerk reaction, this sweeping you out of everything you know and love. And I am so, so sorry.

"Pearl, that's what I wanted to explain to you. I'm sorry about this. I need to get away for a little bit. You know? It doesn't have anything to do with Ms. Pena . . . who I think is a beautiful woman. I'm simply feeling overwhelmed by some things and need to get out of our house. And I truly would love for you to see the place where I grew up." I pause. "Can you forgive me for this?"

You smile that kind, gentle smile of yours, the one that reminds me so much of Mary. "Grampy, as long as I'm with you, I'll be okay."

Well, that gets me. I pull over to the side of the road, and I don't know if it's this strange disease working its way through my brain or the forty-year anniversary of Mary leaving or your father's birthday or something else, but as soon as the car settles in place on the shoulder and I put it in park, I weep. I've gone from laughing harder than I can remember to all-out ugly crying. I lean forward and put my forehead on the steering wheel.

I hear the click of your seat belt and feel your small hand on my shoulder. Your forehead lands gently on my back. Your little arm slinks around me. "Grampy."

"Yes, Pearl?"

"I really do think you'd be much happier if you married Ms. Pena."

And with that you turn our tears into laughter. I start first, my shoulders shaking. I wipe my nose on my sleeve, and you shout, "Ew!" That makes me laugh even harder.

"Grampy, I'm serious about Ms. Pena."

There's a little pinprick of pain at the future that this diagnosis has stolen from me. I try to say, "I know you are," but I can't stop laughing, and soon you're laughing too. I put the car back in drive, and you scooch over and hastily put on your seat belt. I'm still laughing, gently this time, persistently. Shaking my head, I pull out onto the road.

"You are something, Pearl," I say.

You give me a look that says you know precisely what you are and precisely what you are doing, and that I shouldn't worry because you'll take care of me for as long as I live. Even if it's only anytime to three months.

I should tell you about the diagnosis. I reach up and touch the knot again, thinking this is how an old tree must feel when its trunk begins to rot. I decide that some things can wait a little longer.

"Ms. Pena, huh?" I ask.

"You are very lonely, Grampy."

"Lonely?"

"You're home all day by yourself! You don't have anyone to paint with or read to or play at the park with."

"I have you," I say. The uncontrolled laughter from a few

minutes ago has cut a path into a kind of lightness, a sense that even when facing the worst, there is something shining.

"Not during the day. Do you think she's pretty?" you ask.

"I told you, I think she's beautiful."

"I think she's beautiful too. So are you going to ask her out?"

"Pearl, this is what I've been trying to tell you. We're leaving."

"I know."

"We're going back to where I grew up," I continue. "I don't know when we'll come back."

You are very quiet after that, and miles pass by before I finally ask if you're okay.

You nod.

The Man in the Hotel

We hit a lot of traffic on the highway and pull into a hotel late at night. I considered driving straight through, but we'd arrive in Nysa in the wee hours of the morning, and I want to see it as we drive in. I want you to see the river and the trees and the fields, because I know you'll fall in love with it as soon as you do.

Besides, after so many miles behind us, it feels good to stop, stand up out of the seat, and stretch. You come around the car looking tired and worn but also happy. You are excited about the hotel and sleeping in a room where you can watch TV while you drift off, excited about room service even though I have made no promises.

We walk stiffly into the lobby and up to the counter. It's not a glitzy, upper-crust hotel, but it's not a dump either. There is a small breakfast room off to the side, and an old man sits in a chair reading the paper. A TV is on in that room, volume turned up, but the man goes on reading as if nothing is going on and the angry voice radiating through the room is nothing more than an imaginary buzzing in the ear. The carpet is tan, the walls are a darker tan, and the ceiling is white, but time has stained it a certain shade of tan. There is nothing remarkable about this place, not in the slightest. Which is fine with me, as long as the bed is comfortable.

But still it gives me a strange feeling, as most hotels in small towns do when the hour is late and the space feels vacant. The hallway from the lobby seems miles long, and at the very end of it one of the lights in the ceiling flickers for a few moments and goes out.

The woman behind the desk smiles, and I think I see her eyes flit to the side of my head, to the bulge of the knot. I self-consciously rub it lightly, then drop my hand back down again, because trying to hide it seems more conspicuous than pretending it's not there.

"How may I help you?" the woman asks.

I give her my information, and as we wait for keys, the old man who was reading the paper stands up and comes walking over. The top of his head is bald, surrounded by a fringe of bristling white hair. His eyes purse together in a permanent squint—he is skeptical of what someone might say before they even say it. He licks his lips constantly, nervously, and they glisten.

I think he's going to walk past, but he stops behind us, puts his fingers in each of his pockets, and loops his thumbs around the outside. I glance at him over my shoulder, and he takes me in with a discerning frown.

"Not from around here." His voice is gravelly, his eyes hawkish.

I shake my head, but before I can get a word out, you turn around and declare that no, we are not from around here.

His gaze turns to you, and something in him softens, though he tries to hide it.

"And who is this?" he asks no one in particular, looking around the room. When he talks, it's like he's speaking to an invisible person, someone behind me.

"I'm Pearl," you tell him, walking over to him with three large strides and offering your hand. "And you are?"

Now you've completely unsettled him. He reaches a hand forward hesitantly, as if concerned you might have a communicable disease.

"Yes, yes," he says in a quiet voice to himself, and as you take his hand and pump it vigorously, he tells you his name.

"Pearl," I whisper in a gentle correction. "Not so hard."

But the old man has clearly turned the corner into being amused. His eyes still squint, but there is a glint of mischief in them. "What brings someone like you to this place in the middle of nowhere?" he asks you.

"Someone like me?" you ask abruptly, in an accusatory tone.

"Someone small," he mumbles. "Someone glittery."

You laugh and say, "My Grampy. He's going back to the town where he was born. And he's taking me with him, to show me around. We might stay there forever."

I wince, but I'm not sure why. Your honesty is sharp.

"That's a good Grampy," the old man says with astonishment. "And what town is that?"

"It's a small town," I interject. "I'm sure you haven't heard of it." But you jump in, as you always do.

"There's a lake and a cabin," you say, excitement flashing in your eyes. "Right, Grampy?"

I nod.

The man finally turns toward me. "Try me."

"I'm sorry?"

"Try me. Where are you from?"

"Nysa," I say. "We still have a little ways to go."

He frowns to himself, nodding. "I know Nysa. Anyone within a hundred miles of Nysa's heard of the place."

"Really?" I ask. That seems strange to me. When I was younger and we left town, we didn't have to go far before finding people who had never heard of Nysa their entire lives.

"It's a wonderful place," you say. "I drew a map of it."

"That's not what I heard," he mumbles.

"What have you heard?" I ask, curious.

"Oh, all sorts of odd things. Something about the lake. Drownings. Heard recently the whole place is basically a ghost town."

"No," you insist, your voice chirpy and innocent. "Nysa is wonderful. A friend told me about it."

"Your Grampy?"

"No, a different friend. Besides, Grampy's not my friend. He's my Grampy."

"Of course," he says, suddenly serious, but in that mock-serious tone that adults take with children. "Who is this friend?"

I sigh. Here we go.

"A woman with silver-white hair came to me and told me where to put everything on the map. Well, not everything. Some of the things she asked me to put on. She's very nice. She cares very much about me and Grampy. And she needs my help. She lost something very important to her, and I'm going to help her find it."

The man's expression changes from whimsical to serious. His squint sets in. "Did you say a woman with silver-white hair came to you?"

You nod.

"She came to you, just like that?"

You nod again, clearly delighted at this conversation.

"Did she have a name?"

You think about it. "I don't think she told me her name," you finally reply.

"Did she . . ." the old man begins, his voice unsteady. He glances at the door, then back at us. "Did she come with you here, to the hotel?"

"No," I say in a flat voice. "She did not."

You give me that cute little glare. "Grampy," you mutter before addressing the old man. "No, she didn't come with us. But she said she would meet me there, in Grampy's hometown. In Nysa."

I sigh. You turn and glare at me again—my clear disregard for the existence of the woman is ruining the story. I nearly say, *She isn't real*, but I bite my tongue.

"Would you both be so kind as to join me for breakfast? Seven o'clock sharp?" the old man asks in a hesitant, distant sort of voice.

I'm inclined to turn down the offer. I've been very tired lately, probably because of the disease sprouting a knot on my head, and besides, I'm not one to visit with strangers. A polite hello is usually as far as I allow such interactions to progress. But once again, before I can speak, you interject.

"It would be our pleasure." You give him a half curtsy.

I nearly groan, but now the old man is walking off, and you turn your face up to me.

"Pearl," I begin, but the woman behind the desk says my name. I turn, and she gives us our room key while listing the amenities. We pick up our travel bags and head to the elevator, all the way up to the sixth floor. We find our room and settle in, and although you have been so eager to watch television from your bed, within minutes you're asleep.

I stay up for another hour or so. All the lights in our room are turned off. I pull the desk chair over to the window and stare up at the stars, take in the acres and acres of forest we drove through to get this far, and imagine the trees shifting in the wind, their shadows swaying.

I can't stop thinking about what the man said about Nysa. Drownings?

I had only ever heard of two.

Driving Away

Tom and Shirley and Mary and I became inseparable, spending afternoons and evenings anywhere but in our houses. Tom was the first to get his driver's license, and that opened up a new world of exploration for us. How many nights did we drive long into the darkness, Shirley leaning her head against Tom's shoulder while he drove, Mary leaning her head against mine in the back seat, our fingers entangled? How many times did we stop and park somewhere, take blankets up on the roof of Tom's old car, tuck ourselves in against the cold, and stare at the stars?

"What's up, old boy?" Tom asked me on a warm summer morning. It was around eight months after the four of us had first met, sometime in June. My life was unrecognizable when compared to what it had been like before those friends swept in and pulled me out of my lonely existence. I felt like I was finally awake to life.

Tom stood over my bed, shaking me by the shoulder. He had taken to calling me "old boy." I can't remember where the phrase had come up, although we had recently read *The*

Great Gatsby in school, and I have a feeling it was his version of "old sport."

"What are you doing?" I groaned, rolling over to face the wall.

Tom pulled the covers off. "We're going out to the lake today. Did you forget?"

I sighed. I had forgotten.

"C'mon, old boy."

I made some other sound of protest, but the truth was, I was ready to wake up. Thoughts of Mary filled my head constantly. Everything I saw reminded me of her, and when I closed my eyes, her face was there, offering that same bashful, hopeful grin.

"Don't call me that," I said as I put my feet down beside the bed.

Tom laughed. "Okay, old boy."

Within a few minutes, Tom and I were in his car, windows down, the morning air fresh and new and warming up. Everything smelled like it did in the summer on a day that would soon be extremely hot. Tom's face was sleepy and happy and free, everything you'd expect to find on the face of a teenager who was in the middle of discovering life and all it might have to offer. I laughed and punched him in the shoulder. He only grinned harder. I put my arm on the window, leaned my head into the rushing stream of air, and closed my eyes.

In that moment, life was perfect.

We picked up Shirley first. She gave Tom a peck on the cheek before climbing into the back seat, over my protests.

"I want to talk to Mary," she said, "not be the passenger in between you and Tom gabbing."

"Hey!" Tom protested, but he winked at her in the rear-view mirror, and she laughed.

"Where are we going, anyway?" I asked.

"The lake," Tom said.

"I know that. But where?"

He laughed. "It's a surprise, old boy."

"What?" Shirley exclaimed, sounding genuinely offended.

"Whoa, whoa, easy now," Tom said. "Don't worry, babe. You're going to love it."

I glanced back at Shirley, and she crossed her arms in mock protest. It didn't last long though. Sullenness never clung to Shirley.

Five minutes later we stopped in front of Mary's house. Tom beeped the horn once, and Shirley slapped the back of his seat.

"Thomas Avery James, are you kidding me?" she snapped, glaring at me—I could feel it.

"You'll make quite a mother someday, Shirley," I said.

"You get up to that door this instant and ring that bell like a proper gentleman."

"Okay, okay," I mumbled reluctantly. I climbed out of the car, turned toward them, and raised my arms in surrender. But by the time I was halfway up the sidewalk, Mary came through the door. I stopped in my tracks. She was a vision.

"Hey, Mary," I said, my voice running away from me.

"Hey, Paul," she said with her customary bashful look, eyes flitting here and there.

"You're real pretty today," I managed to choke out.

"Paul!" she exclaimed, red rushing up her neck. She pushed her hair out of her eyes, smiled, and shoved me away playfully, then trotted to the rear passenger-side door and climbed in. I followed her and got back into the passenger seat.

"Where are we going?" Mary asked, rolling down her window.

I wished I was sitting in the back seat with her. I noticed she was glancing nervously at her house. "Let's go, Tom," I said.

"Okay, okay, old boy. Relax," he said, putting the car in gear.

"It's a surprise." Shirley rolled her eyes, saying "surprise" like it was the most fake word in the world.

For some reason, Tom didn't pull away. He was lost in his thoughts, or something else, but as we sat there for an extra moment, I could see Mary getting more and more uncomfortable.

"What's up, Tom?" I asked. "Let's go."

"Tom," Shirley insisted from the back seat. "C'mon."

Out of nowhere, Mary shouted, "Go!" and there was panic in her voice.

Tom jumped out of his reverie and looked at Mary like she had lost her mind. Shirley and I were stunned, not knowing what to do. I turned toward Mary to see what would cause her to cry out like that, and she was staring out of her window with fear in her eyes.

"Go, Tom. Please go," she whispered.

"For goodness' sake, Tom," Shirley said, her voice quiet and flighty and trembling. "Mary said go."

I turned to Tom to tell him to put his foot down, but as I did, he took off, and my head flew back against the seat. The sound of gravel pinging the underside of the car blended with the sound of the air rushing in the windows.

Tom drove at breakneck speed for at least two miles, winding precariously along the back roads between the edge of town and the lake. But before we had gone too far, he hooted a loud cry of freedom.

"How about that, old boy!" he said, laughing.

I grinned. "What were you waiting for?" I asked, but his laugh was contagious, and soon I was laughing too. I heard Shirley giggle.

How easily we forget things when we are young. How quickly we move from one moment to the next. Our laughter rang out, and we basked in the sunshine, the warm air, the empty, open roads. We weren't thinking about Mary's unfounded fear anymore, or the silver-haired woman she had seen in the shadows the previous Halloween. We weren't worried about the future or the past or anything outside of that moment in the car, racing through summer. We were young and in love and had made our way out into the world, out where no one could stop us.

But what had she seen? I was young and careless. I never asked, though now, years later, I could probably guess.

"So where are we going?" I asked Tom again.

"It's a surprise, old boy!" he shouted, pressing on the accelerator once more.

Gone Again

I wake up and the hotel room is still dark, but there is a glow around the heavy curtains, so I know I slept later than I wanted to. I sit up in the darkness, rub my eyes, clear my throat. Instinctively, as I have done every morning for the last three months or so, I reach up and gently touch the knot on my head. It feels harder this morning. It feels like it has taken root.

There have been times when the knot makes me feel almost claustrophobic, desperate to rid myself of it. When it was smaller, I considered shaving it off with a razor—anything to flatten that side of my head back to normal. Recently, as it grew, I considered shooting it off.

Yes, I know.

But you have always kept me here.

Thinking of you, I look over at your bed. Strange, because in the darkness your bed appears empty, but that must be because of the way the dim light flattens out the blankets. You must be hidden in there somewhere. I reach over and turn on the light. "Pearl?"

But you're not there. Your map sits on the desk, partly

unrolled. I put my feet down on the rough carpet, stand, walk quickly to the bathroom. You're not there either. I open the door to our room wide enough so that I can stick my head out and look down the long hall. I don't see you anywhere.

"Pearl," I say again, this time with exasperation. You don't make anything easy.

When I pull back into the room, something is different. The darkness feels heavy, loaded with something that makes me walk quickly to the windows and pull back the curtains. The light erupts, pushing back the shadows. But still, the room makes me feel like a foreigner, like I'm staying somewhere I'm not welcome.

Your shoes are by the bed, side by side. I sweep the blankets away, wondering if it's possible I overlooked you, if the bed is so soft that you are still there, sunken into the mattress. But no. The bed is empty.

I throw on some clothes, slip on my shoes, and get ready to leave the room. But a wave of nausea hits so heavy that I bend over inside the door and feel my whole body tense. I dash back into the bathroom, bend over the toilet, and throw up, over and over again, without stopping.

Finally, I wipe my mouth with a small hand towel and throw it in the trash. I stare into the toilet, because there it is, a small thread of ruby-red blood among the vomit, and other threads of black. My breath is taken away with how long I might have. One less day than I had yesterday. One day closer to the end of my anytime to three months.

I clean up and go out in search of you, feeling unsteady. The long hallway is quiet and still, which seems strange for this hour of the morning. Shouldn't people be up and around? Shouldn't parents be herding children to the continental breakfast or businesspeople be moving efficiently on the cheap carpet, their roller bags leaving small tracks behind them?

The emptiness of the hallway is unnerving.

I turn the corner, and at first all I notice is the empty lobby. There isn't even anyone at the reception desk, so I pause. I reach up and touch the knot on my head. Decidedly bigger.

I see the old man we met the night before sitting at a table for two, and you across from him, listening intently while eating a piece of toast. I walk over.

"Pearl," I say in a firm voice.

You seem surprised, like I was the last person on earth you expected to find there that morning in that hotel, in that small dining area, surrounded by the smell of bacon and biscuits and waffles. "Hi, Grampy," you say, and there is nothing defensive in your voice, nothing ill at ease. You clearly have no clue that I am ready to give you a stern talking-to.

The old man turns and looks at me dismissively, only nodding the briefest of acknowledgments.

"Where have you been?" I ask you.

"What?"

"Where have you been?" I ask again, quieter this time, slower. "When I woke up and you weren't there, I was worried."

"I thought we had agreed to meet here," you say. "For breakfast. At seven a.m."

"Yes, but you're eleven years old. You shouldn't walk around on your own in a strange place."

The old man turns and gives me a look that clearly communicates, *What's wrong with you, mister?*

I shake my head. I grab a chair from a neighboring table and pull it over, but the old man stands, gathers his things.

"You two go ahead," he says, his morning voice scratchy. "I should be getting on."

I don't say anything, not even when you get up, walk around the table, and give him a hug, the kind where you wrap yourself close and hold on for an extra moment. Tears gather in the man's eyes. He clears his throat, pries himself away, and walks out the front door.

"Pearl," I begin, but to be honest, I don't know what to say to you. These kinds of things—you disappearing or running off or leaving for hours at a time—have been going on for so long that I've given up on reforming you in any way. So I change direction. "How was breakfast?"

You smile as you sit down. "He's seen the woman too. The one helping me with my map," you say, focusing on your toast while you talk. "That's why he's afraid."

"The woman?" I ask.

You nod.

"The one you've been seeing at school? And in the building in the alley?"

You nod again. "The one who helped me with the map, the one who needs my help," you say again, insinuating that I am clearly not operating on all brain cells. "But I told him not to be afraid. There's really nothing to be afraid of."

I think of the woman Mary started seeing, first on that Halloween night in the field, then over and over again after that. But I don't know what to say to you. Could something like that be genetic? Can visions pass from one generation to the next, like black eyes or arthritis?

I go get a cup of coffee and sit back down at the table.

"Are you excited to go home?" you ask me, light in your eyes.

I give a wry grin. "I don't know," I say, and it's true. The closer we get to my old hometown, the more questions I have about why I thought this was the thing to do, why I thought this was a good idea. I think again about what the old man said. Drownings. Ghost town.

"Well," you say, "I can't wait."

I'm glad. But your visions of the woman have unsettled me. I can't help but wonder if this time she has come for me.

No Trespassing

Tom's driving slowed uncharacteristically, and I glanced at him to see what was going on. In the back, Mary had fallen asleep, her head on Shirley's lap, and Shirley's head nodded as she drifted off. It was only thirty minutes or so after we had left Mary's house.

"I know it's here somewhere," Tom mumbled to himself, sitting up straight in the driver's seat, his eyes scanning the woods on either side of the back road we were on.

"What's here?" I asked.

But he refused to say. When I was ready to make some kind of threatening statement about boxing his ears if he didn't tell me what was going on, his eyes lit up, and he fell back into his seat with relief.

"There it is," he said. And somehow the simple proclamation woke Mary and Shirley. Both of them stuck their heads into the area between the front seats. I could smell Mary's shampoo, and I closed my eyes, took it in. I thought I might collapse under the weight of my infatuation.

"There's what?" Shirley asked, and that's when I saw the

break in the trees and the metal livestock gate blocking the way, and on it a sign: "No Trespassing."

There was enough length of driveway between the shoulder and the gate so that Tom could pull off the winding back road, get out, and walk over to the chain that held the gate closed. He wiggled his eyebrows up and down at us, the way he always did when he knew something spectacular that we weren't yet privileged enough to know, and proceeded to untangle the chain from the gate.

"What is he doing?" Mary asked.

"Just Tom being Tom." Shirley sighed. She leaned her head out through her window. "Tom, what in the world are you doing? You're going to get us all arrested."

But Tom kept at it until the length of chain was pulled clear of the gate. There wasn't even a lock. He walked the gate open and propped a rock against it, then came back. He hopped into his seat energetically.

"This is it," he said, and the sound of victory was in his voice.

He pulled far enough forward so that he had room to close the gate behind us, and I watched through the back window as he wrapped the chain all around the gate and the post. He ran back to the car, and I thought he was going to drive us farther down the lane, but instead he reached in and fished around under his seat, eventually pulling out a large padlock with a key sticking out of it. He removed the key and held up the lock.

"Just in case," he said, grinning. He ran back and clicked the lock in place. No one could follow us, at least not in a vehicle. They could climb the gate easily enough, but when he attached that lock onto the chain, it felt like he was blocking out the entire world.

I glanced at Mary—she was also watching Tom lock the gate—and I thought I caught a small glimpse of the anxiety she had shown at her house, as if Tom barring the way with a locked gate somehow wasn't enough.

He drove carefully down the rutted lane, and the trees pressed in close on each side. We drove for about five minutes, the car heaving this way and that, the occasional branch reaching out and screeching along the length of the car. We were all quiet—we knew that any question we asked would be answered with Tom's cryptic, "You'll see," or maybe we didn't want him to tell us. We were holding our breath, wanting to discover this new and fabulous thing together.

We came around the last corner and there was the lake, a flat slate gray under the light blue Saturday morning sky. Farther up the lane, perilously close to the water, rose a kind of cabin—two stories clad in dark wood with oversized windows and a long back porch that reached out over the gentle waves. I could see the dock from there too, a long, straight line into the water.

"Wow," Shirley said in a hushed voice.

Mary stared at the house, her eyes bright.

"Whose place is this?" I asked.

Tom smiled, shrugged. "Ours, I guess."

"Thomas Avery!" Shirley exclaimed. "Have you lost your mind?"

"Whoa!" Tom said, and his laugh made Shirley even more disgusted with him.

"You can't take over houses," Shirley spat. "Not even if they're abandoned. And in fabulous locations."

"Well, if you would listen once in a while, I'd have a chance to talk," Tom said.

Shirley's eyes squinted as if she was trying to pierce through him with her gaze.

Tom laughed again. "Geez, Shirls. This is my family's place!"

"No way!" I exclaimed.

"No way," Shirley said matter-of-factly, the voice of reason.

"It is," Tom replied, shrugging. "It is. My grandparents built it like fifty years ago. All their kids moved away from this crazy town—I guess they had more sense than us. All of them except my mom. And she hates the wilderness. And places without air-conditioning. My dad too. Their last idea of a relaxing weekend is coming out here and chopping wood and clearing the driveway and cleaning off the dock."

Shirley's defenses seemed to be crumbling.

"C'mon," Tom said.

Into Nysa

The morning drive is long and slow and sleepy, and you drift in and out beside me in the passenger seat. Out of nowhere, the bridge to Nysa appears. I had lost track of where we were, my mind wandering through all of these long years, and then the bridge emerges, rising up above the tree line. It's a lumpy old arc of metal and concrete, but I have to admit that seeing it brings a tear to these old eyes. I reach up and touch the knot. I look over at you. You have been sleeping for at least an hour.

"Pearl," I whisper almost reverently. "Pearl. Wake up. We're almost at the bridge."

You yawn and stretch, your limbs unfurling like one of those fiddlehead ferns in time-lapse, and you rub your eyes. "Where are we?"

"We're nearly at the bridge that goes over to Nysa," I say, and we drift off the exit and make a right onto the simple two-lane road that leads toward the bridge.

The forest in those parts is dense and dark, so when we drive down the exit ramp and off the highway it is like we are submerging underwater. You, however, rise. You press your nose against the window, and I can see a mini caldera of steam form on the glass. We drive through the deep shadows, and sharp flashes of light fall through gaps in the trees. I put my window down a few inches, and I can smell the water. I feel suddenly like I'm home. It's been forty years since I felt this way.

We arrive at the bridge, begin driving up its long span, and the whole sky opens up. There is one lonely boat droning its way upriver, to the left and away from us, its hull smacking the water over and over. I have such a strong longing to be in that boat, to feel the spray, the sun, the almost violent up-and-down movement, being tossed, to close my eyes and smile at the expanse of the river.

You turn downriver, looking to our right, your face open to every possibility offered to us by the wide world. We get to the top of the bridge and begin another descent, this one down onto this strange terrain, this Nysa. The forest that waits for us on the far side of the bridge is even more dense than what we've already driven through, if that's possible, and far beyond those trees I can see the flat expanse of farmers' fields, but I can't yet see the small town. I can imagine it. I can see it how it used to be, forty years ago.

Strangely enough, so far nothing has changed. Yes, the bridge is crumbling, the cement barriers missing chunks, the pavement cracked and pockmarked. I had prepared myself on the drive for developed land, perhaps mansions along the river with their own docks slicing the water and cell phone towers rising through the trees. But the woods are exactly as I remember them, the river the same, the sky as endless as it ever was. I can easily imagine that I am eighteen again.

You retreat down into your seat so that you're almost prone. You look surprised, taken aback.

"Pearl, what is it?"

You lift your head slowly and peek back through the passenger-side window, and it sounds like you might be crying.

"Pearl," I say again.

You look at me, and now the disbelief, the amazement, is clear. When you talk, your words come in whispers.

"Why didn't you tell me?" you ask.

"Tell you what?"

"It's so sad here. So sad."

You turn, facing straight ahead, and I experience a flash of memory, the quickest vision. I was approaching the bridge again but driving the other way. Leaving. Your father was only a couple weeks old, and he was in a kind of bassinet wedged into the floor space in front of the passenger seat. That was in the days before car seats. He was crying, his voice raspy and dry. And I was driving as fast as I could.

The trees had felt heavy, and they leaned in over us as we approached the bridge, but your father and I made it into the clear air, rising up onto the bridge. As we entered into that bright daylight, the sun streaming in, I rolled down my window and felt the warm breeze, smelled the fresh air. Immediately, your father stopped crying and fell asleep.

In the rearview mirror I saw the forest churning, a green so dark it was nearly black, the shadows boiling up over the surface of the treetops. I felt an immense amount of relief that day, leaving Nysa with your father.

As if we had barely escaped.

We are across the bridge now, down among the trees, and

I pull over onto the shoulder of the road, the trees so close you could roll down your window and stroke the bark if you wanted. But you are still crouched in your seat, quivering now, whispering to yourself.

"Pearl," I whisper. "Pearl." I reach over and hold on to your shoulder, and my touch seems to ground you somehow.

You reach up and hold my hand in place, swallow hard, and nod, saying to me without words—reassuring me—that you can do this thing.

"Pearl," I say again, this time a little louder. "This place . . ."

I look away from you, across the street, into the woods on the other side. Everything is still. I see a single leaf fall from one of the trees and spin, fluttering, all the way down until it rests on the road. Nothing else moves. There are no cars.

"This is a good place," I say, trying not to sound like I'm convincing myself. "It can be a lonely, dark place, yes. It can be sad. But there are good people here." *People who could take care of you*, I want to say.

"It's okay," you say, your voice trembling. "It's okay, Grampy. I know."

"It's kind of scary," I admit. "But that's probably because you grew up in the city. You're not used to these wide-open spaces, not yet. Or all the trees—they can crowd in on you sometimes, if you're not familiar with them. But you'll get there. You'll love it, Pearl. I know you will. You'll be playing in these trees soon. And there are streams and fields and even a beach. I'll take you there. You'll see."

You nod again.

"Pearl, what's wrong?"

But for the first time in a long time, you refuse to say. You shake your head, purse your lips. After I try to press you for information one more time, you shake your head in tiny, quick jerks. "It's okay, Grampy. It's okay."

I pull back onto the road and close my window, the silence between us like an extra passenger in the car. I know you well enough to know that you saw something you didn't expect. This isn't a surprise—you've been seeing things like that since you were a little girl.

What's surprising to me is that you don't want to talk about it. You have always been eager to tell me about your latest imaginary encounter. You have always gone on and on about the things you see, the inexplicable friends, the fairies, the mythical creatures bounding along the skyline of our small city.

The road turns in a sweeping motion to the left, and as I glance in the rearview mirror, the light from where we came down the bridge vanishes. All around us is nothing but the dark wood. In front of us, the road is worn and crumbling. There are no lines. I know the woods will give way any minute—soon we'll be in farmland, out in the wide-open day. I hope you'll be okay once we get into the light.

I drive faster.

No Cares in the World

We'll fix the place up," Tom said in a convincing voice as we stood inside the front door, taking in the dust and the animal droppings and the cobwebs. But there was such unguarded optimism in his voice, such hope lifting his face, that the three of us couldn't say otherwise. "All the inside needs is a good cleaning and a little paint. We can tear out the old carpet—it's wood floors underneath. I checked it all out. It'll be fun."

"A good cleaning?" Shirley asked skeptically.

"You'll see," he said. "You'll see."

"I bet it gets hot here during the day," I said. The midday heat made it hard to breathe inside the house, although the open front door did let in some air.

"Thus the lake," Tom said, laughing. "And the nights are cool. We can sleep on the porch."

"I think it sounds wonderful," Mary said almost breathlessly. "Can we stay here all summer?"

Tom laughed again, and this time it was completely unreserved. "That's the spirit, Mary."

"What's the alibi?" I asked.

"What do you mean?" Shirley asked.

"If we're going to stay here all summer," I said to Tom, "what do I tell my parents?"

He shrugged. "School trip? You're working at a summer camp in Connecticut? Me and you are heading out for the summer before our senior year?"

"I don't know."

"So pick one they will go for, Paul! I'm telling my parents I'm taking a road trip—not exactly a lie. This is the chance of a lifetime. The four of us! No cares in the world!"

You Should Turn Around

*T*he roads are all the same.

I keep thinking this over and over, almost in disbelief. *The roads are all the same.*

The same old curves, the same pin-straight stretches, the same farmers' lanes (although some are overgrown now), the same winding streams and narrow, one-lane bridges that span them. There is the steep dip on South Creek Road and the nonsensical winding on Old Schoolhouse Lane. I laugh to myself. I could drive these roads all day. But it is noon now, and we need to find some lunch and a place to stay.

Galen's gas station is still here. I can hardly believe it. I pull into a parking space and sit there. You seem relieved.

"You okay?" I ask.

"I feel better now."

I'm not sure what to say to that, so I reminisce out loud. "This old gas station was here when I was a kid. Forty years ago. Used to be run by a man named Galen. He was so big he used the garage doors to come and go out of the gas station. He didn't fit through the normal door."

I shake my head in wonder. This does take a man back.

I catch some movement out of the corner of my eye, and I feel a chill race through my body. A very large man shuffles across the pavement.

Galen?

But as he gets closer I can see it's not quite him. It couldn't be him, anyway. This man is much too young, seems to be about my age. Galen would be in his eighties or nineties by now.

He taps on the window and I roll it down. His eyes squint suspiciously. "Help you?" he asks. He wears a limp ball cap pulled down low, the shadow hiding his eyes.

"Do you know Galen?" I ask.

His squint deepens, grows shadows. "Who's askin'?"

"I'm Paul Elias. I'm from here. From Nysa. Grew up here, anyway."

"Paul," he says, and it comes out in a deep croak. He stands up as straight as he can and pulls a pack of cigarettes from his back pocket. He slaps the small box four or five times against his meaty hands and twitches the pack so that one peeks out. A lighter emerges from his sagging pockets. He lights, inhales, and exhales my name.

"Paullllll." He scowls to himself before asking, "What year'd you graduate?"

Smoke clouds out of every hole in his head like there is some inner fire.

"Seventy-nine."

He shakes his head. "I was a year behind you. Can't say I recall your face."

"Does Galen still own this place?"

"Galen was my pop. Guess he still is, but he's dead now. Has been for six years."

"I'm sorry."

"That's life," he says, and the squint returns. "Why'd you come back?"

"This is my granddaughter." I gesture over to you. "I wanted her to see the place where I grew up."

He grunts, seems to communicate that this is perhaps the dumbest thing he has ever heard.

"Doesn't seem like it's changed much," I say hesitantly. "The old town still the same?"

"When did you leave Nysa?"

"Right after graduation," I say, not wanting to get into the details.

"Summer of '79?" he asks.

I nod.

"You really haven't been back, have you?" he asks.

I shake my head.

"Some things happened back in the day . . ."

"Things?"

"Things," he says, and that word is like a period, ending that conversation. "You need some gas?"

"Sure," I say, though we have half a tank. I turn the car back on and pull in front of the pump. I move to get out, but he has already shuffled over.

"I gotcha," he says, waving me back into my car. "I gotcha."

Galen's son is pumping my gas. We probably went to school together, but I don't remember him. Everything about this feels so odd. I think of the old man's words from the hotel—it does feel like a ghost town. I realize I haven't passed a single car since we came over the bridge.

I hear the loud click of a full tank. He tells me the total.

"You take cards?"

His mouth scrunches up, twists, and he jerks his head back and to the side. "Inside," he mumbles.

I turn to tell you that I'm going in to pay and see you've fallen asleep. Across the street from the gas station is a field. There's a house in the distance, though I can't see the road that goes to it. A grove of trees wraps around the gas station on three sides. I decide to leave you. I lock the doors.

Inside, he swipes my card four times before it works. When he hands me the receipt, he says something I don't understand at first.

"I'm sorry?" I say, signing the receipt.

"This place isn't no good no more," he says in a nonchalant voice that doesn't seem to go with the message.

"I'm sorry?" I say again.

He squints at me again. "Nysa," he begins, but his words devolve into mutters. "You know, when we were kids, this was a good place to be. The town was hopping. Community. Stuff like that. The little fair that came around in the fall."

I smile and nod.

"Not anymore. Stopped coming. Not enough people. And things happened out by the lake. Bad things. Around the time you left, and it hasn't stopped since. Don't go out there."

He stands there as if he's waiting for something from me, but I already paid. Everything is so quiet. Through one of the back windows I can see a squirrel jumping from limb to limb and then climbing onto an old barrel. From there it scampers into the shadows.

"You really should turn around, head out," he says again. "I would if I were you."

Our gazes meet, and there's a sadness in his eyes, and regret.

"I think we'll check out the town," I say hesitantly.

"It's all dead, Nysa. The whole island. Nothing's left." He clears his throat.

I decide to pretend he never gave me this advice. "We need a place to stay. Anything downtown?"

"Downtown?" he asks in a husky voice, taking out his pack of cigarettes and going through the same routine as before. "Downtown?" Now he's laughing through the smoke.

"No motels?"

"None suitable for a kid, 'specially not a little girl," he says.

"What about the old Highway Inn?"

"Like I said."

"So there's nothing?" I ask, skeptical. It's a long drive back over the bridge, south on the highway. The last hotel we passed was a good hour away.

But even more discouraging is that I am beginning to doubt my entire premise. I had hoped, perhaps unreasonably, that Nysa had grown into a certain quaintness, that the gentrification I railed about in the city might have positively impacted our small town, our small island even. I thought mansions would line the lakefront. All I'm seeing so far is a crumbling place, a place left behind by the rest of the world, and it gives me an aching sense of loss.

What if there is nothing here for you?

I shake it off. I'm making this judgment based on Galen's son and what he's telling me from a gas station outside of town. I rediscover my optimism.

"Thanks anyway," I say, turning to go. I stop. "I didn't get your name."

"Junior," he says. "Just Junior."

On the way to the car, I panic. What if you ran while I was inside? Where would I even begin to search?

But there you are, still asleep, your hair pushed flat against the glass.

I climb in and turn the car toward town.

When Everything Started Happening

The two-lane road widens into three as we enter town, the middle being a turning lane, and you are staring out the passenger-side window again, your fingers on the ledge, your nose against the glass. An old Chevy pickup passes us, going in the opposite direction, out into the countryside. The driver appears to be in his sixties, white tufts of hair slanting out from under a green baseball cap. He stares straight ahead, doesn't even make eye contact with me as our cars pass.

Driving through town feels like an out-of-body experience. Everything is arranged precisely as I had left it forty years ago. On the right is the tire store and the small grocery and the in-town gas station that is Junior's only competition. The Nysa Diner is on the corner of Main Street and North Bay Road, which runs north to south, all the way up the island. There are other small shops and offices at the intersection, but the buildings thin quickly to either side of Main.

It's the same but different. Nothing seems to be taken

care of as it used to be—the weeds are high in the alleys and even in some places along the street, the roads themselves are rutted and pockmarked, and I can't tell if the Nysa Diner is open. I try to think of some kind of explanation or apology for the state of things, but you're still staring through the glass.

"We should grab some lunch," I say. "Hungry?"

You nod, and your skin makes a squeaking noise against the glass. I eye the diner warily, but there's nothing else close. There is the seafood place at the southern end of Nysa, and somewhere between here and there is a burger joint. Was a burger joint. It was in a terrible state of deterioration even when I was a kid, so if it has followed in the footsteps of the rest of Nysa, it is probably nothing more than a pile of dust.

Again, I am overwhelmed when I think about why I'm here. Finding you a home feels less and less likely. For the hundredth time since my diagnosis, I wish Mary was here. I would feel completely at peace with dying if I knew she could watch over you.

But would I? If she was here, would I be so willing to say goodbye to this old lump of dirt circling the sun? And if she was here, would your parents have even met? Would you even be here? Now that's a sobering thought. If Mary hadn't left me on that day long ago, your father's life would have been so different. Would we have ever left Nysa? Would your father ever have met your mother and vanished? Would your mother have overdosed? It's hard to imagine the endless twists and turns in life that would be different if Mary hadn't left.

I pull into the diner's parking lot and turn off the car.

You give a half smile and climb out. I shake my head, weariness from the drive weighing on my eyes. I see you in the rearview mirror, walking up to the door of the diner like an adult going in for a table for one. I rub my eyes.

Some food and a good night's sleep will make all the difference, I think, racking my brain for reasons the town feels so empty. It's a weekend—perhaps everyone has gone to the coast or is taking the day off of work. That's it. It's quiet because everyone is off work or off school, and most of these businesses are probably closed for the day.

I follow you into the diner, and again I find myself disoriented, unable to tell between past and present. A cowbell rings quaintly above the door. The same old bar with the same old bar stools. The afternoon air inside the place has a slow feel to it. Two men sit with their elbows on the bar, a mug of black coffee in front of each of them. One man wears eyeglasses with dark lenses and a John Deere ball cap. The other man is dressed more professionally, wearing a collared shirt with the top two buttons undone and a tie that's been loosened so much it resembles a noose. They both swing their heads and look at me when I walk in, size me up, and go back to staring at their open newspapers.

The booths are tucked up against the wall, and the large sheets of glass that make up the upper half of the outer wall let warm sunshine in. A handwritten sign propped on a folding table says, "Please Seat Yourself," and beside the sign is a large pile of sticky notes made specifically for the diner with a watermark on each page: "Nysa Diner." I see that you've taken a booth in the far corner, the same one the four of us always used to sit in. Of course you did.

I walk over and sit down. The booth's seats have that

same brittle plastic feeling. There is a jukebox between us and the server's area behind the bar, but I can see the cord has been unplugged and the selector buttons are coated in dust.

A waitress comes out from the kitchen, the door swinging behind her. She's about my age, I think, wearing jeans and a red T-shirt. Her gray hair is pulled up in a ponytail, and she speaks through a throat tuned by years of cigarette smoking. She drops a few sticky menus down on the table in between us.

"You ever plug that old thing in?" I ask, smiling, trying to be friendly.

She stares at me like I'm speaking a foreign language. "Anything to drink?" she asks.

"Hi," you say with a smile.

Mild surprise shows on her face.

"I'll have a water," I say. "Pearl?"

"Do you have lemonade?"

"We do, but it's not very good."

"Oh. Root beer?"

The waitress stares at you. "Coke, Diet Coke, Sprite," she says, listing them off in tart fashion.

"I'll have a water," you say, still smiling at her like you're expecting some kind of gift or surprise.

"You ready to order food?"

"I think we'll need a minute," I say. You nod.

The woman scribbles something on her notepad, although seeing as how we only ordered two waters, I'm convinced she's writing down all the ways we've annoyed her so far. Thinking that makes me grin, and I smile at you as she walks away.

"This is where you grew up?" you ask in a hushed voice. Your eyes are wide.

"This is it."

"Is this how it was when you were little?"

"Yes and no," I reply. "Everything seems a lot older. But the diner is the same. Actually, my friends and I used to sit in this very booth."

"Really?"

I nod. "We'd better figure out what we want to eat before our waitress comes back."

You smile, and your eyes scan the large menu. I glance over at the men at the bar, and they barely move. Every so often one of them will turn the newspaper page, and it makes a crinkling sort of wispy sound. I look longingly at the jukebox. It's much too quiet in here.

The bell above the door rings again, and we both turn to see who is coming in. Another older man, but he seems friendly. He catches my eye and nods, gives a half smile, walks over to the bar, and sits beside the man wearing the ball cap.

"What's up, Danny-boy?" he asks good-naturedly.

I can't hear the man's reply, but the two of them chuckle and the friendly-looking man settles onto the stool. The waitress comes out, smiles when she sees him, and pours him a cup of coffee. Everyone suddenly seems more relaxed, and sunshine slants in through the windows and warms me on one side. I feel all of the mortgaged tiredness from the last few days coming due, and I take a deep breath, lean back in the booth, sigh. My knot throbs.

"Know what you want?" the waitress asks, sliding up beside us.

"Pearl, any ideas?" I ask you.

"A grilled cheese, please."

The waitress grunts quietly.

"What's good?" I ask.

"What?" She seems taken aback.

"What do you like? Do you have a specialty?"

She glances at her notepad, then back up at me as if I haven't said anything at all, and sighs impatiently.

"Let's do the grilled cheese," I say. "Can you put bacon on that?"

When she writes, it's like the pen is her weapon, the paper her enemy. I'm surprised she's not tearing right through it. She grunts again and plunges through the door to the kitchen. The door swings in wide arcs behind her.

"You know what she is?" you say. There's a mischievous glint in your eye, and I know what's coming. But I pretend I don't. I try not to smile.

"No. What?"

"That waitress is the secret witch queen of the island of Nysa." You're whispering now, your voice hissing and hesitant.

"Is that so?" I ask.

You nod, your face serious. "This is the entryway to her secret lair. Back in the room where they keep all their ingredients, there's a secret door behind one of the shelves."

"Like in Nancy Drew?"

You nod again. "Only better. It only swings opens if you lift up one of the ketchup bottles. There are a thousand steps down into the earth, and at the very bottom is where she keeps her prisoners."

"Who does she take prisoner?" I ask, feigning seriousness.

"Only people with one name."

"One name? What name is that?"

"Paul!" You start giggling.

"Paul?" I pretend to be offended, but I'm unable to keep the smile from my face. "Paul?"

"Yeah, Paul!" you say, laughing so hard now you almost can't speak. "She takes all the Pauls prisoner." You're rolling around on the booth, holding your side.

"Why all the Pauls?" I ask, but you can't answer. You're laughing too hard. Finally you stop, wiping the tears of laughter from your eyes.

"Oh, Grampy," you begin, then stop talking.

"You're a good storyteller," I say.

You get a strange look on your face, a kind of earnestness that's akin to pleading. "You know, not all of my stories are made up."

I reach across the table and place my hand palm up. You put one of your small hands into mine. I stroke the top of your hand with my index finger, and for some reason I'm feeling emotional now, feeling the smoothness of your skin, the tiny bones in your young hand.

"I know, Pearl. I know."

"Do you really believe me? Do you really believe that some of my stories are real?"

To be honest, I don't know what to think about your stories. You're so earnest when you tell them. I know you were making up this one about the waitress, but I still find myself wishing I could search the back room of the diner, check the ketchup bottles, make sure there are no secret passageways to the underworld.

"There's a lot in this world I don't understand, Pearl."

You nod, but you take your hand from mine gently, and I can feel you withdrawing.

"I can't believe we're here," she says. "This is really the same town where you grew up? This is where you met Grandma and where my daddy was born?"

"I don't know, Pearl, I have to be honest. It's the same town where I grew up, but it's not the same. It feels different."

"How's it different?"

"It's quieter, for one thing. People used to take care of things, but now the buildings are falling down." I pause. "It's kind of sad."

You are staring through the window again. I reach up and touch my knot, and I wish I would have sat so that it was facing the wall and not the inside of the diner. It seems bigger again, swollen somehow. I wish I could rip it off.

"It's a nice place," you say. "It's quiet, but I like that. It's not like the city."

I chuckle. "No, nothing like that."

"Did you come here a lot?" you ask.

"You mean to the diner?"

"Yeah."

"Once my friend Tom had his license, we came here all the time. This place was open twenty-four hours. You know your grandma Mary? Well, her mom worked here. I guess she would be your great-grandma."

I hadn't thought of that before. Considering all the generations you've missed out on makes me so sad I could cry right there in the diner.

"She used to give us free French fries. We almost always came here late at night or in the wee hours of the morning. Usually to this booth, unless it was taken."

"Tell me about her again," you say.

The cowbell rings, and everyone's head swings to see who came in. Another man. I guess he's about my age, but something about him seems older too. Worn. He has a long face and short hair, and his clothes aren't business formal, but they're sharp. A button-up shirt is tucked into suit pants, all held together with a classy belt. He pulls reading glasses from his pocket as he makes his way to the end of the bar opposite us, as far away as he could be from the other three sitting there.

A silence settles in the diner. The three men, who had at some point started chatting, are immediately silent. The waitress comes out, and I see her glance toward the new arrival before spinning around and going right back in, timing the swing of the door. I check to see if you notice the presence the man brought when he came in, but you're staring out through the glass again.

I can't shake the idea that I know this man. From high school? But that was a long time ago, and I can't get a good look at him anymore—where he's sitting, a shadow falls across his face.

"That man?" you say to me.

"Yeah?"

"He's in league with the witch waitress. Together they rule the island of Nysa. You've been brought back here to overthrow their evil kingdom." The whole time you're saying this, you're gazing out through the glass, out into the town.

I shake my head and sigh. The thing about you is, you don't really know when to stop. When to come back to reality.

"Nothing happens in Nysa, not really," I say unconvincingly. I remember that icy vein of fear we all felt after the drowning of Gillian Hudson, the rush of adrenaline I felt the night Mary saw the woman in the field, the way anxiety gathered in me when I saw Tom and Shirley paddling home without Mary. Those things happened. They happened here, in Nysa. How can I tell you that nothing ever happens in Nysa?

"I saw the woman again," you say. "On the drive here."

"The one with the silver hair?" I try not to sound dubious.

You nod slowly. "The one who helped me with the map. She was walking across the bridge as we drove over. She was coming here, to Nysa."

Now, I know for a fact no one was walking that bridge when we drove across. They would have been impossible for me to miss. But I stay quiet.

The John Deere ball cap man stands up. He pulls out his wallet, retrieves a single bill, and lays it down on the counter. He pats the man wearing the loose tie on the back and walks out. The man in the tie shakes his head, clears his throat, closes his paper, and also puts some cash on the counter. He shakes the hand of the happy one who had made everything feel lighter.

After the man wearing the tie walks out, the lighthearted man stands up and seems to think about leaving but has second thoughts and comes over to you and me. His eyes are quizzical, his hands fidgety and restless. What I first mistook for glib happiness when he walked in? It's more of a nervousness, a jittery sort of pep.

"I'm Gerald Mills," he says, holding out his hand, which I shake.

"I'm Paul. This is my granddaughter, Pearl." At the mention of the word "granddaughter," he visibly relaxes. Maybe he thought I was a kidnapper or something. I don't know.

"Hi, Gerald Mills," you say. Your happiness and the enthusiastic way you shake his hand seem to bathe him in a second round of relief.

"What are you kind folks doing here in Nysa? That is, if you don't mind me asking."

"Of course not," I say. "I grew up here and wanted to show Pearl my old homeplace."

The man who came in last, the one who sits in the shadows, seems to shift in his seat. I can tell he's listening to us.

"Is that right?" Gerald says, now appearing genuinely interested. "What's your last name? That is, if you don't mind."

"Sure. Last name's Elias. My parents had a place outside of town on Vintage Road. You know, the house up the hill, past the bridge."

Now I can feel the man across the diner staring at me.

"Up on the top?"

"Yeah, that's it."

"Well," he mutters. "I'll be. I know it well. I used to live down that way a little further, over on Pendrick."

It's a road name I've not thought about in forty years, but I can see it now. I know how it moves with the countryside, the bends, the dips, as it follows one of the streams.

"It's been years since I've been here," I say.

"Your folks still here?" he asks.

I shake my head. "No, sir, they are not. They both passed quite a while ago." A sharp regret stabs me in the chest. I never came back for their funerals. After Mary died, I left everyone behind. Everyone except your father.

"May their souls rest in peace," he says, the superstition thick in his voice.

I nod, not knowing what to say to that.

He stands there awkwardly while the waitress brings our grilled cheeses. Still he stands there, more than a little bit in the way as she tries to unload her tray.

"Need anything else?" she asks, and I glance at you but have to look away quickly so I don't start laughing. I know you're sizing up the woman for real now, wondering if it's possible she might actually be a witch or a sorceress.

You clear your throat and speak in an even voice. "No thank you, ma'am."

"We're fine. Thanks," I say.

She walks over to the bar and talks to the man in the shadows in hushed tones. I have a sneaking feeling they're talking about us, and I want to stand and walk out calmly and drive away, back past Junior's, back over the bridge, back to somewhere that isn't here. But I don't. We're both hungry. And I have no other plan for you—it's Nysa or bust.

I lift the grilled cheese and take a bite. It's delicious. The melted cheese is hot and the bacon crunches between my teeth. I close my eyes in ecstasy.

Gerald Mills is still standing there beside the table.

"I'm sorry?" I say, not sure what he's waiting for.

"Of course," he says. "I should be going." He hesitates.

"Is there something . . ." I begin, but again it all feels awkward. Why is he still here, staring at us? At you? What does he want to say that he's not saying?

He looks nervously over his shoulder, in the direction of the man sitting at the bar. "We don't get many visitors."

"In the diner?" I ask, wiping my mouth with a napkin.

"In the town." He whispers the words, and something about the faintness of his voice makes my mouth go dry.

I reach for my water. Your eyes are wide.

"What year did you leave, if you don't mind me asking?"

"1979," I say.

He nods slowly. "That's about when everything started happening. It's strange you've come back now."

"When everything started happening?" I ask.

"Out at the lake," he says, sort of coming back from wherever his mind had escaped to. "That's when all the drownings started. I wouldn't go out that way if I were you."

An Unexpected Encounter

Gerald Mills walks away, out through the door, and the cowbell rings. I turn back to see how you took the odd message, and I widen my eyes to emphasize the strangeness of the situation. You give an excited kind of grin, anticipating some new adventure.

"That was weird," I whisper, and you lean in.

"He's in on it too."

"In on what?" I ask.

"He's in cahoots with the witch queen. Except he's been in a feud with that man over there for a long time."

"Cahoots?" I laugh. I can't help it. Your imagination is running wild now. "So why did he tell us, 'We don't get many visitors'?"

"He's trying to warn us," you say in a serious voice, all the joking gone. "He's trying to tell us to get out while we still can."

I feel it again, that sudden rush of saliva to my throat, a

swelling of something in my gut, something that wants out. I think I'm going to vomit right there on the table.

"Sorry, Pearl. I need to use the restroom."

I assume it's where it always was, through the swinging kitchen door to the right, more of a closet than anything else. And I'm right. I catch a glance of that old kitchen before I go through the bathroom door, and it's not changed at all. Except nothing's quite as shiny as it used to be—the stainless steel is clouded over, and the large stove has rust patches down around the bottom corners. I doubt the health department even comes out to Nysa anymore.

I stand over the toilet and wait, but whatever it was that stirred up my stomach starts to settle. Maybe moving around was the cure. I think getting outside for some fresh air might be a good idea, so I flush the toilet, wash my hands, and walk back out.

Standing there by our table is the man from across the diner. The man from the shadows. The first things I notice are his expensive shoes and how his pants are pressed in a perfect crease. The sunlight glares off the shined leather of his belt, and the brass buckle nearly glows. Every line of his shirt is sharp, he is clean-shaven, and his eyes . . .

That's when I realize who he is.

"Tom?" I whisper, barely able to formulate the name, and when I do, so little air escapes that it's more me shaping his name with my mouth than actually saying it.

"I thought it was you when I heard your voice," he says, but the words barely register because his tone is unexpected. There's no joy there at seeing a long-lost friend. He seems somehow flat, like the old Tom I knew had been pressed out when his shirt was ironed.

"I thought to myself," he continues, "'I know that voice. Where have I heard it before?' And it's really you, right here in front of me."

Here I am, standing in front of Tom, a friend I haven't seen for forty years, shortly after Mary died. And because his voice sounds so vacant, I'm not sure what to do—hug him? Shaking hands feels too formal. Standing here feels like the worst option, but that's what we do—stand in the narrow diner aisle and stare at each other.

"It's me," I say, putting my hands in my pockets. Why is he so emotionless?

"I never thought I'd see you again," he says, his words more a statement of fact than any kind of accusation or relief.

Is he angry at the sudden way I left Nysa all those years ago? That fits. That seems to make sense, and I consider apologizing. Should I say I'm sorry for how I left things? Should I take the conversation in that direction and see if that's what he wants? An apology?

That's when I hear you sliding out of the plastic booth. You stand behind me.

"Tom," I say again, and I don't have to pretend that I'm shocked, because I am. I don't know why I didn't consider it before, the fact that I might run into people from my childhood. "I can't believe it's you. I can't . . . This is my granddaughter, Pearl. This is John's daughter."

You hold out your hand, and he stares at it, turning his head to the side, examining it. He crouches down so that his eyes are level with yours, and he finally reaches for your hand.

"You look exactly like your grandmother," he states, and a

recognizable softness is there this time, something creeping through the flat exterior.

Time has treated Tom well—he seems like he's in good shape. He dresses like someone who has found a great deal of success. I angle my head so he can't see the knot that's growing. It's suddenly embarrassing, this weakness. I raise my hand and pretend to scratch my scalp, cupping the knot in my palm.

"Join us?" I ask.

"Of course," he says, his voice still sounding like it's coming through gauze. "Of course."

I sit back down and slide over, but he walks over and sits in your side of the booth. You slide all the way to the wall and stare up at him with something like amazement.

"Where do we even begin?" I ask, trying to keep it light but not succeeding. We sit there in the quiet, the warm sunshine radiating in on us, you staring up at him, the waitress bustling around in the back room. There is the never-ending clatter of dishes and silverware, and something sizzles on the grill.

"Why'd you come back?" he asks, and I can sense it—genuine interest.

I shrug. "I wanted to show Pearl where I grew up." I've said this half-truth so many times, it's beginning to feel true. Perhaps there is no diagnosis, no knot on the side of my head, and this is only an innocent trip in which an older man wants to show his granddaughter where he learned how to ride a bike or catch his first fish.

I reach up and touch the knot again, to be sure. It doesn't seem like Tom has seen it—if he has, he's kept his eyes from wandering back to it.

"When did you get in?" he asks.

"We drove across the bridge, oh, about an hour ago."

He nods, taking it all in. "Where are you staying?"

I give a half-hearted, wry smile. "No plans. Any recommendations?"

He glances down at his expensive watch, grabs on to it, and turns it this way and that on his wrist. "You should come stay with me," he offers, and his voice is still so neutral I can't tell if he'd genuinely like that or not.

"Oh, I don't know," I say, looking out the window, squinting in the sun.

"You've got no other options. Trust me. Not anymore. Unless you want to go back out to the highway."

I glance over at you. Your plate is empty, the grilled cheese polished off long ago. You nod eagerly, smiling first at me and then at Tom. "I'd like that."

"There you have it," I say, trying not to sound too relieved. "I guess you have houseguests."

There's a banging in the kitchen, someone swears loudly, and someone else complains.

"What about Shirley?" I ask suddenly without thinking. "How is she?"

But Tom doesn't hear, or pretends not to. "Jenny!" he calls into the back.

"Jenny?" I ask.

"The waitress."

"Oh." I glance over at you. "Pearl thinks she's a witch queen."

Tom gets a peculiar expression on his face, and it's the closest he's come to a smile since we first saw each other. "Is that so?"

You nod, your eyes wide, eager to see how this adult will respond to your imagination.

Tom leans in close. "You're not far off," he says, and now his eyes are definitely smiling.

You grin from ear to ear.

"Jenny!" he shouts again, and this time there is something playful in his voice. He turns to us. "We eat things besides grilled cheese in Nysa, you know."

Night Swimming

We spent the rest of that summer before our senior year of high school cleaning up Tom's family cabin. His parents gave him a chunk of money for his "road trip," and those were our funds. The four of us ripped out carpets, tearing up our knuckles, and laughed after we pulled so hard we fell backwards. Tom and I did light roof work, mostly patching the obvious holes and splits. We reinforced the dock and replaced some rotted boards on the deck. We trapped mice inside the house and groundhogs outside. We mowed and mowed with a mower we borrowed from our closest neighbor, about five miles away. We found four old kayaks at a garage sale.

The stories we told our parents, regarding the road trip or that we were all working at a summer camp in upstate Maine, were absorbed without incident. We told them it was a wilderness camp, so there would be no mail. No phone calls. Nothing. When I told my parents, I think my dad might have nodded while he turned the page in the newspaper, and my mother said something like, "Okay, honey, have a nice summer," while staring wistfully out the kitchen window.

Neither Tom's nor Shirley's parents had any concerns. Mary told her father, but he was so drunk when they had the conversation that she wasn't completely sure he took it in. She told us her mother was happy she could get out of the house for a time.

While the projects we did might make it sound like we were hard workers, let me settle that point at once—we spent the majority of our time lounging in the water, taking naps, going on hikes, swimming, kayaking, lying on the dock and staring at the stars, making out with our respective significant others, and falling asleep on the deck or in the living room to the sound of the crickets and the loons and the cicadas. We slept in until noon almost every day, worked until dinner, and relaxed late into the night.

On one of those late nights, when the air was warm and the waves came in off the lake in steady ripples, Tom and Shirley and I sat on the dock, staring at the moon. Mary stood up and stretched, her form a reed bending here and there. She started walking the long dock back to the cabin.

"You going to bed?" Shirley called after her, disappointment in her voice.

"I'll be back." She laughed, her words floating back to us.

Her departing form was backlit by the single outside light that hung by the rear door of the cabin. She was a gracefully moving shadow, and I couldn't take my eyes off of her.

"Man, you've got it bad!" Tom shouted, hooting out into the dark void that hung over the lake. It felt like we were the only people left on the planet.

I grinned and lay on my back, staring up at the sky. Shirley laughed. The heavy summer air swallowed the sounds we made, left me feeling melancholy and reflective. It was hard to believe how quickly my life had changed—the previous summer I had been aimless and on my own.

"What a summer," I said.

"I don't want to go back to real life." Shirley sighed.

Even Tom was serious. "Nothing like it," he said, and I thought I could almost detect a huskiness in his voice, a depth of emotion he usually managed to cover up with something boisterous.

I stood up.

"You too?" Tom asked.

But I didn't turn for the house. I walked the ten steps between us and the end of the pier, stared out over the water, and dove in.

The water was cool but not cold. I hovered there in that other world, paddling to keep myself under, my hair drifting like seaweed. If I could have survived underwater, I might have stayed there forever—everything was silence and peace and darkness. When I came up, I swam away from the dock, out into the night.

"C'mon," Tom called after me. "Don't go out alone, Paul."

But I kept swimming. Pure, youthful energy had gathered in me, collected from Mary and the melancholy night and the moon, and I swam harder. Soon the porch light was a dot, like some star far behind me. A stiff breeze came and went, and the surface of the lake was brittle, choppy. When I tried floating on my back, the small waves came up over my mouth, and I coughed the water out, treading darkness.

Something came up out of the water, something large and frantic and direct. I stifled a shout, but it was only Tom.

"There you are," he said, trying to catch his breath. "Idiot.

You didn't grow up around water, did you? Don't go out by yourself at night. Not like this. C'mon."

He swam back to the dock, and for a moment I considered going out even farther, leaving all of them behind, even Mary. Why did I want to keep running? What was I running from? Could I see us getting older, the years gathering around us? Maybe I could sense that summer was the end of our youth, the last time things would be that way, carefree and light. I wanted to swim away from whatever it was that was coming for us, whatever it was that would take it all away.

But I didn't keep swimming away. I followed Tom back, the small, single porch light leading us home. By the time I got to the dock, Tom was already sitting beside Shirley, and when my head peeked up over the edge of the wooden boards and I pulled myself up, he shook his head.

"You are such a—"

But he never finished, because that's when Mary, still inside the house, screamed.

Shirley

You and I follow Tom out of the diner parking lot, sufficiently stuffed. Jenny, aka the witch queen, at the continued requests of Tom, had brought out various plates of diner food for us, and what we didn't eat, Tom packed in Styrofoam clamshell containers and carried out with him.

"For tonight," he said. "I love leftovers."

Now he turns onto Main Street, away from the diner, the golden light flickering from his BMW's turn signal. It's a beautiful car, and with the clothes he wears, I'm beginning to think that Tom has done very well for himself.

"I like Tom," you say, and I can tell the food has made you sleepy. I could use an afternoon nap myself.

I don't reply. I always liked Tom. I liked him a lot. But there is something about him now that seems far away. The man we sat beside in the diner, the one who told you funny stories about me from when I was a teenager, the one who insisted on buying the food, the one who wrote his address on the back of a napkin in case we get separated—that Tom is somehow an outer layer. I can tell the old Tom is in there somewhere, but he's buried deep.

"So, you were old friends, huh?" you ask.

"We were. Inseparable."

"Only the two of you?"

"Well, your grandmother and I spent a lot of time with Tom and Shirley. But I left Nysa with your father . . ."

"After Grandma went away?"

Have I told you that already, or is this one of those strange facts you seem to pull out of thin air?

"That's right. After Grandma went away, I scooped up your daddy and left Nysa. I couldn't bear to stay."

"That must have been sad," you say, and it was—the saddest thing ever—but I can't put that into words.

I nod, clear my throat, and keep following Tom's car as he winds his way into the countryside. At first it feels like we're going to the old cabin—we seem to be heading in that direction. Am I ready for that so soon? I think again of the things the man in the diner said about the drownings, about staying away from the lake. I make a mental note to ask Tom about that later.

But we turn off the roads I recognize and drift through fields I don't remember. There are road names I am unfamiliar with—did I know them at one time? Forty years ago, would I have known where we are?

At some point we turned onto a private lane with fewer potholes than the country road. Tom slows down, the lane narrows, and tree branches reach in over us like fingers. His car is sleek in the afternoon shadows, and slants of sunlight fall through the forest. Even though the windows are closed, I can smell the fall leaves and the fields we left behind and the approaching lake.

You are peeking up over the edge of the window again.

"What do you see, Pearl?" I ask, but you won't answer.

The narrow lane with trees pressing in on all sides suddenly opens up into a large clearing, and we arrive at Tom's house. We have also arrived at the lake. There is green grass on both sides of the drive, and the lane which widens into a small parking area. His BMW pulls lazily into a yawning garage door.

The house is massive, part cabin, part stone house, and laid out in an irregular way. There are strange peaks and dormers and windows in places you wouldn't expect, like some of the floors of the house are in between the main floors. It looks more like a stretch of uneven, ancient row homes than one house.

Beyond the grass, beyond the house, is the lake. This is not the lake house where we spent the summer, but that is the same lake. I feel the weight of the past.

"Oh, Grampy!" you squeal, clicking the door handle and hopping out.

I know you're taken by the water and the size of the house—I should probably call it a mansion. I can hear your footsteps on the pavement, but the sound vanishes as your feet enter the grass.

The longer I examine the house, the larger it seems. I have an empty feeling inside of me, an uneasiness. Part of it was the sadness I saw in Tom's eyes at the diner when he first came over, as well as the fact that my mission of finding you a place to stay in Nysa seems more and more outlandish the longer we are here. Then there's the stillness of the trees, the removed choppiness of the lake, the way the candy-blue sky drapes around us all the way down to the tree line, placing us in a bubble.

And always, there is the knot on the side of my head.

I reach up and touch it. It feels bigger. A wave of nausea comes and goes, much faster than the other times. I grit my teeth. That's the last thing I want to do, throw up all over Tom's manicured lawn.

He emerges from the side door of the garage, and I stand where the driveway meets the yard. I expect to see him grinning, proud of this beautiful house, the view, the exclusivity that seclusion can bring. It's the way I imagined him the entire drive here, speeding along in his expensive car the way he drove when he was eighteen, grinning, hand out the window. Did he roll down the window while we drove here from town? I didn't notice.

But he's not smiling. In fact, his face is drawn, and he seems even sadder than at the diner. You come around the corner of the house, run across to him, and grab his hand in an unexpected show of affection, and he reaches up with his other hand, pulls down gently on his chin.

"Can I show you the house?" he asks in a weary voice.

If the day outside is bright and blue and winsome, the inside of the house is nearly the opposite. Its floors are cold stone tile and dark hardwood, the walls covered in rich colors that surely took many coats of paint. The curtains are thick and swollen and keep out the light. There are old paintings on the walls, each with its own dim light above it. Some of the interior walls are brick, and I wonder if this was once a smaller home Tom added on to. I'll have to ask him.

We follow him through a winding maze of hallways, up half a flight of stairs, back down, and around a corner.

"This will be your room, Pearl," Tom says, and as you and I enter, I can sense the wonder rising between us.

The room is large, sits at the front left corner of the house, and would be long enough to have three beds side by side, although there is only one, right inside the door. The rest of the room stretches out in a long rectangle away from us. The ceiling is much higher than the ceilings in the other rooms, and it is painted light blue, so at the edges of my sight it feels more like the sky than a ceiling.

But the walls—there are no walls, not exactly. There are only bookshelves. The walls are covered in books from floor to ceiling, from corner to corner, the only break being two tall, narrow windows that face the driveway and another window at the far side of the room that faces the side yard and, beyond it, the forest. The shelves are stained a light, almost transparent stain so that the wood comes alive. Light comes through the far window in a long, shining beam.

"Oh," you say, and that is all. You take two or three hesitant steps into the room, waiting for Tom to say it's a mistake, this is not your room, you shouldn't go any farther. But he doesn't say anything. I glance at him, and he is watching you, his face placid, his eyes sharp.

The floors of the room are a light wood, but the wood is only visible around the edges, because the floor is covered in the most incredible Persian rug I've ever seen, bright red with swirling patterns of blue and green and tan. The short ends of the rug have long, ancient-looking tassels that are tangled on each other. Your feet sink into the rug.

"That's why we take off our shoes before we come into the house," Tom says in an emotionless voice.

You nod, your face serious, looking slightly embarrassed because you have your shoes on. You slip carefully out of them and place them beside the door. There is a round table by the far wall of books, and you move toward it. Three books rest on the table, and you sit lightly in one of the two chairs, your eyes sinking into the book you open.

"This is the room I built for Shirley at the end," Tom says in a quiet voice. The room is so long and he talks so quietly that I doubt you can hear us. "She lived her last days in here, reading, sleeping." He pauses, and his voice is without emotion. "Don't tell the girl. I wouldn't want her to be afraid."

"Shirley's . . . gone?"

He sighs. "Yes."

"How?"

"She had cancer. But that's not how she died."

I look at him, waiting.

"She drowned," he says, and I can feel my pulse quicken.

"Drowned?"

He nods. I think again of what the man told me in the diner, but I'd rather talk about that with Tom when Pearl isn't around.

"So, you were married all this time?"

"Nearly forty years," he says.

I sense his disappointment that we weren't together all that time, that he and Shirley and Mary and I weren't great friends for all of those decades. Disappointment that I left them. That I never came back.

"So, we just missed her."

"She would have loved seeing you." He glances over at Pearl. "And her."

I am penetrated by a deep guilt. "This room. It's rather incredible."

"I don't come in here much."

I nod, walk to the table, and check out the three books.

One is called *Pan's Labyrinth*. It has a blue cover with a girl in the middle and tall trees growing up around the edges. I fold over the book you're reading and see it is a worn paperback called *The Golden Key*. The third is a beautiful, sky-blue, hardback book embossed in gold lettering: *The Light Princess*.

Tom walks up behind me. "Shirley's favorites."

I look around at the floor-to-ceiling shelves, the endless books, and the rich red rug. I didn't even look at the bed as we walked in. I guess the walls of books distracted both of us. But even the bed is perfect, sitting a little lower than most, with a post at each corner and pure white sheers rustling in the light.

"Are you sure?" I ask Tom.

He looks at me with questions in his eyes.

"She's eleven years old," I explain. "It's very nice. I'm afraid she might ruin something. This rug is incredible."

He waves away my concern. "Everything in here is very sturdy. Even the rug's attached to the floor."

"My main concern is not that she's going to remove the rug," I mumble.

"Does she wet the bed?" he asks in a loud voice.

"Wet the bed?" you say from the table, indignant, suddenly coming up out of the book.

"Yes," Tom says without any hint of humor. "Do you wet the bed?"

"No!"

"Can you follow simple instructions?" he asks.

"Yes," you say, still indignant.

"Simple instructions," Tom repeats, "such as, take off your shoes before coming inside?"

Your pale skin blushes red, and you stare at the carpet,

nodding. You murmur something that sounds like, "Of course."

"Do you know how to read a book without breaking the binding?"

You look at him. You don't know how to read a book without breaking the binding.

"All right," he says in a stern voice. "I'll show you."

Tom crosses the room and pulls out the chair beside you. He shows you how to hold the book so that the spine doesn't crease, and that you shouldn't press down on the pages when the hardback is open. But I can't hear him because he's talking in almost a whisper, or perhaps it's the room and all the books are swallowing up the sound of his voice.

I stand there and watch him with you, and I think of all the things I won't be able to teach you after I'm gone, all the things you'll have to learn on your own or from people I don't even know. It's a source of pain, the idea that important people will enter your life who I will never know.

I turn and walk out of the room.

The Woman at the Window

I ran as fast as I could to the house, the rough wood trying to push splinters into my wet feet. The summer air was so heavy it held me back as I ran, the way dreams can keep you from lengthening your stride. Behind me, I could hear Tom catching up and Shirley shouting right behind him.

"Mary!"

The lone light above the deck entrance flickered as I flung open the screen and shot into the house. Mary screamed again, and her voice came from some muffled place.

"Mary! Where are you?"

I scanned the living room and the kitchen. Nothing. I ran through the small entryway and into the downstairs bathroom. She wasn't there.

"Mary!"

But she wasn't returning my cry. I ran up the stairs to the two small bedrooms.

We rarely slept in the bedrooms—they were mostly for storing our clothes for the summer and where we'd go to change, and they were normally too hot at night. More often than not, we slept on top of sleeping bags on the dock, or on the couch or floor of the living room.

I had not been in the girls' bedroom very often, but when Mary let out another cry, I could tell that's where she was.

"Paul!" she screamed, and I barged through the door, not sure what I would find. An attacker? A wild animal? Something worse? At first I didn't find anything—only a dark room, the shadowy outline of two single beds, a window that didn't let in any light.

"Mary?" I asked.

A whimpering made its way across the floor. Mary had tucked herself in the far corner of the room, behind one of the beds, and I moved quickly through the darkness, banging my knee on the bedpost, crawling over the mattress, reaching for her.

"What's wrong?" I asked. "Mary, what's going on?"

"There was a woman outside the window," she whispered, and her eyes flashed in the dark. "The same woman I saw in the field at your house last fall."

A chill raced along my spine. "Mary, we're on the second floor."

Her eyes remained wide open.

"How did you know it was her?" I asked.

She closed her eyes and leaned her head against the wall before whispering, "Paul, I feel like I'm losing my mind."

"Tom!" I shouted, but he was already bursting into the room and turning on the light. "Tom," I said again, "some strange woman is outside the house. Mary saw her through the window."

Shirley's mouth dropped open in horror, and she came across the room and tucked herself in the corner with Mary.

"Stay here," I told them both. Tom and I took the steps down from the loft two at a time, turned the corner, and went out through the front door into the warm summer night.

One might think that being in the middle of nowhere meant silence, but it seemed like those lakeside summer nights were the noisiest places on earth. Crickets in the undergrowth and cicadas in the trees and other insects I couldn't identify whirred and chirped and sang. Bullfrogs along the lake's bank were bellowing, giving their loud assent. Occasionally, bats would swoop through the light, snagging gnats and moths and mosquitoes. When the breeze gathered and moved among the leaves, there was the sound of a thousand trees, their leaves green and fluid, rustling.

We did a quick walk around the house, and the night was still warm. We were both wiping the sweat from our eyes. When we didn't see anyone, we continued up the lane, into the deepest shadows under the trees, night within night. I tried to walk quietly, but every so often my bare foot caught a rock in the driveway and sent it diving into the leafy underbrush.

"What do you think?" Tom asked.

"It's dark. We should have brought a flashlight," I replied.

"I mean about Mary," he continued.

"What do you mean?"

"Do you think she really saw someone?"

We kept walking, and I moved ahead, farther into the dark, leaving Tom behind.

What's Real?

You don't come out of the room all afternoon. Tom makes us dinner, some kind of fish and green beans served on beautiful pottery plates that each have a small blue square filled with a red infinity symbol. I guess the diner leftovers are being saved for another time. The house feels empty as the three of us eat in the large dining room that opens up into an even larger living room. Expansive glass doors on the other side of the living room go out onto the deck and face the lake. I can't imagine how lonely Tom must feel in this place, by himself, with Shirley recently passed.

You are quiet. I find the silence unnerving.

"Enjoying your room?" I ask you, and you nod, your mouth full.

You swallow and say, "The knives are scary."

I recall a glass case of various knives hanging on the wall down the hallway from your room.

"I can take them down if you'd like," Tom says, tilting his head.

"No, it's okay," you say.

"Which book did you start reading?" I ask, changing the subject.

You chew vigorously and swallow hard before speaking. "I read a little from both of the George MacDonald books."

"Ah, yes," Tom says with a smile.

"I love Mossy," you say.

"And what did you think of the flying fish that they ate?"

"A little weird."

"Yes, yes," Tom agrees, his voice trailing off. "I always thought that was rather strange."

The rest of the meal passes in relative silence. We learn that Tom was a psychiatrist, now retired. He and Shirley never moved away from Nysa. They never had any children. He started a successful practice in a neighboring state, opened five locations, and some years ago sold to a large hospital conglomerate. Thus the mansion. The car.

What that doesn't explain to me is why, after all these years, he and Shirley remained here, in Nysa, so far from everything.

I notice three or four hallways that all branch off from the living room, as well as a stairway that leads downstairs from the kitchen. What possible use could Tom and Shirley have had for a house like this?

"May I be excused?" you ask.

"Where are you off to?" I ask.

"My room." You don't wait for an answer to your question, leaving Tom and I sitting over empty plates. I stand up and carry yours and mine to the sink, watching you skitter off into the expansive house, down the hall that leads to your room. It is nice being under the same roof while simultaneously giving you some space to explore, to be on your own.

"I guess we won't see much of her," I say as I set the plates in the kitchen and go back out to clear the rest of the table. Tom stands and joins me, and we go back and forth, table to kitchen, loading the dishwasher, neither of us saying anything. I smell coffee. Five minutes later, Tom hands me a mug.

"Come outside," he says.

I follow him out through the double doors that lead from the dining room onto a wide deck that stretches along the entire back of the house. On one side is an outdoor kitchen complete with a grill, a sink, and a stone island with a refrigerator in it. In the middle are a few benches facing east, over the water. It is a perfect deck for parties, for entertaining, but Tom doesn't strike me as the entertaining kind, not anymore. And even if he was, who from Nysa would he invite to his house? Junior? Jenny the witch queen from the diner?

One section of the deck has two comfortable chairs with a small table in between. Tom motions for me to sit in one of them. I do, staring into the forest off to the side of the house. The sky is dark in the east. Tom walks soundlessly along the edge of the deck, lighting small torches that flicker and somehow make the night outside of the light seem that much darker.

He sits in the chair beside mine, and for a long time we say nothing. I am very aware of my own breathing. I can sense the lost presence of Mary and Shirley in a tangible way.

"How long since Shirley passed?" I ask.

"One year," Tom says, and I can't tell by his response if this is something he wants to talk about.

Again, an apology forms in my mind alongside this growing sense that I somehow abandoned Tom and Shirley, that things would have worked out differently if I had stayed. But I keep it to myself.

"It's forty years since Mary," I say, unable to add a verb onto the end of that sentence. Died? Disappeared? Left?

"Yes, I know," Tom says. "And how is John?"

I take a breath. "Not well. Haven't heard from him in a long time. Four years now, give or take." Saying it, I feel like a complete failure. Here we sit in Tom's mansion, with its accompanying garage that holds his expensive car. Meanwhile, back at home, I live in a falling-down row house raising my granddaughter because I failed at parenting the first time around. Even my own body, with this knot growing out of my head, is somehow evidence of my failure.

"I'm sorry," he says.

"Addicted to drugs."

"I'm sorry," he says again. "Happens a lot these days. I see it all the time."

"I have Pearl. Every day I ask myself how John can keep himself away from her. She's the most beautiful thing in my life."

"Maybe he doesn't want to spoil her. I've known people dependent on substances who leave their lives because they think they'll destroy the people they love." He moves in his seat and the wood creaks under him. The night is quiet around us. "She's a fascinating girl," he says.

"You don't know the half."

He smiles. "Is that so?"

"Tom," I begin hesitantly. "Do you remember the woman Mary saw in the field that night? The one she kept seeing every so often after that?"

Tom doesn't answer.

"Or did I make that all up in my head?" I ask, adding a dry chuckle.

"No, no," he says. "I remember. Of course I do."

"I think Pearl's been seeing her."

"Who?"

"The same woman. I think Pearl's been seeing her. You can't pass that kind of specific thing down through your DNA, can you? She keeps talking about this silver-haired woman who's been helping her with various things. I'm used to her making stuff up—she's met with more than her fair share of fairies, gnomes, elves, and autonomous shadows. She has an extraordinary imagination. But this one, this 'kind, silver-haired woman,' as she refers to her, has me a bit unsettled."

Tom stands and walks to the deck rails, staring out over the water we can no longer see in the darkness. The red-orange of the torches flickers on his back, dancing his shadow around us in many different forms and angles.

"You must have mentioned it to Pearl at some point," Tom says in what I imagine is his diagnosis voice. "That's the only explanation. Pearl heard the story, and now she's taken it on as her own."

I shake my head. "I've never talked about that with anyone. Not a single soul."

I wish I was having this conversation with Tom inside, where I could read his face. As it is, his back faces me, and the darkness keeps me from noticing even a slump in his shoulders or an uncomfortable shifting of his weight.

"Shirley saw the woman in the weeks before she died," he says.

"What do you mean?"

"As she was dying, she said she was seeing the woman Mary had always talked about, the one from the field the first night we met." He paused. "The woman we all knew was imaginary."

"Maybe you knew that. I was never so sure."

He clears his throat but doesn't say anything. I hear a splash in the lake where it edges up against the woods.

"How'd Shirley know it was her?"

"I asked the same. She said she just knew."

I reach up and touch the knot on my head tenderly with my thumb. "Is it a psychological thing?" I ask. "I mean, Pearl hasn't had a father. He's been gone for a long time. Her mother died when she was a baby."

"She has you."

"You know what I mean. Could be she's wishing for a parent?"

"It's possible."

"But you don't think so? In your professional opinion?"

"I'd have to spend some time with her to get a better feel for what's going on."

"The woman isn't real," I say. "Is she?"

"That depends on what you mean by 'real.'" He is still facing the water out beyond the trees. "If you mean something that everyone else sees, I would guess not, or someone else would have seen this woman by now. But if you mean something that actually occurs to someone in their own mind, then yes. I would say what Shirley explained to me was very real to her."

"Real to her? Isn't that the definition of insanity?"

He turns away from the darkness and returns to his chair,

giving me a slight smile. "Perhaps. Do you think Pearl is insane?"

"It's something I've thought about at times." I pause, gather myself, take a breath. "Maybe not insane. Not quite that. But ever since she was little, she's been very different. Brilliant in some ways. In other ways . . . just different. For a few years, she would run off almost every day. I tried meeting her outside her school so that she couldn't leave without me, but she'd find some other exit. So I started coming to her room at the end of the day, with permission from the principal, and she'd have already gone to the bathroom or for a drink or slipped out the window. Out the window, Tom. Eventually, I let her do it. I let her run off. In the city." I shake my head.

"She sounds like a clever girl," Tom said.

I look down at the chair I'm sitting in. The cushions are burnt orange. I look up. There are stars in the sky, far away, their light coming at us from a thousand years ago.

"You've done well for yourself here, Tom. I guess I should have been a psychiatrist too."

He laughs. It's the first laugh I've heard from him, and it takes me back forty years. That is the Tom I knew, that Tom in the midst of laughter. Tears rise to my eyes, because at the sound of that laugh I am reminded of everything he has lost with Shirley's death. I think about her laugh, the way she would come up behind him and give him a bear hug, refusing to let him escape, and the way she'd peek around him and smile at me from that safe spot, wink, and laugh again.

"I'm so sorry for your loss, Tom," I say.

"Grief is hard and good. It is the disease and the medicine, all at once."

"It's been a long time since I've grieved Mary," I admit. "I moved on long ago. Here I am."

"You must throw yourself in. There is no other way," he says in a far-off voice.

"What?" I ask, confused.

"I'm sorry," he says, and when he shakes his head it's like he's coming back from somewhere far away. "It's a line from one of the books your granddaughter is reading."

"I think I'd like to go over to the cabin tomorrow," I say, and something in my chest flutters uncomfortably.

"We could take the boat over," Tom suggests.

"I'm sure Pearl would enjoy that. She's fascinated by the water."

I wish I hadn't said that, because I know that now we're both thinking about the afternoon when Mary left us.

"The man we saw at the diner said some strange things," I venture.

"Gerald?"

"Yeah, that's his name."

"What did he say?"

"That Nysa went through a strange time right after I left, in 1979. He said something about drownings, that we should stay away from the lake. Junior said the same thing out at the gas station."

Tom nods hesitantly. "Yes. Soon after you left, it did seem inexplicable what was going on. A few teenagers vanished. Another one was found in the lake. Drowned. And another. And after that, an elderly couple. Because they came so soon after Mary, when everyone was still going out to search the lake for her, it started to feel like there was something ominous going on."

"But you don't think so."

"I think teenagers run away sometimes. We did, for a summer. I think accidents happen. There were a lot of people at the lake who had never spent much time around water, especially during the search for Mary, so it seemed expected that people who weren't strong swimmers might fall in. I think Gerald Mills is one of the superstitious few who would like there to be a deeper story, some other reason for the failing of this small town."

"Nysa is as empty as it looks?"

Tom nods. "It's dying, Paul. Twenty years from now, I don't know if there will be anyone left. Those disappearances were the beginning. They frightened people off. Since then, all the young people have left—it's a town of geezers. When we're all dead? I don't know who will remain."

So I am correct. My hope is crushed. What will I do with Pearl?

"I have a breakfast meeting in the morning," Tom says, an obvious attempt at changing the subject. "My weekly catch-up with some friends in town. You're welcome to join us."

"That's okay," I say. "I think I'll take a slow morning here."

Tom stands up. "I should be home by ten. We can have lunch out on the boat."

I stand too. "Thanks, Tom." We both know I'm thanking him for more than a boat ride, for more than a promised lunch on the lake.

He nods, and the shadows dance around us, congealing as he makes his way from lantern to lantern, snuffing them out. I follow him inside.

It takes me a little while to get to your room—I get a bit lost, but then I see it. Your door is open slightly, and I press on it, peek inside. The only light on is an antique lamp with a green glass shade and a golden pull string. You are lying on the carpet at the far end of the room, almost under the table, sleeping on your side with a book close to your face. I walk across the room, and the carpet feels like thick moss under my feet. I can understand how you fell asleep on that luxurious floor.

The book beside you is the third one, the one you hadn't yet read, and I lift it carefully and place it on the small table. I lift you even more carefully and carry you across the room. You seem both light and heavy, both floating and weighing me down. Your hair is loose around your face, and your eyes don't open, not even when I half drop you onto the mattress. I take off your socks and adjust the pillow under your head, and you cuddle deeper into it. I pull the thick comforter up over your shoulders, take one last look around the room, decide not to close the blinds, and walk out.

The Question

When Tom and I came back from our search for the woman who had been peering in the second-floor window, I found Mary asleep on the sofa in the living room, her head in Shirley's lap. Shirley watched Tom climb the stairs, cross the loft, and vanish into the boys' room.

"What's up with him?" she asked.

I shrugged. "I don't know."

I stared down at Mary's dark hair, spread as it was on Shirley's lap. It was hypnotic, the movement Shirley's fingers made through the dark strands, the way she started close to the scalp and moved ever so smoothly outward.

"Will you sit here with her for a little bit?" she asked. "I'm so tired." She yawned to prove her point, then smiled.

"Go ahead," I said. "We'll be okay. I'll make sure she gets to bed soon."

Shirley slid out from under Mary the way a mother eases herself from a child's bed, and I took her place, Mary's head now on my lap. I took her in, didn't even notice Shirley making her own way to bed. All I could see was Mary.

Have you ever examined someone so closely that you see their pores, the particular designs in their skin, the path of a single hair, the tiny wrinkles in their eyelids that make blinking possible, or the bundles of skin that form their lips? I watched Mary that way. What did she want out of life? What did she dream about? Who was this woman she kept seeing? I wished she would leave Mary alone. We had this whole future spread out in front of us, and it felt like this woman might be the only thing in the way.

Mary's eyes slid open, and it was in that moment that I knew something.

There was a small twist tie from one of our bread bags. I took it and wrapped it around one of my fingers, making the most insignificant of rings.

"Mary," I said. "Are you okay?"

She nodded, and her face was innocent, like a small child's.

"Do you want to talk about what you saw?"

She shook her head this time.

"That's okay," I said. "It's okay." I stroked her hair, not the way I had seen Shirley doing it, like a comb, but smoothing it, pushing the small strands behind her ears. She closed her eyes, relaxed.

"Mary?"

She opened her eyes again.

"I don't ever want to leave you."

She smiled faintly.

"I mean it," I said. "I don't ever want to leave you. When I heard you screaming, I knew I always wanted to be close enough to help. Close enough to come running."

Her eyes glazed over with tears, but none ran down her cheeks. "Oh, Paul," she said, taking my hand.

151

"I'm serious, Mary. I always want to be with you. Would you marry me?" I held up the small wire ring, and she giggled.

"Paul!" she said, emotion in her voice, her eyes searching mine to see if I was serious.

I met her gaze with such earnestness that she knew I meant it. I didn't say anything else. She nodded eagerly. I slipped the ring on her ring finger.

It was nearing the end of our first summer in the cabin, and we were both seventeen.

The End of Me

The smell of coffee lingers in the house, and besides that there is only silence. Tom left early to go meet with his friends, and in the massive emptiness of the house, I never heard him stir. I walk through the stillness. It feels so strange to be here, to be waking in a place that is not our home, and even more strange not to know how long we will stay or what the end will be. I should talk to Tom about that. I should tell him my diagnosis, go over how long he's okay with us staying here.

I reach up and touch the knot on my head, and it feels as though it has grown overnight. Tom, in his kindness, still has not asked about it, but I'm sure he has noticed it. How could he not? And even you still have not asked, which is a relief to me, because I don't know how much to tell you, if anything. I feel weary, although I don't know if it's from the illness or from the long night or from yesterday's drive. It could be anything, I suppose, though it is hard not to see the end of me in all these small changes.

I walk the winding hallways in search of your room, and at first I can't find it. I somehow end up on the second floor, in a room with large picture windows that face the lake. There is a large couch and a few plants in the room. Who waters the plants? Who cares for the home? Tom must have help, maybe a maid, some cleaners. I walk over to the large window and look out at the water. The far side of the lake isn't visible, even from the second level, and a stiff autumn breeze rustles up narrow whitecaps all across the blue-green skin of the water.

She Went Under

id I grab Shirley by the shoulders after passing John to her? Did I shout my questions at her, or did they come out in desperate whispers? Some memories are forever lost to us.

"Mary? Where is Mary?"

Shirley shook her head, tears falling, so I asked, "Where were you?"

"By The Point," she whispered.

"Did she jump?"

But Shirley was crying into Johnny's neck, and his little arms were flailing.

"Shirley," I said again.

"No, she didn't jump. She . . . fell in."

Even in the chaos of that moment, I recognized the unnatural pause between "she" and "fell."

"Where is she?" I asked, feeling the edge of something frantic beating in my chest, throbbing its way up the veins in my throat.

"We don't know," she sobbed. I could barely understand her. "We don't know. She went under."

Maybe that's how it went. I do know that I paddled as hard as I could, felt the entire lake alive under me. Soon I was skimming over it, my eyes on the horizon.

"No, no, no," I muttered with each stroke of the paddle, with each pull.

The Point was where a rocky outcropping jutted out into the lake, a thirty-foot-high piece of granite that the lake could not wear away. There the lake was deep enough for someone to jump from the top, if they had the courage. I saw it long before I got there, that bony knob poking up out of the gray water. A cloud passed over the sun, and I could see its shadow move, turning the water from gray to green.

"Mary, where are you?" I whispered, my arms aching. I was gasping for breath.

That's when I saw it: her kayak, all alone, drifting away from The Point, toward the middle of the lake.

Desecrated

I pull myself away from the view of the water. Why did I bring us back here, really? Was it to find you a new home, a new set of parents, a future? Or did I really return to Nysa to find out what happened to Mary? To find Mary? Was that what brought me here, this tumor and a desire for closure after all these years?

We can never trust ourselves, never know our true motives. There is always something deeper at work, something unseen pulling us along to hidden ends. We paddle where we think we want to go, but all along it's the hidden current that takes us.

After more searching, more wrong turns, more empty rooms, I find myself finally in front of the door to your room. I feel like I should knock, which is a first, because at our house in the city I never felt the need to knock. In fact, I don't know that you ever closed your door, and I start to feel a strange sense of foreboding. Why is your door closed? Did you close it? Are you hiding something?

I don't knock. I simply push the door open, and it swings in. There you sit on the floor in the middle of the room, on the rug. The beautiful red oriental rug that Tom had purchased to furnish this special room. My breath is taken from me because the rug is ruined, cut into pieces, and you hold a knife in your hand. What hasn't been destroyed, which is most of it, is covered in muddy footprints.

I can't even say your name. I can't speak. I am too shocked and disappointed, and anger simmers, begins to boil.

You stand and run to me and fall into my arms, weeping. "Grampy, oh, Grampy," you say.

I'm still not sure what to say. Your name finally comes to me, and it contains all the questions I want to ask but don't know where to begin. I stare at the rug. The word that comes to mind is *desecrated*.

"Pearl?" I can barely speak, barely say your name. What have you done? And why?

Through your sobs, you tell me a story. The words come fast at first, through hiccups and sobs and sniffles, but soon your voice steadies. You do not look at me, but I wish you would, because I feel like I would be able to check for the truth of the story in your eyes.

The Carpet

Grampy, the room was so quiet and dark, and I tried to close my eyes and go back to sleep, but someone whispered my name. At first I thought you had come into the room, but the door was still closed. That's when I knew the silver-haired woman was in the room with me, standing still in the corner. The woman from my school. She wore a kind of hooded coat, and the only reason I knew it was her was because the moon coming through the window lit up a few of her stray silver hairs. She asked me if I had finished the map. I said I had, and she sighed like it was the best news, like I had done something very important and she was happy instead of sad like she had been up until then. She asked if I would show it to her, so I reached down under my bed and brought it out, and when I turned she was right there. I hadn't heard her coming across the room, and I jumped. The carpet makes footsteps so quiet. Her face was still in the shadows of her cloak.

I handed her the map, and out of nowhere I felt this fear that she wouldn't be pleased, that maybe my drawing was too much like a little kid's or my words weren't spelled right. But she nodded and drew a sharp knife from her pocket. It was one of the knives from Tom's knife collection, the scariest-looking one in the case, the one with the black handle and the curving, smiling blade. She held that knife up to me in between two fingers so that she was barely touching it. I knew she wanted me to take it, but I was afraid of it.

The blade flashed in the night and reflected the moonlight coming through the window. Sometimes I think the tall windows are more like doors than windows, and sometimes the light that comes through feels more like something I can grab on to.

"Go ahead," she said. At first I wasn't sure what she wanted me to do with the knife, but I took it in my hand, and it was much, much lighter than I thought it would be. So light, like it might float away. I held it extra-special tight so it wouldn't float, because I knew Tom wouldn't be happy if we lost his knife.

"How did you get this?" I asked. I hadn't seen an easy way to open the glass case on the wall, but of course this woman is taller than most women I know and it was probably quite easy, so I felt stupid after I asked. But she didn't make me feel stupid. She pretended I hadn't said a thing.

"The only thing your map is missing," she said in a kind, quiet voice, "is the location of the door, and it's a very important door, one we need to find together. I know it leads down into the ground, and I think it might be . . . under this carpet."

She knelt down on the floor of my room, right there on Tom's red carpet, and drew a big rectangle with a long, pointy fingernail. I stared at her finger because I had never seen anything so long and thin, and I had never seen such white nails. And sharp. She drew the rectangle again, and I knew without her saying so that she wanted me to cut a hole in the carpet.

Oh, Grampy, I didn't want to. I didn't even kneel down beside her at first, but I could tell she was very serious and very sure it was what I needed to do. I came down off the bed, and at first I tried to pull up the sides of the rug, to see if we could move it, but the rug is fastened to the floor somehow. I got on my knees beside her, and that's when I noticed that she hadn't taken off her shoes when she came in, and the rug was covered in muddy footprints ground into the redness.

"Oh," I said. "You didn't take off your boots!" I was so sad about the mud on the carpet and so sad about how upset Tom would get when he saw.

She smiled at me like that was the silliest thing she had ever heard. We were both on our knees on the floor, but her back was to the window so that the front of her was still in shadows, and even though we were close, I couldn't see her face. I so badly wanted to see her face—I thought if I could, it would help me do what I needed to do. She leaned forward again and traced the same large shape in the red rug with her long fingernail.

"You do it," I whispered.

She told me this was very important and that it would be a great help to you if I did it. To you, Grampy.

"Someone took something from me a long time ago," she said in a kind, faraway voice. "It means quite a lot to me. I've asked so many people to help, and no one has been able to bring this thing back to me. But I think you will. I think you're the one."

Still, it was the fact that this might help you that made me do it. Oh, Grampy, I was so sad to do it, but I held the knife tight in my hands and slid the blade along the carpet. I expected it to be very tough, but the carpet almost melted under the sharpness of the knife, and it only took two trips around the rectangle before I could peel it away. It came back like a thick slab of skin, and a hardwood floor was underneath. I could see that by cutting through the beautiful rug I had also scratched the floor, and I had to catch my breath. I felt so horrible about what I had done.

There was no door.

The woman stared at the square, and I could tell she wasn't sure why the door wasn't there. She stood, took a few steps away, and chuckled to herself.

"Of course," she said in a quiet voice. She reached out one arm—it seemed a very long arm—and beckoned for me to come to her again. My feet were very heavy and I wanted to go back to sleep, but not because I was tired anymore. I wasn't tired at all. I was scared. I thought cutting the rectangle out of the carpet was the hardest thing to do, but I could tell she wanted something else now, and it worried me.

She knelt again and drew another rectangle, this one bigger than the first. That's when I started feeling sick to my stomach because I knew how much the carpet meant to Tom, but the woman was depending on me, I could tell. I started to cry, Grampy, but quietly, because I didn't want her to see. I thought that if I only had to cut out the first small rectangle, I could fix the rug so that no one would see. I didn't know how, but I thought I could figure something out. But cutting out another piece? This was no good. I was ruining the rug for sure.

But she told me again it was for you, that I would be doing it for you, and that it was very important. Her voice was so sincere and kind, so I cut again. This one was harder. I went around three times, four times, and each time I couldn't quite find the same line, so the rug was sliced and the material started to fray and the edge was raw. This piece was not like the last one, cut nice and neat, but torn so that I would never be able to fix it. I'm so sorry. I cried and cried while I cut it.

When we peeled and tore that piece away, there was nothing but hardwood, and the floor was even more ruined than the first time. I'm so sorry.

She stood, and we did it over and over again, and each time the woman grew more and more frustrated and sad. After I cut the last piece and pulled back the carpet, only to see there was no door there either, she was gone.

Gone.

And there were no doors. No doors anywhere.

I'm so sorry.

The Boat

Oh, Pearl.

My anger subsides in light of your story, replaced by a sick feeling in my stomach at the state of the carpet and a deep, deep sadness at the realization that something is very wrong with you, with your mind. How could you do this? Why? What would bring you to this?

But I don't ask any of these questions out loud. I start gathering the scraps of carpet and piling them beside the bed. "Where will we go, Pearl?"

"What?"

"Where will we stay? Tom won't let us stay here anymore, not after this."

"We could go home," you say, and clearly that is where you want to be. "Do you believe me?"

"Pearl," I reply, not knowing what else to say.

"Do you believe me?" you ask again.

Morning light drifts down through the windows. "It doesn't matter if I believe you, Pearl. This"—I open my arms, indicating the destruction—"this is what we have to deal with right now. What am I going to tell Tom? That you destroyed a room that was precious to him because a 'kind woman' told you to? That doesn't sound very kind to me. Should I tell him that there's a door in his floor, under this carpet, but apparently there isn't?"

I feel like shouting. I feel like crying. I feel like leaving. But I keep picking up strands of carpet, chunks of carpet, not even knowing what to do with it all.

I hear you whisper something, but I can't hear the words.

"What?" I ask in a sharp voice.

"It does matter whether or not you believe me," you whisper. "It's all that matters." You get down on your knees and, through your tears, begin to help me.

After some time, I go into the kitchen and find a bucket, fill it with soap and hot water, and return to your room, settling in to clean the remaining scrap of rug. The worst of the dirt comes up, but even after I've cleaned it as best as I can, there is still a tan effect to it, a kind of tint of the lightest brown that covers everything. Scrubbing only made it worse. We try to piece the squares and rectangles of cut carpet back into their original spots, but as we stand there beside your bed and look over the massive rug, I sigh.

It is completely ruined. There is nothing we can do.

I walk back to the kitchen and dump the brown, soapy water down the sink. I stand there and watch it swirl around, listen to the sound the water makes as it vanishes. I rinse out the bucket and the sink and put it all back. I return to your room.

You come out and stand in the hall. There are tears in your eyes.

"Come," I say. "Don't worry." I walk you into the bathroom

and start a bath. "Sit in here for a little while. Relax for a minute. I'll tell Tom when he comes back."

"But he'll be so mad. He'll ask us to leave."

I think about Tom. I think about Shirley and the room he created for her. I think about the cabin farther up the lake where the four of us stayed and The Point where Mary left us, and the life I lived in this small town seems a million years ago.

"We'll see," I say, and I really have no idea if he will or not. He is so different from the Tom I knew as a teenager. No reaction would surprise me.

I close the bathroom door and hear three things: you getting into the bath, Tom's vehicle coming down the lane, and the distant rumble of the garage door opening. A nervousness rises in me.

I don't know if I can tell him about what you've done.

He comes into the house carrying a brown paper bag of groceries, sets it down, and takes in the expansive interior of the house, almost like he's enjoying the view for the first time. He seems . . . not happier, but perhaps less morose. The day before, when we arrived and even while he and I sat on the deck, there was something deeply sad about him, something that clung to him like a heavy coat. But now he is almost light.

"What a morning it is," he says.

I am thinking the same thing. What a morning indeed.

"Were you able to find some food?"

"I haven't gotten around to breakfast yet," I say slowly.

"Did you just wake up?" He smiles, crossing the room and putting the groceries down on the granite countertop.

"I've been up," I reply elusively.

He begins putting things away.

"How are your friends?" I ask.

"My friends? Oh, yes. They're fine. They rarely talk about anything new—that's why I like them. Every morning it's the same old, same old—local roadwork, trees down, people who died, children living far from Nysa who are now a disgrace to their parents. You know, the sort of local news that means the world to no one except the dozens of people who live within ten miles of it happening."

With that, he nearly laughs. I can see it start up around his eyes, and his mouth pulls back. For a moment I see the old Tom, but then he clears his throat and turns away quickly. He folds the empty grocery bag neatly and puts it in one of the cabinets.

"How's Pearl?"

"She's in the bath," I say.

"A peculiar time to take a bath, right before we go out on the boat."

I nod. Now's the time. If I'm going to tell him about the rug, now's the time.

But he interrupts my thoughts. "I saw she's already drawn a map of the place."

"A map?"

"Didn't you see it? I found it on the coffee table in the living room this morning."

I see the map there, as Tom said, spread out. I hadn't noticed it before. I walk over and sit down on the sofa to examine it.

"Pretty incredible for a young girl. Have you told her all those stories?"

"What stories?" But even as I ask, I see how she labeled some of the various points.

The cabin where Grampy proposed.
The house where Grampy grew up.
Nysa Diner.
The Point where Grandma died.

"I don't know," I say, my voice lost and wandering. The map is completely covered in detailed identification, places labeled, some with events that took place there. It is a hand-drawn version of the first eighteen years of my life.

"Absolutely incredible," Tom says again, and now he is standing right behind me.

That's when you emerge from the hallway. Your dark hair is shining and braided perfectly. You're not wearing anything particularly fancy, only blue jeans and a gray T-shirt, but there is something about the flashing of your eyes, the sheen of your hair, and the way you bounce as you walk that scream "life!"

Tom and I are taken aback.

"Hello," you say bashfully, your eyes suddenly dropping. You glance up at me long enough to see if I have said anything about the rug, the floor, the disgrace of a room. I subtly shake my head. You purse your lips and look as though you might tell him yourself.

"Tom showed me your map, Pearl," I say. "How did you do it?"

You give me a serious look. "I had help."

Tom walks back over to the kitchen. "Your drawings are very detailed. Do you like to draw?"

"Sometimes."

"You're very talented."

You come over and stand beside me. I can't take my eyes off the map, and that's when I see a tiny red X on the detailed sketch of our old cabin.

"What's that?"

"That's where she wants to go next," you whisper. "That's where she thinks the door might be."

The same old chill races down my spine. I glance over at Tom to see if he is listening. He's not.

"Did you tell Tom?" you whisper.

I shake my head.

"Now, now," Tom calls from the kitchen. "No whispering. No secrets."

You and I look at each other, not knowing what to do.

"Let's go," he says, pulling some things from the refrigerator and tossing them into a bag. "It's a beautiful day to be out on the water."

And he's right.

We walk out onto the deck and go down a flight of wooden steps I didn't notice before. Tom goes ahead of me and you come along behind, your footsteps light, barely touching the ground. I glance at you once, and you stare at me with hesitant eyes. I can still see the guilt there, and I don't have any more anger, only sadness that you did it, that you destroyed something precious to Tom. I nod, reach back, give your tiny shoulder a squeeze. You give me a sad smile.

At the bottom of the steps is a wooden pier, about forty feet long, that goes straight out through a boggy, swampy area of high grass and marsh. It leads out into the lake and ends where the water is deep and a small motorboat thumps against the wooden posts.

"Here we are," Tom says in the flat voice I have come to recognize as his. It is nothing like the voice from our teenage years, when it was always on the edge of laughter or teasing or sarcasm.

He reaches for your hand and helps you down the short ladder and into the boat, beckoning me to follow. It's awkward backing off the dock and onto the ladder and taking that first swaying step onto the boat. He follows us both down, bringing along the rope that had tied the boat to the dock. He drops it onto the floor, where it curls up like a dead snake.

"It's a little cool out here today," he says. "Sit at the front if you want to stay dry."

We slide along the bench seats toward the captain's chair. He chokes the engine and starts it up, and the gurgling roar of the motor erupts in a cloud of smoke, chasing off the silence that had hovered along the edge of the lake. It feels like there are things hidden in the wooded shore, living things, that watch us leave before slinking away into the late morning shadows. You move closer to me, and I put my arm around you.

"So who owns the old place?" I have to shout my question so that Tom can hear me.

"I do!" he shouts back without turning around.

"You?" I ask, surprised.

"Shirley and I decided to buy it from the rest of my family about twenty years ago. We never used it though. We wanted to keep it out of the wrong hands."

"The wrong hands?"

He shrugs. "It's a beautiful location. We were worried someone might try to develop it, or tear down the cabin and replace it with something modern. It seems unlikely now, with the direction the town is going."

I reach up with one hand, clap him hard on the shoulder. "Thank you," I shout into the wind.

As we ease out into the deep, I close my eyes. All I have is the sound of the motor and the boat slapping the water, the scent of the lake and the cold air, the feel of the wind blowing over us, misty and fresh. There is a particular feeling of the sun on my face that takes me back to those days just before your grandmother left us.

Sinking

The heat leaked in around the doors and windows, soaked in through the glass. Mary had been up with Johnny through the night, so early the next morning, she woke me up.

"Can you take over?" She yawned, handing me that little bundle. "I can't keep my eyes open."

He floated down into my arms, not yet a week old, fragile, so light it felt like his bones must be hollow, like a bird's. I got out of one side of the bed while Mary walked around and collapsed into the other side. We were so young. So young. We were kids, barely eighteen. How were we supposed to know? How were we supposed to see clearly?

Mary fell asleep before I even left the room. I carried John out into the living room of the cabin. I heard someone else waking up, a door closing gently, a toilet flushing, a sink running. I lay down on the sofa with John on my bare chest—he was asleep, sucking on his bottom lip, his eyes flickering with dreams.

It was still early on a Saturday morning, which usually meant we slept as late as we could. But Shirley was rubbing her eyes and sitting on the rocking chair, pulling her feet up underneath her as she normally did.

"What's wrong?" I asked. This was the life we had all been dreaming about, planning for. There we were, finally finished with high school and with nothing to stop us. And yet she looked forlorn.

"It's Mary," she said, and those two words sent a ripple of fear through me.

"Mary?"

She nodded. "She's not doing well."

"What do you mean?"

"I was up with her late last night, Paul. She's . . ." Shirley fidgeted with her hands. She rubbed her eyes and stared through the glass, out over the lake. "Not well."

Not well.

"C'mon, Shirley," I said, trying not to wake John. I could feel him breathing on my neck, up under my jaw. His hands jerked open. What dreams flash through such a new mind?

"She's seeing that woman again."

My insides dropped. "She told you that?"

"She didn't want to worry you. Doesn't want to worry you. Now that the baby's here."

"When did she tell you?"

"She said the woman needs her help. That the woman wants her to go with her somewhere. I don't know."

"She said that?"

"She said she keeps telling the woman she won't do it. But apparently she's very persistent."

"Who do you think this woman is she's been talking to?"

"Paul, she's not well."

"How long ago did she tell you, Shirley?"

"A few weeks ago."

"A few weeks ago? Why isn't she telling me this stuff?"

"She doesn't want you to worry."

"Worry!" I shouted, and John squirmed, his little head jerking up and then lying back down slowly. "Worry?" I whispered.

"She loves you, Paul. What do you want me to say?" Shirley stood and walked over to the kitchen counter, moved around in the kitchen like she was going to make some food, searched the fridge, gave up, and came back over and fell onto the couch. She was clearly spent. "You need to think about getting her some help," she said.

"What, like a shrink?" I asked.

"Call it what you want. She needs help, Paul. She's . . . sinking."

The worst part was, I knew she was right. I had convinced myself with the same old stories.

She's tired.

She's stressed out about starting this new life.

She's pregnant.

She had a baby.

Had it only been a year since our weightless summer at that very same cabin? It had. But landmark events had come and gone, and things were definitely not the same. Mary never came back up. She was never the same old Mary. Her eyes were empty.

"We should talk to her," I said, pressing my face against the side of John's head. His hair was so fine, so new, and it smelled like something from another world, something alive in its own right. "This little guy needs his mom."

I felt tears welling up in my eyes. I sniffed, wiped my eyes with the back of my wrist, and stared out through the glass at the lake.

The Weight of Memory

And this is that same lake. The same shoreline. The same far-off horizon. For a second, I want to lean forward and shout at Tom to turn the boat around. I don't think I can do it. I don't think I can go back to that cabin.

But I want you to see it. I feel this strange, deep desire for you to see the last place I saw your grandmother, the last place your father was held by her. There is something important about place, something that grounds us deep into our memories. And without memory, we might float away.

You lean in closer to me, and I squeeze.

"Grampy!" you say, laughing. "Not so tight."

Tom looks over his shoulder. "Almost there," he says, and his emotionless words come across more as a warning than an excited announcement.

I see it from a long way off: The Point. I feel like I might have a panic attack. *Breathe in your nose, out your mouth. In your nose, out your mouth.*

"Grampy," you complain again, shrugging away from my tight grip around your shoulders.

The rocky promontory rises out of the water, above the trees.

The Point.

That was where they said she went under.

The boat makes a wide turn around The Point, and we rotate toward a deep inlet. In the midst of that inlet, like a shining jewel in the dark, glimmers the cabin. The almost-midday sun glares off the east-facing windows.

I stand, take a few wobbly steps to the front of the boat, and sit in the seat beside Tom. Approaching that cabin is like approaching the past at light speed from a galaxy away. I see the four of us skinny-dipping under the moonlight, much farther from shore than we should have been. I see Tom and me fishing from the boat, the sun burning our skin, our one-gallon water jug empty. I see Mary and me sitting on the dock, my hand on her pregnant stomach. I lean down and sing against her skin, making her laugh. Somehow I see the three of them heading off in their kayaks, leaving me behind on the couch, holding one-week-old Johnny.

I don't see Tom's face, but I can feel his gaze. You are standing in between us, bouncing with each wave, leaning forward involuntarily as the boat slows and the motor dims into a low rumble like distant thunder. The three of us drift forward like that, right back into the past, and I have a panic-filled moment. What have I done? Why did I bring you here? What monsters might still be lurking in the deep water of those long-ago years?

Strange thoughts to have when the sun shines so bright, when the air is so clear.

Mary, where did you go?

We drift up against the cabin's pier with a thud, and Tom cuts the engine. I don't stand up. I don't know if I can't or if I won't, but I sit there staring at the bright glass windows of the cabin. Tom takes one large step up onto the pier and winds the rope around one of the posts before reaching back and lifting you up by one arm.

"Whoa!" you say, laughing. Tom can't help but grin too, even though he lets it slide quickly from his face.

I watch all of this without moving. I'm still sitting, feeling the rock of the boat, the gentle swaying, the up and down, and the occasional knock as it bumps the dock.

"We'll head inside," Tom says. "You take your time, Paul."

You follow him along the wooden boards, looking over your shoulder twice to see if I'm coming. You seem nervous, skittish, ready to bolt. I recognize it, because that's how I feel. This place is too familiar to feel strange, too long ago to feel like home.

I pull myself up onto the dock, and the firmness of the world under my feet feels comforting. The boat rocks up and down in the small waves, the rope going back and forth between slack and taut. I wipe my wet hands on my jeans and take a deep breath, breathing in that place. Up ahead, Tom opens the back door to the cabin, and the two of you disappear inside.

I walk slowly up the dock. The outside of the cabin has been recently stained so that the wood shines, and the glass in the oversized windows is so clean it's almost invisible. The grounds around the cabin have been cleared, at least more than they used to be, and there's a small patch of grass off to the side. I can't see the lane from there, but I expect it's been widened slightly and properly maintained. It seems

Tom has become a very responsible adult. Perhaps having money makes that a little easier, if you can hire out the work you wouldn't normally do yourself.

All in all, the place looks good. Well kept. Tidy. The dock feels firm, not flimsy at all. I slowly open the door.

I can see Tom has renovated inside. All in good taste, of course—nothing over the top. The countertops are a plain, beige granite, the appliances are all stainless steel, and the living room furniture is new. The floors are hardwood.

"What do you think of the place?" Tom asks, coming out of the hallway.

"Where's Pearl?"

"Exploring."

I smile. "It's nice. You've done a great job on the place."

He seems relieved. I get the feeling he cares more about my opinion of the cabin than my opinion of his huge, glorious house.

"We wanted to keep it sharp, Shirley and I. Nothing too fancy."

"Did you ever stay here?"

"Not often. A handful of times. One of her cousins brought their family here for a week every year, and I had an uncle who used it as a writing getaway. Besides that, not much." He pauses. "Every so often we'd find beer cans out on the dock. I guess the high school kids camped out here from time to time."

"Sounds familiar," I say, thinking back on our first summer fixing the place up. "You've done a better job of renovating than we did that summer."

He laughs, and it sounds nice. It's quiet, not full, but a laugh nonetheless. "That's because I'm not doing the work.

You know, one funny thing we realized is that this place has a basement."

"Really?"

"Well, more of a crawl space, really. When we discovered it, we dug it out, made a proper basement."

"Wouldn't it flood, being so close to the lake?"

"It did," he admits. "It does. There's nothing down there now except a few empty shelves and, occasionally, some standing water that my guy has to pump out."

It doesn't surprise me that Tom has a "guy." I glance around the place, again taking in the simple class of the décor, plain and yet somehow perfect. There is a bookshelf against the wall that separates the main living area from a small entryway, and the books are lined up like little soldiers. I walk over and run my fingers along the titles, most of which are classics.

"Nice collection," I remark.

"Shirley's," he says, and that one word, her name, is filled with longing. It's the most emotion he's shown yet, and it gives me hope that the old Tom is still in there somewhere.

"She always did enjoy a good story."

On one of the shelves, completely out of place, sits one of those Russian nesting dolls, the kind that you can break in half to find a smaller doll inside, and another, and so on. I reach up and take it from the shelf. It's so bright, painted with reds and oranges and greens, that it seems almost garish there among the beiges and grays and pastel blues.

"Another one of Shirley's favorites," Tom says, but his voice is flat again. So flat that I look over at him to see if there's a problem. He gives me a tight smile and almost imperceptibly glances at the doll.

I look at it again, spinning the top half around without removing it. "Where did she get this?"

"She liked to travel," Tom says, and again I think his voice seems strained.

Maybe it brings back memories of Shirley, I think, placing the doll back on the shelf. "I'm sorry," I say, but I'm not sure what I'm apologizing for—Shirley's death? Handling something that has personal meaning? Simply being there?

Tom shakes his head. "It's okay."

"I love it here," Pearl says.

We both spot her standing by the bannister, and I have this vision of her, that she's a bird getting ready to fly away. It feels like Tom and I stand there for a long time looking up at her, not saying anything.

She smiles down at us. "I love it here," she says again.

"We lived here for almost two whole summers," I say to her, but I'm also saying it to Tom, reminding him for some reason, as if he might have forgotten. "Tom, Shirley, your grandmother, and me."

"Really?"

"Really. It was . . . We had a great time."

"A million years ago," Tom reflects.

"A million," I repeat.

I see it again—that morning—and even with the new furniture, the vision is strong of me standing there, passing Johnny to Shirley, the sound of Tom's vehicle kicking up stones, me running down the dock, jumping into my kayak so recklessly I nearly tip before I can get going.

"I think I'll wait outside," I say.

"You don't want to see the rest of the place?" Tom asks. Hidden in his voice is the understanding of how hard this is for me, but there is also a twinge of disappointment. Maybe he hoped I had left those memories somewhere else, somewhere far away.

"Another time," I say. "I'm sure we'll be back."

He nods, and I turn, push open the door, and walk down the long dock. I don't get in the boat though. I sit and let my feet dangle, and because this dock is lower to the water than the one at Tom's house, my feet nearly graze the lapping waves.

Why am I here? I wonder for the hundredth time.

I hear the pitter-patter of little feet skidding along the dock, feel a small hand on my shoulder, and sense the restless sitting of an eleven-year-old.

"Hey," I say.

"Hey," you reply, your hand moving to mine. Your fingers are so small. "I know why we're here."

I feel alarmed, though I don't know why. "You do?"

There is a solemn expression on your face. "The woman told me last night."

"The woman?" Every time you mention her, sadness and disappointment rise in me, holding a small dose of anxiety. I keep thinking something must be very wrong.

"She told me why we're here. And Grampy? She needs my help, but she's going to help me too. We're going to make it all right."

All right. Wouldn't that be nice.

"I saw there was a red *X* on your map where this cabin is," I said.

You nod eagerly. "Yes! The silver-haired lady put that mark on the map last night. And now I think I know why—the door must be here! In your old cabin! I'm going to go look around."

"That's fine, Pearl. But stay out of the basement."

"There's a basement?" you ask, your eyes lighting up.

"Pearl," I say in a warning voice.

"Hungry?" Tom calls out from the cabin.

I look over at you. "How about you?"

You nod, grinning, but I can tell the excitement of searching the house is distracting you.

"Sure," I shout back.

"Can you bring in the bag of food from the boat?"

I help you climb down into the boat, you grab the bag, I hoist you up, and we walk back up the dock. And for just a moment I think I can see it: a life for you here in Nysa. The sun is shining and the trees are rustling in the breeze and the lake is all around us, blue and shimmering. You wouldn't need a lot of people around—Tom would give you a happy home, make sure you get a good education. You would like it here, even alone, roaming the woods and spending days out on the lake. It would probably be safer for you than the city.

You skip ahead, and I follow you inside.

Tom is in the kitchen—I can hear him taking plates from the cupboard. "I hope you guys like ham and cheese," he says.

You have vanished again. I think I hear you upstairs. But that isn't what gets my attention.

The Russian nesting doll? It's not on the bookshelf anymore.

It's gone.

Photographs

We stay at the cabin long into the afternoon. I even take a nap while Tom shows you some trails in the woods. By the time we're loading up the boat, the sun is lower in the western sky and the shadows of the trees reach out far into the water, rippling, waving goodbye.

The boat's engine roars to life, and we pull away into the lake, racing the darkness home. You cannot take your eyes off the cabin, and even long after it is out of sight, you sit at the back of the boat, watching it retreat behind us.

"We'll tell him tomorrow," I reassure you. I'm beside your bed, tucking the blankets in around you. "Will that make you feel better?"

You nod. The carpet is awful.

"Should I roll that up and move it over beside the wall?" I ask. You understand what I'm saying. The room might not seem so bad if we get the carpet out of the way.

You nod again. I take the cut-out squares of carpet, put them in a small pile, and place them in the closet. I have to wrestle with the rug to peel up the edges—it was attached to the floor with some kind of glue, and it takes me a long time to free it from the wood. After a long battle, I roll the carpet the long way and slide it over so that it's up against the wall.

The whole time I'm doing this, a heaviness presses against my chest. It was a good day. It was a good day with Tom. What will he say when he sees this?

The knot throbs on my head, so much that I don't even reach up to make sure it's there. I know it is. And with each throb comes the question.

What will you do when I'm gone?
What will you do when I'm gone?
What will you do when I'm gone?

Tom seems to have a soft spot for you, but what will he do after he finds out about the carpet? And do I even want you to stay here in this dead town, grow up in this dying place? We didn't see a single child when we were in town. It's beautiful out here, but would that be enough for you? Each hour seems to bring a change in my perspective, and right now I'm skewing pessimistic.

I wander over to the small table and flip through the books you've been reading. Then I step over to the window and stare out into the country darkness. I envision taking the boat out at night, roaring around the lake, docking, and going inside the dark cabin. Where did that nesting doll vanish to? Did Tom put it somewhere? Why?

"Grampy?" you call from the bed.

"Yes?"

"Will you tell me about Grandma?"

For a second I have trouble catching my breath. I am still

looking out the window. "What would you like to know?" I manage to ask.

"Was she like me?"

"In what way, Pearl?"

"You know. Did she see stuff no one else saw?"

I think of the silver-haired woman she saw in the field that dark night, and again in the cabin that first summer. "Sometimes she did. She had an imagination, I guess. Like you."

"But I'm not imagining things, Grampy. These things are real."

I pull my eyes away from the window and look over at you, so small in the bed made for Shirley. I reach up and tenderly touch the knot on my head. For a moment I do not hate the lump. For a moment it feels as much a part of me as my heart or nose or kneecap.

"I know, Pearl," I say. "I know. But when you see things no one else can see, you have to accept that it might be hard for people to believe you."

"Do you believe me, Grampy?" you ask.

"About what?"

"About everything."

I sigh, walk over to your bed, bend over, and kiss your forehead. "I love you, Pearl. Good night."

"Did you believe Grandma?"

I pause.

"You know," you continue, "when she saw stuff?"

I take a deep breath, staring at the long rows of books. I wonder where they all came from and how many of them Shirley read before she died.

"For a long time, yes, I did," I say.

"'Night, Grampy," you say, but the light in your eyes has dimmed.

I turn to walk out. I turn off the light, and darkness fills the room with a kind of warmth. I begin drawing the door closed behind me when you call, "Grampy?"

"Yes, Pearl?"

"I didn't find anything in the cabin today. I didn't find the door."

"It's okay, Pearl." I turn to go again, and again your voice stops me.

"I know you're very sick." You pause. "I know you're dying."

Your words leave me blinking, my mouth hanging open.

"And we're going to help you get better," you insist. "The silver-haired lady can help us."

I wander through the house, distracted by your latest proclamation.

I know you're dying. And we're going to help you get better.

I'm so taken by your words that I lose track of where I am, get lost again, and find myself somewhere in the basement. The ceilings are lower here, the hallway long and straight with a sprinkling of doors on either side. I look over my shoulder, debating if I should go back the way I came, but at the far end of the hallway I can see stairs leading back up. They head up into the middle part of the house, maybe the kitchen. I head in that direction.

But my curiosity overcomes me at the first door, so I open it slowly, reach inside, and fish around on the wall for the light switch. When I find it, the room lights up, and I see that it's another spare bedroom. The carpet is cream, and the comforter on the bed is navy blue. There are no windows, not even the small window wells that some basement bedrooms have. I don't know how Tom keeps the water out with the lake being so close. A door, partially open, leads into a bathroom.

I turn off the light and close the door.

I find myself wanting to check each and every door, spend the rest of the evening searching all these rooms. For what?

The next door that I open creaks, and two recliners face a large screen on the far wall. A kind of home theater. I close the door.

I manage to walk the rest of the way down the hall without opening more doors. Then I notice a gleam of light coming from under the last door on the right, just before the stairway, which climbs half a flight before turning. I listen for the sound of footsteps, but there's nothing. The basement is almost completely silent, apart from the humming of some distant appliance.

I turn away from the steps and open the door to the last room. The floor is different from the other rooms—it's unfinished concrete, and the room is some kind of storage area. It's lined with row after row of well-organized metal shelves. Some hold shoeboxes with white labels; some are lined with binders, each labeled with black marker in exaggerated handwriting. Accounting boxes take up a few rows, apparently full of tax documentation. At the far end of the room, the shelves hold large plastic bins, also labeled.

When I enter the room and pull the door closed behind me, the rest of the house goes completely silent, like I'm sealing myself into a crypt. Even the distant humming I could hear from the bottom of the stairway shuts off, and again I strain my ears, listening for the approach of someone, anyone, but there isn't a sound. I walk through the aisles of shelves, my socks scratching quietly on the cement floor.

I run my fingers along the shoeboxes, and while I can't tell what they are from the way they're labeled, when I lift one of the lids and take a glance inside, it looks like they are all filled with letters or printed-out emails or notes. One person's handwriting seems to dominate—Tom's or Shirley's or perhaps Shirley's mother's. Why so many letters, and what could they possibly have had to write to each other about? Didn't Shirley's parents live here in Nysa? Didn't Tom's?

I drop the lid of the box and turn, taking in the rows and rows of binders. One is marked "Jan–Jun 1980." The year after Mary left. I pull it from the shelf and open it—it is full of photographs tucked into plastic sleeves with only an occasional caption. But I don't need captions for most of them. This is close enough to the time I remember, and although I wouldn't have been in Nysa anymore, I can supply the captions myself.

Tom and Shirley on the couch with her parents.
Tom and Shirley fishing in a boat in the middle of the lake.
Tom holding up a bass.
Shirley smiling, shielding her face from the sun.

I page through the notebook, photo after photo after photo, mostly of Tom and Shirley but also of friends I recognize but whose names I can't recall. I close the book. What would those years have been like for me if Mary hadn't gone away? Would the three of us, John included, have thrived here in Nysa? Would we have stayed even as things deteriorated, as people moved away, as Nysa shrank? Would we have grown old alongside Tom and Shirley, spent Labor Days and Memorial Days together on the lake, eating burgers and watching John (and maybe more of our own children) jump off the dock or water ski or jump off The Point?

A shot of curiosity moves through me, something like adrenaline mixed with dread and hope all at once. I slide the notebook back and look to the left of it, my eyes roaming the shelves.

There it is.

A book from the summer before John was born. The second summer that we lived at the cabin.

I take it down and hold it in my hands. I imagine the photos Shirley must have taken that summer, pictures of Mary's swelling stomach and of me, baby-faced, standing beside her with my baseball cap on backwards, grinning awkwardly. Eighteen years old.

I turn the notebook over and over. I can open it if I want—there's nothing keeping me from it—but there is something inside of me that's afraid of those days, afraid of going back. I've run from that time of my life for forty years, and even when it's right here in front of me, those years waiting to be viewed, mulled over, I can't make myself do it.

But I have to.

I open it, and a sob catches in my throat. There are faded photos tinted orange of us at the cabin that summer and fall. John is a baby. These are photos Shirley took days before Mary left us. One of them in particular grabs my emotions. The two of us are sitting at the end of the dock, and the sun glares off the water. Our bodies both face out over the lake, but we're looking over our shoulders at Shirley and the camera. I'm grinning and holding up a hand ("Stop, Shirley!"), while Mary tilts her head and smiles. At the bottom of the photo, I can see our hands resting on the splintered wood of the pier, our fingers barely touching.

I don't see any sign of John in the photo. Was this taken in the weeks before his birth? It's hard to tell—I can't see Mary's stomach.

Of all the things taking place in the photo—the sunny day, Shirley stealing another photo, me protesting, and Mary calmly letting it all happen—the detail that remains is the touch of Mary's fingers on mine. Whenever our hands touched, her fingers were always moving, grazing over mine so lightly I could barely feel them. Yet there it was—her touch. It was like magic.

I take the photo out and tuck it in my pocket. I reach up and touch the knot on my head. Is it all a dream? Is it all a memory? Will I wake up soon, in my bed in our small city, or perhaps even longer ago? Maybe I'll wake up and Mary will still be here, John will still be a baby, and life will somehow be back to the way I had always imagined it would go.

I slide the notebook back into the empty spot and grab the previous one, also from that summer but earlier, with photos of Mary clearly pregnant. As I page through, I notice a shift in the style of photos, as if someone else was behind the shutter. The pictures I had seen from later in the summer caught us all from a distance, and there were usually two or three of us in the photo, Shirley normally missing since she was taking the photos. But this album is different.

This album contains almost exclusively photos of Mary.

There are photos of her from far away as she stood at the end of the pier holding her swollen stomach. There are photos of her sitting on the sofa in the cabin, her legs crossed beneath her, staring through windows lit by the sun. There are photos of her asleep on the deck, and I remember how restless she became in those final weeks, how at night she slipped from the bed and wandered the cabin, sometimes pacing the kitchen, worried about the impending labor, too uncomfortable to sleep.

The thing about these photos is that they are beautiful, well taken by someone who clearly had an eye for how to frame a shot, how to catch that intangible thing that skilled photographers will sometimes capture. What first appears as a stray line of light is crucial to the image. Nothing is accidental.

Who took these intimate photos of your grandmother? It wasn't Shirley.

Could it have been Tom? It had to have been. There was no one else there.

I hear a door slam somewhere down the hallway, and it scares me worse than a gunshot. I close the notebook gently and slide it back into the vacant spot on the shelf.

Was It You?

I race over and switch off the storage room's light, feeling embarrassed that I'm snooping around and hoping Tom doesn't come into the room. The door is still open about an inch, and a blade of light from the hallway shines in. I look through the crack and into the hall. As far as I can tell, it's empty. It must have been Tom, right? Who else would be wandering through the house at this hour?

I take a deep breath.

I open the door, walk through, and close it behind me.

I exhale.

As I'm about to climb the stairs, I hear it again—another door slams. I look quickly over my shoulder and see a shadow vanish around the corner at the far end of the hall, the direction I came from. I pause, consider going on my way, following the stairs up to wherever they might lead, but my curiosity gets the better of me, and I jog the long length of the hallway and follow whoever raced around the corner.

After a moment, I slow to a walk and realize I'm somehow in a part of the house I haven't been in before. When did I take a different turn? This hall seems narrower than the hallways in the rest of the house, and it's lit by lights that come out of the side of the wall like upturned hands. There is another hall to the left, and I decide to take it. But there's no sign of the person who slammed the door.

"Hello?" I venture. My voice vanishes in the empty spaces. Nothing returns.

I keep going, and soon I have to go up a flight of stairs. I come to a short hall with two doors. I consider opening them but am scared of what I might find. The photo is stiff in my pocket. I go up another flight of stairs, and I find myself staring at a plain door with a dull brass knob. I open it.

I'm in the kitchen.

How did I get so turned around?

The transition from the basement hallway, which felt almost otherworldly in its stillness, to the very normal kitchen disorients me, and I stand there with my hand on the knob for an extra moment, the stairway door still open. What is this strange house? How long until I know my way around? How many secrets can one residence hold?

"Hi, Paul," Tom says in a steady voice, approaching from what I assume is the direction of his bedroom, over by the garage. The kitchen and dining room and large open living room seem to be the axis around which the rest of the house rotates.

"Hey, Tom," I say, closing the door, my heart still pounding. The photo feels conspicuous in my pocket.

"Looking around?" he asks in a disinterested voice, glancing at the door as he walks past and stops at the kitchen counter.

I nod. "Yeah. I hope you don't mind."

"Not at all. Find anything interesting?"

"This place is huge," I can't help blurting out.

Something like a dim smile flashes across his face. I still find something about him uncomfortable, but I can't pinpoint it. Is it because he's so different from the teenager I was friends with? But if that's the case, should I hold it against him? Don't we all change significantly as the years go by?

There's something else, though, something besides age. He's so staid, so emotionless most of the time. Except when it comes to you—he seems to have a genuine interest in you.

Am I jealous?

The knot throbs on the side of my head. Now that I'm here, I'm finding it difficult to imagine giving you over to him. But it would be difficult no matter who it was. Giving you to someone else is unimaginable.

I miss him. The old Tom. I miss his big laughter and his teasing, his audacious claims and the way he ruled the room. This Tom seems a deflated version of my best friend, and I want that guy back.

"Yes, I suppose it is rather large," he says. "Shirley always thought the place was too big."

He pours two mugs of coffee and hands one to me. "Let's drink it out on the deck," he says, and it's not a question, not really.

He moves steadily away, and I take a sip of the hot coffee, scalding my tongue. I glance at the doorway that leads down the hall that eventually winds its way to your room. I should check on you once more before I retire for the night, and I think of veering off, going to your room. But I don't. I follow Tom through the unlit living room, through the glass doors, and outside onto the deck.

I'm surprised by how warm it is tonight at the edge of the water. I sit down in the same spot as the night before.

Out of nowhere, I think of the doctor who gave me the diagnosis. What is she doing tonight—sitting on a porch with her husband, enjoying one of the last warm nights of fall? Perhaps drinking a glass of wine? I wonder if she thinks of me at all, if my diagnosis weighs on her, or if, when she closes the file folder, she forgets about me. I hope she thinks of me. I'm not sure why. It's not romantic, this desire of mine to be thought of by her. I think I want to know that someone else who knows about my diagnosis is swimming these dark waters beside me.

Tom doesn't turn on the large floodlights—there is only a small porch light shining from the back door of the house. We sit among the slanting shadows, steam rising from my cup of coffee. Above us, the stars are bright, and the forest sounds very alive.

"Pearl is . . ." he begins.

"Yes?"

"She's . . . quite the little girl."

"That she is," I reply. A breeze picks up and swirls a few leaves around on the deck.

"When we got back tonight, she asked me if I would teach her to swim."

"Really?" I ask.

He nods, laughs to himself. "She said she needed to swim the entire lake, that she wanted to soak it all in."

"That sounds like her."

"Is that okay with you?" Tom asks.

"If you teach her to swim? Or if she swims the entire lake?" We both chuckle. "I don't mind."

I picture the two of you in the water, Tom holding you afloat, and an ache soaks into me. But this is why I came, isn't it? This is why I dragged you across the country, over the bridge, all the way into Nysa—to find you a new home, a new guardian. I reach up in the shadows and feel the lump. It feels almost like another lump is starting to grow right beside it, the size of a pea. The wind is knocked out of me.

Oh no.

"How was your evening?" Tom asks, interrupting my thoughts, sipping from his mug.

I pause. "Interesting."

"Interesting?"

I'm not sure how much to tell him. How comfortable will he be with me sneaking around his house, exploring the rooms he never showed to you and me? To be honest, it wasn't completely deliberate—most of it was simply the result of me getting lost. I decide to start there.

"I actually got lost in the house. It's quite a place you have."

He chuckles. "You should start leaving a trail of bread crumbs."

Bats swoop down into the low light, flickering here and there, barely missing our heads. I decide to tell him.

"Tom, it was completely by accident, but I found myself in the long hallway in the basement. I happened to open one of the doors, trying to find my way back, and I ended up in the room with all the photo albums."

"I should've taken you down there before. There are some great old photos in those boxes. Shirley was quite the historian of our friendship. And then, afterwards, of the life that she and I created together."

"Pretty amazing, actually," I admit. "I felt like I was back there."

A melancholy silence drifts down between us, and I know that Tom and I are thinking through the same old memories. It's like we're sharing a mind, sifting through those two summers at the cabin, reliving all of it.

"Was it difficult, not having children?" I ask, peering cautiously at him to see if I've caused any offense.

"For a time."

I wait for more of an explanation, but he lifts his coffee mug and takes another sip. I could only be imagining it, but I think I see a flash of regret drive his gaze lower. It takes less than a second to pass.

"You know . . ." I continue, because I can't stop talking. My curiosity is too great. "You know, I found the album of the summer Mary was pregnant, right before John was born."

"Seems like a dream," Tom replies.

"It does."

"A dream," he repeats.

"Shirley was quite the photographer," I say in a steady voice. "She really knew how to capture all of us. In fact, there were so few photos of her."

"I always told her she needed to be in more pictures herself."

"Yeah." I pause. "But I also looked in the album of photos taken earlier that summer."

Tom doesn't say anything. I can't see his face in the shadows.

"There were some really beautiful photos of Mary. Absolutely stunning."

"That was Mary," he says, which seems like a strange thing to say, but I keep going anyway.

"They were so different, those photographs. I don't think Shirley could have taken them. Completely different style."

The cicadas and crickets are chirping, and the lake seems to have grown rough, perhaps from the wind that sweeps through the trees. Tiny waves lap against the dock. The trees whisper.

"Did you take those photos, Tom? The ones of Mary?"

He doesn't reply. In the shadows, he turns his face away from me toward the trees, away from the house. I keep waiting for him to say something, to admit that he had spent those months looking at Mary in such an intimate way.

Unexpectedly, he stands, not making a sound. At first I think he's going to walk right past me and disappear into his endless house, but as he passes me he stops. He stands there for what feels like a long time, and his hand comes down to rest on my shoulder. When he speaks, his voice is tired and soft.

"If you want, send Pearl out to the dock early tomorrow morning. Around eight. I'll teach her to swim. If she'd like."

I think about you jumping off the dock, vanishing into the cobalt water.

I nod, not saying anything. When his hand lifts from my shoulder, the movement is so subtle that at first I don't realize he's taken it away. It's only when I hear the back door of the house open and close that I register the absence of his touch.

I sit on the deck for a long time.

So, it was Tom who took those photos, Tom who captured Mary in that loving gaze. He saw something of her in those photos that I never saw. Everything about that time of my life—everything about Tom and Mary and Shirley—it all shifts in my mind. Questions knock on the door of my brain, but I don't want to let them in.

We have a certain way of recalling the past. Our mind relives those old days in particular ways, travels comfortable paths, but do we ever really know the whole story?

I stand up and dump my coffee over the deck. I need to check on you.

A Wedding and a Ring

Maybe I got the suit and tie from Tom. He would have had to sneak home to retrieve it, out from under the nose of his parents. The pants and coat were navy blue, almost black, and the tie was a yellow paisley. This was, what, thirty years before you came into this wild world?

I was waiting with Mary in the back of Tom's car on that hot day. My skin flamed up, and sweat gathered around the tight shirt collar and under my arms and trickled down the small of my back. Mary was in a plain white dress that made her look like a fairy or a princess. Her dark hair was braided, and the two braids formed a crown around the top of her head. When she smiled at me, when she reached over and took my hand, my heart soared.

"Are you sure you want to marry me?" I asked her, so earnest it hurt. "If you want to wait, we can wait."

"I'm so sure," she said, leaning over and putting her head on my shoulder as we waited for Tom and Shirley to come out. I could see her forehead and the small rivulets of sweat welling up.

It was the end of that first summer we'd spent at the cabin, a month after I proposed with the twist-tie ring, and Mary and I had persuaded Tom and Shirley to drive us across the state line to get married. In Nysa, you could only get married before you turned eighteen with your parents' permission. I knew my parents wouldn't give me permission, and Mary knew her mom would be depressed and her dad would kill us. Or at least he'd kill me. We had to drive about four hours, into the next state, where the legal age was seventeen.

Tom and Shirley took some convincing.

"Where are you going to live?" Tom had asked.

"We'll live apart until next summer, when we'll both be eighteen and finish school," I said. "After that, we'll tell our parents and get a house, or run away if we have to."

"So why not wait to get married until next summer? What's the point in being married if you can't live together?"

"Don't you want a proper wedding?" Shirley asked Mary with concern in her eyes.

"I don't care about that. We couldn't pay for it anyway, not now, not next summer. That won't change. I'm ready, Shirley," she insisted.

"You don't have to take us," I finally said. "But we're going, one way or another. We're getting married. We'll walk there if we have to." I searched Mary's face for some reassurance that we weren't crazy, that what we were doing was right. Her smile was enough.

Happiness found its way into Shirley's eyes as she came around to the idea.

"Married. My two friends. Kind of hard to believe," she said, smiling shyly and wrapping Mary in a hug.

But Tom didn't change his mind. I could never figure it out at the time, why he had such a problem with it. Eventually, it took Shirley talking him into it, and I had overheard them arguing about it the night before.

But all of that was in the past. In that moment, in the heat of the car, in the glaring sun and the August air heavy with humidity, it was only Mary and me. I dug in my pocket for a tissue and dabbed the sweat from Mary's forehead. She sighed.

Shirley came out, sat in the passenger seat with a nervous smile. When Tom climbed into the car, he didn't even give us a backward glance.

"All set?" That was all he said.

"Yep," I said. "Me and the missus are ready."

Shirley laughed at that, and Mary smiled. Tom grunted, whipped the car around, and sped down the drive.

"Tom!" Shirley protested. "Slow down!"

It was a long trip, and I dozed off and on along the way. I dreamed of swimming in the lake, Mary off in the distance. The water felt amazing, but a sense of frustration grew and grew as the various dreams progressed and I couldn't find my way to her. In the end, my limbs were exhausted, and I gave in to the water, sinking into its coolness.

I woke with a start, gasped for breath. Tom's eyes met mine in the rearview mirror, but neither of us said anything. Shirley's head rested against her door, bobbing with each bump in the highway. At some point during the drive Mary had leaned away from me, against her own window, sound asleep.

In that moment I had an overwhelming sense of panic. It was like I suddenly recognized how young we were—only seventeen! A stirring anxiety itched deep inside of me, a place I couldn't reach. My hands were the hands of a kid. I became strangely aware of how large Tom's suit was on me, how ill-fitting his shoes. The disappointment of my parents, should they find out that I had eloped, threatened to take my breath away.

I put my hands down to my sides, stared out through the glass. When I was about to tell Tom in a quiet voice that he should stop the car and turn around, I felt Mary's cool fingers intertwine with mine. She didn't look at me. I don't even know if she was awake. But her hand held lightly on to mine, and all of my doubts melted.

The town where we went to get married was called Deen, and it was much farther across the state line than we thought. We drove along the main street, where there were only a few shops: a pizza place, an antique store, an auto parts shop. Behind the line of stores, I could see a baseball field full of kids playing. Through the open car window, I could hear the ping of the ball on the bat, the shouting of the children, the protests about whether or not the batter was safe. I felt so old, watching that scene.

Tom muttered something about being lost.

"Why don't you ask those kids?" Shirley said hesitantly, and Tom must have been suitably frustrated because he actually pulled to the side of the road where a boy and a girl walked slowly along the shoulder.

"Hey, kid," Tom shouted through his open window. "What's your name?"

The boy was skinny, his baseball glove much too large for him. The girl's blonde hair was long and swirled around in the summer breeze. She pushed it aside and stared at us.

"Sam," the boy said.

"I'm Abra," the girl added, in a tone full of confidence and daring that said, *Who are you and what do you want?*

"Well, Sam and Abra, we're late for a wedding and looking for a little chapel." Tom wiped the sweat from his forehead. He said the name of the preacher and asked if they knew where the chapel was.

The boy thought about it for a minute. "I think if you keep going the way you're going, it's outside of town, on the right."

Tom pulled away.

"Thank you!" Shirley shouted.

"This town gives me the creeps," Tom muttered.

The boy was right—the chapel was beyond the town. Actually, it was a double-wide trailer where a small church congregation met, and the pastor was a larger-than-life Pentecostal preacher wearing a gray suit and black shoes that shone like the deepest reaches of space. He was balding ungracefully, the way someone does when they refuse to admit it and no one around them has the heart to break the news. Long, wispy brown hair was gathered from every corner of his skull and combed up and over the dome. During the entire ceremony, which didn't last more than ten minutes, he kept reaching up with a yellow handkerchief and wiping the sweat from his face and forehead.

When he asked for the rings, Tom reached in his pocket and handed me the green twist tie. Mary giggled as I slid it on her finger.

"I'll get you a real one soon as I can," I whispered at the end of the "with this ring, I thee wed" portion.

"I don't want another one," she whispered back.

When it was her turn to put my ring on my finger, Shirley handed her a small cloth bag, an inch square. Mary turned it upside down, and out of it fell a small gold band. My eyes must have bulged out of my head.

"Shirley picked it up for me," she explained. "It's probably too big, so I got you a chain so you can wear it around your neck."

I started crying. It was embarrassing. Tom put his hand on my shoulder, and I reached up and grabbed it. Shirley was crying too, and Mary.

"I now pronounce you man and wife," the preacher said, his face red from the heat. "Go ahead, give her a kiss."

We kissed, and it was salty from sweat. Her lips were cool, and the ring clung loosely to my finger. We must have gone on for too long, because Tom pulled me away, chuckling with embarrassment.

"Easy there," the preacher mumbled.

The four of us laughed and cried together, and in some ways it felt like something about our friendship had also been consecrated, as if we had all been officially joined to each other. Tom was better now that the deed was done and there was nothing he could do to persuade us otherwise. He was going along with it in his normally chipper way. Shirley kept putting her arm around Mary and hugging her. At one point, Shirley put my face between her hands, pulled me down to her, and kissed me square on the mouth.

I was shocked.

"Whoa!" Tom shouted.

"This girl is practically my sister," Shirley said earnestly, not letting go of my face. "That means you're practically my brother-in-law." She paused, and tears rose in her eyes again. "Take care of her." Her voice choked up, and she shook her head. "Take good care of her."

We drove back to Nysa, crossing the bridge only nine or ten hours after we had first made the crossing that day, but

I felt like a completely new person, like decades had passed. As we reached the apex of the bridge and I stared out over the island, the river, and the trees, it felt like the four of us were arriving as completely different people. Tom seemed larger somehow, transformed into an adult during the drive. Shirley hummed to herself, tapping one of her fingers on the edge of her door. Mary rolled down her window and sat there with her eyes closed, her dark hair blowing chaotically around her face, floating.

Dreams and Open Windows

checked on you last night, and all was well. Now it's the morning after, and I can't stop thinking about how Tom didn't answer my question about taking those photos of Mary. His lack of an answer was a good enough answer, as far as I'm concerned. It makes me feel strange, the idea that he paid such close attention to her during those summers. I'm not sure how to feel about it.

I slept a fitful sleep. I did not dream. Now I stand here, outside your room. I should wake you. I wonder if Tom will still want to give you those swimming lessons, or perhaps, after the way I grilled him last night, if he might possibly come out and ask us to leave. And of course there's the rug, which we still haven't told him about.

The knot is throbbing. I can no longer sleep on that side of my head, and there is an ache that spreads all the way down behind my ear, halfway to my shoulder. I've had no nausea recently, so hopefully that was a passing thing. It feels very real this morning: the end. What will I do if Tom sends us away?

I ease the door open to your room and immediately sense

a change. The air smells like the outside—like the woods, like the swiftly arriving fall—and it's much colder than the rest of the house. I can hear the morning breeze in the trees through the wide-open window. I walk past the rolled-up carpet, all the way across the room, and gaze at the forest. I even peek my head out and glance to the right, toward the lake.

It is a gorgeous, crisp fall morning. Geese fly overhead in a lopsided V, honking, and the sunlight hits the water at a shallow angle. I slide the window closed, and I notice leaves and dirt on the hardwood floors we cleaned the day before. They lead in a trail all the way across the room, to you.

"Pearl," I say, turning and standing over your bed. "Pearl."

You are so deep in sleep that you don't even move. I reach down and pull the comforter back, gently hold your shoulder, and give you a subtle shake. Your nightgown is damp, as though you had a fever that broke in the night. But the small patch of your nightgown that I can see has dirt smudges on it, and there are leaves in your hair.

"Pearl, wake up," I say, sounding stern. What have you been doing?

You moan and roll away from me, licking your lips.

"Pearl. Where were you?" I ask.

You take a deep breath, roll back to face me, and smile. "Good morning, Grampy."

"Pearl, your window was open."

"It was?"

"And there's dirt on the floor and leaves in your hair. Where have you been?"

A flash of memory moves across your face. "I thought it was a dream," you whisper.

"What was a dream?"

"She came again last night." You look at me, clearly nervous at what my reaction will be.

"Who?"

"The woman. The one who told me to cut squares in the carpet."

I sit down on the edge of the bed and take you in. You're so little under the covers, your face so innocent.

"Pearl," I begin, not knowing what to say after that.

"It's not my fault, Grampy. I can't stop her from coming."

"The window was locked, wasn't it?"

"That's true, but it seemed very important."

"So you let her in."

You nod reluctantly.

At this point, I'm at a loss as to what I should do next. Give you a good talking-to? Go find Tom and see if he'll give you a psychiatric examination on the spot? Pack everything up and leave? Instead, I do what I've always done.

"What happened, Pearl? What did she tell you?"

A subtle relief relaxes your face. This is what you tell me.

New Developments

At first, when I opened the window, she looked like a shadow, and I thought it had only been my imagination. Had I really seen her through the glass? Had I really heard her tapping? But she shifted from side to side, and I knew it was really her, and it made me scared and glad at the same time. I told her she got me in a lot of trouble, and why shouldn't I close the window on her right there and go back to bed? I was very stern with her, Grampy. You would have been proud of me.

But she said there were "new developments." That's what she called them. "New developments." She said there were pressing issues. Her words, not mine, Grampy. Pressing issues. She asked if I had the map with me, the one I had drawn.

I said that was fine, but why couldn't we do all of this during the day? She laughed at that, not a nice laugh, and said that she didn't do things during the day. That was no time at all to do the kinds of things she needed to do.

When she laughed like that, it was the first time I was afraid of her. I told her, fine, come in, but if she started making a mess like last time, I was going to run and get you, Grampy, and that would be the end of all this. She nodded and acted sad about it, but I knew she didn't really care.

That's what scares me the most about her, Grampy. She doesn't seem to care at all about the things we care about. When I saw her in the city, she seemed nothing but kind, but now I'm not so sure. Here, closer to this thing she needs to find, she seems kind of desperate.

I pointed at the small table not far from the window. My map was there—I had been working on it after you said good night to me. She bent over and stared at it like she was looking for something, and she laughed a loud "Ha!" and pointed at the cabin and the red X. She asked me in a quiet voice when I had added that, and I told her I thought she had added it yesterday.

She leaned in over the map. "Interesting," she said in a whisper. "Maybe I did."

She told me again that she needed my help, that there was something she had lost a long time ago. I told her I wasn't so sure that I could help, that I'm only a girl and most people call me flighty. A lot of people don't believe I see the things I see. I told her all of this.

"Well," she said, "you sound like the kind of person who can do what needs to be done."

She made a quiet sound kind of like a laugh and said she had "enlisted" many people to try to help her through the years, but none of them had been successful. She was sure I could do it though, and again she told me that if I helped her and we were successful, she might even be able to help you.

You, Grampy.

Anyway, when she said that, I knew I had to at least hear her out. I told her I couldn't commit to anything. I think you call that playing hardball, right, Grampy? I played hardball. I told her to tell me what was going on and after that I'd decide. But I really only agreed to listen because I needed to know how I could help you.

She said the island of Nysa is a very old island, older than almost any other place, and that there is a door that goes to some other place, an ancient door. A door that isn't always in the same place. Sometimes it's here and sometimes it's there. Someone who went through the door a long time ago took something of hers along with them. She doesn't think it was intentional—she was standing there helping them along, and they got scared and reached out and grabbed this thing of hers, and now it's gone. She can't follow—she's not allowed to go in there—so she's been trying to find someone who can go through that door, find what she lost, and bring it back.

I know it's hard to believe, Grampy. But this is what she told me. I don't know if it's true or not. I'm just telling you.

I asked her again what was taken from her, and this look of incredible sadness passed over her face.

"You'll know when you see it," she said.

"How?"

"You'll know."

I asked her, "What about the door, the one we tore up the carpet to find?" I told her I had gotten in a lot of trouble for that and she shouldn't go around destroying things that weren't hers. I started to cry. She bent down closer to me, and for the first time I could really see into her eyes, and they were kind. They were also sparking with life. I couldn't decide whether to look away or look deeper in.

She said she had thought the door would be here in the

house, for a few different reasons—something to do with Shirley. But she was wrong, and she said she was sorry. I believed her, Grampy. She was very sorry about it. And she said the door was almost certainly in the cabin where I had marked the X. She said I didn't have to make up my mind right now about whether or not I would help. I could wait until I saw the door, and after that I would have to decide if I was willing to go through it or not. And that if I wanted to save you, I would have to go through it.

So I went, Grampy. I went with her. I asked her if I could please go tell you first, but she turned away and asked me what I thought you would say. She asked me if I thought you would give me permission to go. And I knew she was right. Sorry, Grampy. I knew you would say no.

She helped me crawl out through the window, and when I took her hand it was so, so cold, like ice. When I felt how cold it was, I looked up at her quickly, surprised and scared, but her face was turned away from me, looking out at the lake. She asked me if I wanted to swim the lake or walk through the woods. The lake would be colder but quicker, and the woods would be dirtier and more difficult but not nearly as wet. She laughed when she said this. I said I didn't know how to swim, so I'd prefer the woods.

She paused. "You're going to need to learn how to swim before this is over." She seemed bothered that I didn't know how to swim. She started walking with long, even steps, and she didn't hike through the woods so much as flow through them. I had to run but still couldn't keep up, and soon she was far ahead of me. I think she forgot I was even with her. I shouted out to her to come back for me, and she did. She even apologized.

"If I'm so important," I asked, "why do you keep forgetting about me?"

She asked if I wanted to ride on her shoulders. I said she'd forget about me, probably run me into every low limb in the woods. She laughed and said it was true, she might forget, but if I thought her mind wandered, I could always pinch her hard in the shoulder and that would help. I asked her how she could be so forgetful, and she said she had a million things on her mind, quite literally, and that she couldn't be blamed if she occasionally forgot about one little girl in the middle of the woods.

She crouched down low, which was still high to me, and I climbed up on her back. I felt like a squirrel inching its way up a tall oak tree. When she stood up all the way, it took my breath away, and I grabbed onto her neck. Before I could say anything, she was melting through the woods again, crouching just in time so I didn't hit any branches, weaving in and out of the shadows. I felt like a shooting star.

Faster and faster she went, until the trees were a blur and we were moving quicker than any normal person could move. It rained for a few moments, and the cold drops soaked me straight through. When we passed through a clearing in the woods, I could see the stars rushing along in their paths above us. I thought I could even hear animals talking to one another, and I could understand them. It was so strange, Grampy. So strange.

She slowed down, and it felt like we had only been walking a few moments, but it also felt like a long time. I was cold, but she lifted me down from her shoulders and gave me something warm to drink. I started to walk forward, but she grabbed my shoulder and pulled me back into the shadows where we stood. It was the darkest part of the night, and even the sounds of the forest came to a rest. She told me to wait. Ahead of us was the cabin. The one where you and Grandma and Tom and Shirley spent those summers. I couldn't believe it.

I started asking her where the door was, but she stopped me, putting her hand over my mouth, and I pulled away—her hand was so cold. She stiffened, so I reached over and held on to her arm at the elbow, trying to prove that she wasn't too cold for me. She softened when I did this, even reached up and patted my hand.

"The door must be here," she whispered to herself, and she sounded frustrated. "This door is always causing all sorts of mischief. Would you like to go inside and see?"

A kind of fear boiled up in me so quickly I didn't know what to say, but she told me it was okay, she knew I was afraid, and she would go with me. So I told her yes.

"What will we do if we find it?" I asked.

"Finding it is the first concern," she said in a flat tone. "We'll worry about what to do after that."

The Door

From where we stood, the lake went on forever, shimmering in the night. We crept into the house real quiet and left the door open behind us, which I didn't think was a great idea, but when I went to close it, she snapped her fingers and hissed to get my attention. She shook her head, so I left the door open.

Inside the house, it was beautiful, mostly because of the pale light reflecting off the lake and in through the windows. It seemed like a completely different place than the one you and I had visited. It felt like a dream world. We crept through the house, through an even darker hallway with no windows. I wanted to ask the woman where we were going, but when I started to talk she held one of her icy fingers up.

In that back room, it was so dark I felt like I was floating in space. It even felt like there were rooms and hallways that I hadn't seen when we were there yesterday, like parts of the house were only visible in the moonlight when no one else was there. It was amazing. I heard the creaking of another door opening, and she whispered to me to watch my step. There were stairs, and we started walking down. We walked down the stairs for at least five minutes, not stopping. That's a lot of steps, Grampy. At one point, she stopped and muttered that she could probably risk a match, and I heard a quick scrape and a hiss and the match burst to life. I almost passed out when I saw where we were.

We were standing on a long, unending flight of rickety wooden steps. Behind us, the light didn't go all the way up to where we had started, and below us was a dark hole that the steps vanished down into. There were no walls, only an endless abyss on either side of us. I held on to the rail as tight as I could, because the steps were steeper than I had realized when we had been going down in the darkness. I leaned forward and blew out the match, and she asked me, kind of upset, why I had done such a thing. I told her it was too far down—I didn't want to see. She could light a match when we got to the bottom.

She laughed again, and it was louder than before. It made me start to feel once again that maybe she really did like me, that she really did care about me and you and what happened to us. Her laughter was kind, and it seemed like her own laughter even brought her back to this place, reminded her where she was and what she was doing.

Another few minutes of walking down steps and she asked me in a sarcastic voice if I gave her permission to light another match. I mumbled something about not being a smart aleck. Another match spit to life, and she shielded it with her hands.

In front of us were three doors.

She took in a quick breath and froze, staring at the doors, a smile spreading across her face. "This is it," she said.

She asked me if I could find my way to that spot again, and I said I thought I could. She nodded and pointed at the first door on the left.

"That's the way," she said. "That's the way. You'll have to come back on your own. I really shouldn't go any further."

"Why can't I go now?"

"The night is almost over," she said. "It wouldn't be any good now. You need to come back at night."

I asked if this was the door we had been looking for when we cut up the carpet, and she stood there for a very long time, silent, staring at the door.

"Yes." She hesitated. "I'm almost certain."

"What do I do when I go through the door?" I asked.

"You'll know." But she said it in such a way that made me think she didn't really know herself what I was supposed to do or what I might find there.

"Can't you tell me anything?" I asked. "I don't understand how something can be so important to you but you don't know anything about it."

"I already told you," she replied in a soft voice. "A long time ago, someone took something from me when they went through the door. I can't go through myself—I'm simply not able to—so I need you to go inside and bring it back out, the thing they took."

It was almost morning. She kept saying that. We ran up the stairs as quietly as we could, like cats, but if you walk downstairs for ten minutes, it takes longer than that to go back up. My legs were so tired. I sat down on the steps and cried. I couldn't go any farther. My legs were too tired. I couldn't do it. I thought she had forgotten about me.

A hand grabbed my arm, and I screamed. It was the silver-haired woman—I couldn't see anything, but I knew it was her because of her icy touch. She lifted me up in her arms like a baby, and we rushed up the stairs. She moved so quickly that before I could blink we were outside and into the woods.

I don't know the timing of everything, but the sky was starting to lighten as we swept along through the forest. I fell asleep in her arms, and when I woke up, she was lowering me gently through the window. I tried to see her face one last time as she lowered me down, but she had pulled up her hood, and it cast a deep shadow. And besides, I fell asleep as soon as she put me down. It didn't matter that I was lying on the wood floor. I was so tired.

Going Under

The three of us sit at the table eating a simple breakfast of bacon and eggs. You seem hungrier than normal, wolfing down the food like it's your last meal. You reach for more bacon and moan with delight after each bite, the sounds pulling a slight smile onto Tom's face. He seems to have withdrawn again, acting more like the Tom we met at the diner a couple days ago, and I think it's because of the question I asked him last night, the one about him taking those photos of Mary.

I sigh and push my eggs around. I'm not hungry. Is this lack of appetite a result of the diagnosis or the sickness spreading inside of me, or am I too despondent after Tom's and my conversation last night? I have to admit it was strange seeing those photos and realizing that someone else saw Mary that way. He noticed her. He took her in. This started an uneasiness working its way through me, and it hasn't stopped this morning.

There is no way you could have hiked through the woods at night to our cabin, not through the rain and the cold. And besides that, how would you even have found your way? No,

Pearl, it's not possible. I am worried for you, worried enough to talk with Tom about the things you're saying, even though I'd rather not talk to him at all right now after seeing those photos.

"Do you still want to learn to swim?" he asks you in a disinterested tone.

"Oh, yeah," you say, your mouth full.

"Pearl," I say.

You chew your food and swallow, blushing. "Sorry. I would love that."

"Well," Tom continues, "when you're finished eating, get on your swimsuit. If that's okay with you, Paul?"

"Sure." I shrug, trying to pretend it means nothing to me one way or the other.

At around a quarter to ten on that bright morning, we find ourselves walking out to the dock in our swimsuits, each of us carrying a towel and shivering. The September air is finally chilly, and I hug my arms to my chest. A breeze kicks up, rushing toward us from out over the lake.

We all bumble our way into the boat, and Tom starts it up. He only runs the motor for a few seconds though, long enough to get us about fifty feet away from the dock, out into the lake.

"Should be nice and deep here," he says, and before I know what he's doing, he jumps out of the boat and disappears under the water. When he comes up, he's smiling. It's the kind of smile that can't help surfacing, the kind of smile that I can tell he is trying to keep to himself. It's the old Tom peeking through.

"Can you throw in the anchor?" he asks me, so I do. "Come to the back of the boat," he tells you, treading water.

You sit on the steps at the back of the boat. Some of the water laps up over the edge of the lowest step, rolling over your toes.

"It's so cold!" you protest, hopping backwards, up out of the water.

"Jump in. I'll catch you." Tom puts his hands out in front of him. "Come on. Don't be afraid."

"I'm not afraid," you say, and I have to smile, because those are always words that lead you into action. Afraid? You are the least afraid person I've ever met.

You stand at the back of the boat, and the tiny lake waves barely move the boat up and down. You jump, and you're under.

You come up with a shriek. "It's freezing!"

Tom laughs, a wholehearted laugh, the first I've heard from him since we arrived, and you grin. The sound of it takes me back decades. Even if I couldn't see, had I heard that laugh, I would have known exactly who it was.

For the next ten minutes or so, Tom proceeds to teach you how to float on your back and how to tread water. At one point, he comes over and pulls himself up onto the back of the boat. The two of us watch you float on your back. Your eyes are closed, your face and fingertips the only things breaking the surface. It's like you're dead, or in some faraway place.

"She's a quick learner," Tom observes. "Can you hand me my towel?"

"Is she okay out there on her own?"

"She's fine. She's got the floating thing down."

The morning feels so good, so new. It's inconceivable on this morning how sickness and death and darkness can even exist.

"About last night—"

"I don't really want to talk about it, Tom. It's okay. Let's let it go for now."

Tom nods. "Fair enough."

"There's something else though," I say.

Tom looks at me. I'm still staring at you out there in the water, afraid to take my eyes off you in case you sink down into the depths. I can feel Tom's gaze on the side of my face.

"It's about Pearl." I tell him the story you told me, and when I finish talking, the day is quiet, the morning breeze has died down, and the boat is almost completely still. You are still floating, eyes closed. The sunlight glares off the water.

"Yes," Tom whispers to himself. "Yes, I see."

"So, what do you think?" I ask him, still not taking my eyes off you.

"What do I think?"

"Yes."

"I assume you mean, do I think Pearl is suffering from some form of psychosis."

I bite my lip and nod. "That sounds about right."

"Paul, things are not as simple as that. Psychosis is not an off-or-on switch—this person is, this person is not. Pearl may well be exhibiting subtle signs of psychosis, but I would only be able to determine the extent of that after meeting with her regularly, over a series of sessions."

"She's having conversations with people who don't exist," I whisper. "She's on a mission to save me, and this mission has her flying through the woods and going down endless stairs in a house we both know doesn't have an endless stair-way."

Your arms flutter in the water, and I stand, causing the boat to shift. But you regain your composure, and soon you're floating again, completely still.

"Doesn't that count for something?" I continue.

"Perhaps," Tom admits.

I find myself fuming at him. But before I can come up with another comeback, he speaks again.

"You know, it might do her good to stay out here for a little while. For both of you to stay. Only if you'd like, of course. A change of scenery might be exactly what she needs in order to shed some of these things."

Your delusions feel more serious to me than that. But Tom hasn't seen the carpet. He wasn't there when I found you in bed this morning after you had obviously been wandering the woods late at night by yourself. I don't know what else to say.

"Let's give it some time," Tom says, and I can't help but feel like a placated child.

As we sit there at the back of the boat, your eyes pop open, staring up at the sky. You peek into the water out of the corner of your eye, as if straining to see something barely outside of your vision. Panic comes over your face.

You quickly roll over onto your belly, duck your head under the water, and you're gone, down into the depths of the lake.

The Loss of You

Pearl!" I cry out, getting ready to jump in and follow you. But the boat leans hard into the water and then rises so quickly that I stumble backwards. Tom has jumped in. I take a few sharp steps to the back of the boat. I experience again what I lived through on the day Mary left me. Even in the midst of the chaos, I recognize the smallest details: the warmth of the late morning sun; the far-off edge of the lake where it curves over to meet Tom's house; the way the haze is clearing from the sky, the bright blue taking its place; and the pale, daytime moon hanging wispy and transparent over the trees.

I dive in and go under, and I have to remind myself not to breathe, because the iciness of the lake nearly causes me to gasp. How were you floating there unfazed in this freezing water? I open my eyes, but it's too dark to see anything. I kick as hard as I can to the bottom, waving my arms frantically, searching for you, but I feel nothing—not you, not the bottom, not branches or fish or anything. Only cold, cold water swirling through my outstretched fingers.

I can't reach the bottom. I can't find you. The underwater

world might as well be deep space, and I wish I could stay there for a long time, explore the dark places at the bottom. Is this what death is like?

I stay under as long as possible, until a red haze begins to press in at the edges of my eyesight and I'm about to pass out. I turn and let my sorrow drag me to the top. The cold of the water no longer bothers me. I am numb to it. I burst through the surface and gorge myself with air, unable to take it in quick enough.

Scanning the surface for bubbles, I tread water and gather myself to take another plunge, but as I breathe, Tom pops up lightly from the depths.

"Did you . . ." I begin.

He doesn't answer. He gives me a look that has a warning, one I don't recognize. Is he telling me to be careful? To stay back? To prepare myself for the loss of you? He takes a few deep breaths and sinks into the water, his feet breaking the surface as he kicks his way straight down from the spot where you vanished moments before.

The Glassy Sea

The fall after Mary and I got married blurred past with high school activities that tried to mark our senior year. We spent as many of our days as we could together. I kept promising her I'd get her a small diamond ring as soon as possible, but she smiled and turned the twist tie on her ring finger.

"I've already got you, Paul. I don't need a ring."

Did she prefer the twist-tie ring because it didn't draw any unwanted attention or questions? The truth is, she was changing. The laughing, lighthearted Mary I had met at the Halloween party one year before had begun to withdraw during our first summer at the cabin, and by the time school was in full swing, she'd become almost a recluse. It wasn't that she avoided Tom, Shirley, or me, but when we were all together, I'd so often find her staring off into the distance, eyes glazed over. Those moments always gave me a sinking feeling in the pit of my stomach—they made me feel like I was losing her, that she might leave me. But just as quickly, she'd snap out of it, her eyes clearing, and she'd smile bashfully at me and take my hand. The few times I voiced my concerns, she waved them off gently. I let her do that. It was easier that way.

Autumn in Nysa is always like some kind of golden era in a fairy world. The trees slip from green to the brightest reds and golds you've ever seen. When October hits, the days are suddenly shorter, the darkness gathering in pools along the main road. The four of us spent those chilly evenings in the diner or in secluded spots along the lake, sitting close to crackling fires, our arms around each other. I don't know why, but when I think of that autumn before our final summer together, it seems like a quiet time, an era in our lives when we did more than our fair share of staring into the flames and not speaking, of looking out over the lake with our hands in our pockets, breath becoming visible in the cold air.

Winter followed fall, and while autumn's short days had felt appropriate in a melancholy sort of way, winter's darkness seemed like an affront. I could feel Mary withdrawing into herself even further, and a flat sadness glazed over her eyes as she stared off into the cold distance. We could spend an entire evening together in which she'd say barely a handful of words.

Only the snow snapped her out of it, and we got an unusual blizzard in early December. The four of us even went sledding on the hill behind the school, and Mary gave a real smile for the first time in two or three months. The little children sledding alongside watched us with amazement, surprised that teenagers could enjoy such a simple, childish pleasure.

Whenever I asked if she was okay, she gave a half-hearted

attempt at consoling me, reaching across the table at the diner and forcing a smile that only had the strength to lift one side of her face.

"Oh, Paul, I'm in a blue funk. It will pass."

There were three churches in Nysa: Our Lady of Nysa Catholic Church, Saint John's Episcopal, and First Baptist. It wasn't a full range of churches like most towns have these days, but it was enough. The parking lot of Our Lady was almost always empty, except for a green Ford pickup truck that I assumed belonged to the priest, even though it didn't fit the image I had of what a priest might drive. None of my friends were Catholic; in fact, I didn't know of a single Catholic on the entire island. But I always felt drawn there—maybe by the tall steeple that reached up into the sky, maybe by the way the gold letters of the name shone in the sun, or maybe simply by the emptiness. When it came to God, I wasn't sure what I believed, but I preferred to explore his realm on my own, away from the crowds.

Saint John's Episcopal Church was an old brick church with a bell and a fountain outside that I sometimes saw children playing in. The rector was a middle-aged man who, during the week, sat on a bench on the sidewalk and looked up hopefully at anyone who walked by. He was not a Nysa native and never would be, even though he had lived there for twenty years or so. Even being born in Nysa doesn't confer legitimate Nysa status—for that, you need to have a couple sets of grandparents who grew up there, and preferably at least one set of great-grandparents as well.

First Baptist was the obvious front-runner in our town. On Sundays people had to park on the street because the parking lot was full, and we watched them glide confidently through the wide, welcoming front doors and into the presence of God Almighty. The men wore mostly navy-blue or gray suits with paisley ties while the women swished along in ankle-length dresses and heels. Sometimes we could hear them singing all the way from the diner.

> Holy, holy, holy! Lord God Almighty!
> Early in the morning our song shall rise to thee.
> Holy, holy, holy! Merciful and mighty,
> God in three persons, blessed Trinity!

> Holy, holy, holy! All the saints adore thee,
> Casting down their golden crowns around the glassy sea;
> Cherubim and seraphim falling down before thee,
> Which wert, and art, and evermore shalt be.

"What do you think they mean by that?" I asked Tom one Sunday morning while the four of us grabbed brunch at the Nysa Diner.

"What does who mean by what?" Tom asked, shoveling a forkful of omelet into his mouth.

"'God in three persons, blessed Trinity,'" I said.

Tom shrugged. "Who knows what church people think."

"The Trinity is made up of God the Father, God the Son, and God the Holy Spirit," Shirley recited unexpectedly.

We all gaped at her before bursting out laughing.

"What?" she said, blushing.

"How'd you know that?" Tom asked, admiration and confusion mixing in his voice.

Shirley shrugged. "My parents used to take me to church when I was little, that's all."

"Mine too," I admitted. "But I don't remember any of it."

"What were they saying about a glassy sea?" I asked, hoping Shirley could enlighten me.

But she took another sip of her orange juice and shrugged. I stared out through the window and imagined the cold lake waters on that December morning. We sat there eating and not saying a word, and at first Mary's voice was so quiet I didn't know she was talking.

"It's where you go after you die," she whispered. "Over the sea, and it's where everything wrong is made right."

How quiet we were after Mary said that, none of us even eating or drinking. The only sound was the rest of the people in the diner chatting, their metal silverware clinking against the plates, the old men slurping their piping hot coffee, and the cook in the back calling out orders as they were ready.

Tom tried to say something funny to lighten the mood, but Mary's words clung to us.

It's where everything wrong is made right.

A few weeks later, Tom pulled his car up along the sidewalk, and the four of us walked into Saint John's Episcopal Church. We chose the Episcopal church because the Catholic church was too intimidating and the Baptist church seemed to require a level of dressing up we could not attain to. It was a cold Sunday night, only a few days before Christmas. I guess that's why we were there. We wanted to celebrate our last Christmas as high school students, mark the season outside of our own disinterested homes strung with limp strands of weak lights.

It was a small church and could seat a hundred during a normal service, but because it was nearly Christmas, the wooden, unpadded pews were squeezed full. The walls were painted a bright white, and each stained-glass window seemed to tell a story. I could feel the gaze of all the other people on us as we entered.

We stood when everyone else stood and sat when everyone else sat. We read the words when the cues came, and our voices melted in with all the others.

Why had we decided to go to church? Were we looking for something different in the world, something new?

Mary sat very close to me, holding my hand the entire time. I glanced over at her. We had been secretly married for four months, and I felt a growing connection with her, a sense that we belonged to each other. No, it wasn't quite that—it was that we were becoming each other, that the lines separating what made up me from what made up her were blurring, and what made each of us, us, was mixing.

The rector finished his sermon, and then he and a bunch of other robed people began going through the motions of preparing us for communion. At least, that's what I gathered from the program. Shirley occasionally leaned in and explained things when we had questions (which happened every minute or so). Even though she hadn't grown up in the Episcopal church, she knew some of the terminology.

As the rector waved his hands over the bread and the

wine, Mary's grip on my hand turned into a vise. I leaned over to jokingly tell her to ease up a little, but when I saw her face, my heart sank. Her skin was nearly the color of the white walls, her lips a straight line.

"What's wrong?" I whispered.

But she only shook her head. She didn't let up on my hand.

The priest explained communion and invited up anyone who wanted to partake. I glanced at Tom and Shirley, and they shrugged. *Why not?* That didn't surprise me—they were normally up for just about anything. Mary nodded too, but the fear was still in her eyes.

We stood when it was our turn and waited in the line that led to the front. Mary was in front of me at that point, her hand trailing behind so that she could still hold mine. I leaned forward. The scent of her was intoxicating—she smelled like vanilla and springtime.

I whispered in her ear, "What's wrong?"

"She's here." She cast the words over her shoulder.

"Who?"

"That woman who was looking in our windows at the cabin."

"Where?" Now my heart was racing.

"Up front. Behind the priest."

There was no one behind the priest.

No one. Not a man, woman, or child.

I didn't say anything else. We shifted our way to the front, knelt at the altar, and waited for the priest to press the bread into our hands ("The body of Christ"), then waited for one of the others to tip the cup of wine into our mouths ("The cup of salvation"). The knot never left my stomach, this sense that Mary was ill. She needed something, or someone, that I could never provide or be for her.

When we returned to our seats, the knot turned into an ache.

All I wanted to do was leave. I thought again of Mary's words.

Where everything wrong is made right.

Sometimes everything being made right seems an impossible distance away.

Following Her Down

I follow Tom down again, leaving the sounds above me, and sink into the freezing lake. This passing from one world to the next comes with a simple blip in my ears as they plug against the water. I try to kick my way to the bottom, but I am in no shape for this, and my buoyancy pulls me up. I am momentarily envious of Tom's fit body, his ability to move through the water like an otter. I float unwillingly back to the surface, gasp for air once again. Tom is still under. The clouds float lazily across the sky, indifferent. A gull, miles from the ocean, calls out in a lonely voice.

When the two of you emerge, Tom taking in a long breath, blinking water from his eyes, dragging you up out of the depths, I expect you to be dead. It seemed so long since you went under that I'm shocked to hear you coughing, choking on water. Tom swims gently on his back, tugging you along with one of his arms, speaking soft words into your ear.

"It's okay," he whispers, taking in a deep breath before speaking again. "You're okay."

I swim weakly behind you both to the boat. I say your

name with each sputtering exhale, gasping it out. "Pearl. Pearl. Pearl."

Your eyes are open but dim, your mouth wet with water and drool, your hair clinging to your head like seaweed.

"Hold her while I get into the boat," Tom says.

I grab you with one arm around your chest, my other arm holding on to the back of the boat. You turn, fold your skinny, cold arms around my neck, and start to cry.

While Tom gathers himself in the boat and prepares to lift you, I pull you tighter to me and whisper into your ear, "Pearl, what happened?"

"She pulled me under," you whisper.

"Who pulled you under? Tom?"

"No." You bury your face deeper in the crook of my neck. "The woman."

"The silver-haired woman?"

"She was under the water the entire time. She wanted to show me something, she wants to help me learn how to swim underwater, and she pulled me under."

I think about the look on your face before you sank, the way you glanced down into the water with something like recognition.

"Pearl," I whisper, not knowing what to say.

"She only wants to teach me. She just wants to help," you say again, this time in a neutral voice without fear or regret. "That was all. It's very important."

"What did she show you?" I ask.

Tom reaches down to take you from me, but I hold up my hand, motioning for him to wait.

"Everything," you say, and there is a deep sadness in your eyes.

Something beyond Us

t was cold, so cold, when we left the church and walked out into the winter air. I put my arm around your grandmother and held her tight. It seems funny calling her your grandmother. We were so young, only teenagers at the time, and she had less than one year to live.

She was so shaken by seeing the silver-haired woman in the church that her body trembled when we left, so I put my arm around her shoulders and pulled her in to stop the shaking. Tom and Shirley were in front of us, so they didn't notice. The walk through the parking lot was quiet, and the stars were bright above us. In the western sky a darkness was gathering, clouds bringing in another snowstorm.

"Well, that was interesting," Tom stated as we all found our spots in his car. Shirley sat in the passenger seat, a peaceful smile on her face.

"What are you smiling at?" Tom asked, laughing.

She shrugged. "I don't know. I liked it."

"Liked what?" He seemed to be getting more and more confused by Shirley's obvious enjoyment of the church service.

"I don't know. Goodness, Tom. Why are you being this way?"

"I'm not being any which way," Tom said, his voice softening. "I want to know what you liked about it."

"It was peaceful," Mary offered unexpectedly from where she rested against me in the back seat.

"Really?" I asked, surprised at how quickly she'd forgotten her terror at seeing the woman.

But Shirley had found an ally, and she pressed the advantage. "Yeah! That's it. It was peaceful. Didn't it feel wonderful taking communion?"

Tom turned on the car but didn't make a move to drive away. "Wonderful? I don't know about that." But I could tell by his voice that something about the service had moved him. He clapped his hands to warm them, then blew on them so that his breath steamed out between his fingers. "I mean, I wasn't crazy about sharing that cup with everyone."

"That's not what I'm talking about," Shirley said, pouting.

"That's what I keep asking you!" Tom laughed out loud and clapped his hands against the steering wheel. "What in the world are you talking about?"

We all laughed, even Mary.

"Oh, Tom," Shirley said in a wistful voice. "I don't even know what it was." She paused, but no one else broke the silence, so she kept going. "You guys know how it felt this past summer when we were out on the lake, drifting along in our kayaks, and none of us were paddling or anything. We were floating on the water, under a blue sky, the hot sun shining down."

I knew what she meant.

"You remember how that felt? Like we were the only ones

in the world, but there was something else too, something beyond us, something that cared?"

I felt Mary's head nod against my shoulder.

"That's what I felt tonight, when we took communion." She turned toward Tom. "That's what I'm talking about."

He reached over and squeezed her hand, then adjusted the rearview mirror and pulled away from the sidewalk. I knew what Shirley meant. I knew exactly what she meant. Because that's how it had felt to me too.

"I saw her there tonight," Mary whispered so quietly I wasn't sure if the two up front had heard her.

Shirley's head snapped around. "What?" she asked, her face no longer in that saint's ecstasy.

"The woman who was at the cabin last summer."

"Where?"

"Behind the priest."

"Where should we go?" Tom asked, either not hearing or not caring what Mary was talking about.

"Tom!"

"What?" he asked in a wounded voice.

Shirley turned back to Mary. "Why didn't you say something?"

"I told Paul."

Shirley's piercing gaze darted over to me, and I could feel Tom's eyes searching me in the rearview mirror.

"And?" Shirley asked, directing the word at me.

"And what?" I asked.

"What did you do?"

"What did I do?" I didn't know what to say or how to say it. "I didn't see her." How could I tell them that the person Mary told me she saw wasn't there? That she was a figment of her imagination? That Mary was probably mentally un-stable? This beautiful girl. My young wife.

"Why didn't you tell us?" Tom asked me.

I eased away from Mary and stared out the window at the small town of Nysa as we drove through.

"So we'll go to the diner," Tom said, but Mary spoke up.

"Can you drop me at my house, Tom?"

A heavy sort of quiet settled in the car, and no one said anything. Soon the town was behind us and we were out in the countryside, the trees reaching down over us. Then we were flying through the flat, empty fields. Snow began to fall, swirling at us through the night, strobing in and out of the car's headlights, distracting, mesmerizing.

Let's Not Leave Her Alone Anymore

You are wrapped in a thick down comforter, lying on one of the deck chairs like a sideways cocoon, like a moth waiting to be transformed. The blanket even comes up over the top of your head so that only your face is showing: your sweet, round eyes are closed, your lashes tender and at peace. I panic again, convinced you have died after your submersion in the lake, your near drowning, but then I see the slight expansion and retreat of the blanket where it wraps around your chest. The thought that races through my mind, that you are alive, that you are fine, sends a rush of relief through me.

Tom swoops out of his house and onto the deck carrying three mugs. He bends his knees and manages to place one of the mugs under your chair—hot chocolate with a generous portion of cloud-like marshmallows floating on top.

"Something warm to drink," he says, handing me a cup of black coffee.

I have to admit, the warmth is welcome. Even though the

sun is still shining, this late September day has gotten cooler, and a brisk wind sweeps up off the lake. I look out at the water, and it doesn't bring the same sense of peace that it often has before—I have this sense that something sinister lies beneath its surface. I think of your story, of the woman beneath the water, beckoning to you. I shake my head to clear it away. I have enough to worry about in life without taking on your imaginary stories. Such as this knot on my head. Such as finding you a place to live after I'm gone. Such as dealing with the pit that has resided squarely in my stomachever since I saw those photos Tom took of your grandmother.

"Thanks," I say, taking the tiniest sip of coffee. It is scalding hot.

"She okay?" he asks me.

I glance at you, not because I need to in order to answer the question, but because everything brings me back to you. Always.

"I think she'll be fine," I say, shrugging. "That was strange."

"I don't know how she went so deep so quickly," Tom replies, raising his own mug to his face and blowing. "Especially for someone who can't swim."

The coffee smells comforting, familiar. I take another sip.

Sitting there on Tom's deck, behind his house, at the end of his long lane, fills me with a feeling of isolation like I've never had before. We are so far from civilization. In front of us the lake spreads out, and the far bank isn't visible, even on clear days. We are fifteen miles or so outside of the small town of Nysa, which is a forty-five-minute drive from the highway, which is an hour or two from any other place.

Part of me feels relieved to be so far away, so removed

from the world. It's like the further removed I am from normal life, the further removed I am from my diagnosis. If I can refrain from reaching up and touching the knot, I can almost believe it's not there. Except for the tightening of my skin at the corner of my eye. And the dull ache that radiates down my neck.

But being far away also comes with a certain level of anxiety. What if I need emergency treatment? What if you break a bone or need a doctor?

What if Tom is not who I remember him to be, and we're stuck out here in the middle of nowhere with him? What if he tries to do something?

"Amazing how much she resembles Mary," Tom says.

It's true. Of course I've noticed this before, but I don't like the way he says it, so I take another sip of coffee and hope the subject will change.

"Do you remember when Mary told you she was pregnant with John?" he asks, and there is some strange element in his voice I can't recognize.

"I'll never forget it," I reply, smiling.

"The four of us were in the diner, and it was late, wasn't it? Like one or two in the morning. Someone said something about a baby."

"You said you'd die if your mom had another baby."

"Is that what it was? I guess it could have been. There were so many of us siblings." He laughs, and I can't help but smile.

"One too many, as far as I'm concerned," I say.

He laughs again. "And Mary started crying."

"Yeah, she was pretty upset. That's when she said it. 'Paul, would you die if I had a baby? Because I'm pregnant.'"

"When was that?"

"January or February, I guess. But when she said that, I thought I was going to have a heart attack right there in the diner."

"Wouldn't have been the first person to die of a heart attack in that place," he jokes. He pauses for a minute, seems to see me, really see me, for the first time in the conversation. "Why'd you guys keep the baby?"

"Why'd we keep John?" I ask. His question rubs me the wrong way.

"You didn't know it was John at the time."

"We were married." I can feel myself getting defensive.

"You were barely eighteen. Were you even eighteen yet?"

I try to shrug off the conversation. "That was forty years ago, Tom."

"I don't get it."

I look over at you still sleeping in your cocoon and point to you. "That's why. Right there. Pearl."

Tom stares at you for a long time. A cloud covers the sun, and the breeze picks up, rattling the leaves. There is a yellow tint to the forest—has it been this way since we arrived, or did the leaves start changing color the previous night?

"Fair enough," Tom says, taking a long sip from his mug. "Fair enough."

This is where I'm torn, because even though I'm realizing Tom is not the same person I knew forty years ago (who would be?), even though this new quiet and subdued side of him makes me feel ill at ease, I still need a place for you to be when I'm gone. He seems kind. He seems like he could care for you. I reach up and gingerly feel the knot on my head.

"Tom," I ask hesitantly, "would you consider talking to Pearl later today?"

He looks at me inquisitively. "Sure. Anything specific?"

"You know, all the things I've been telling you about. Her . . . imagination."

"So, you mean, speak with her in my professional capacity as a therapist?"

I nod. "She thought the same woman dragged her down into the lake today."

He frowns, licks his lips, takes a sip of coffee. When he swallows, his sharp Adam's apple disappears. He clears his throat. "I'll talk to her. But let her get some more rest first." He leans his head back on his padded deck chair and closes his eyes. "I'll talk to her."

"I'll carry her to her room," I say. "She can rest there until lunchtime."

"Take the boat out. If you'd like."

"I'm not much of a sailor. Maybe I'll give it a try."

I pick you up. Your hot chocolate is still under the chair. You are almost too heavy for me, and I grunt with the effort.

"Paul?"

"Yeah?"

"Let's not leave her alone anymore. Not until I have a chance to talk with her."

I nod. "Yeah. I'll take her in and let her rest on the sofa."

Too Many Secrets

The day passes strangely. You are in and out of sleep on the couch in the living room. I get you soup for lunch, and you eat most of it. I sit on the floor beside the sofa, reading to you. I pace the room and the deck and the kitchen, looking for food but not really hungry.

The oddest part of it all is Tom. He sits in an armchair in the corner, not saying much. I think I saw him fall asleep at one point, but besides that he simply sits, resting, observing. It all feels rather professional. I have a strange fear that he will charge us for these hours, that I won't be able to pay him. At one point he walks over to the deck doors and stares out over the lake. Other than that, I don't see him get up.

"Do you mind if I go into town?" I ask him. You are still asleep on the couch.

"Go for it," Tom says. "If she wakes up, I'll have a chat with her, try to get a conversation started. We'll go from there."

I walk to the front door.

"Take my car," Tom suggests.

"That's okay. Thanks. I'll just take mine."

I hate to leave you, but a few things compel me to go back into town. First of all, I need to see if it's really as dire a little village as it seemed when we first arrived. I want to see if there's a school, other children, a potential life here for you. I'm feeling more and more urgent with each passing day to find you a landing spot after I'm gone.

Anytime to three months.

Second, and perhaps even more urgently, I have this inexplicable desire to go back to the diner. I feel like there's something there, something I missed. The story you made up when we were there, and especially the things you said about the waitress, have left me wondering.

The drive reminds me of everything I grew up loving about Nysa—the forest that borders the lake, the wide-open fields, the way the roads bend and turn. I'm smiling to myself, and I open the window a few inches. I wish you were with me and think about going back, but you were sleeping so peacefully, and I really do hope Tom has a chance to talk with you about the woman. I press on.

Even in the midst of this beauty, a cloud rises from the direction of the town. Getting closer, I see it's black smoke billowing from a farmer's burn pile. I close the window to keep out the acrid smell, and as I pass the farm, I can see the fire roaring in the middle of a harvested cornfield. An old man and his wife take things from the back of a dilapidated pickup and toss them into the flames, retreating from the heat after throwing each item.

I slow down and look over into the field, and the couple stops what they're doing, returning my stare. He slouches, loops his hands in his jeans pockets, and she leans heavily on a shovel. Their faces are flat, inexpressive, and I instinctively wave. But they don't move a muscle. For as long as I can see them in the rearview mirror, they watch me drive away.

The town emerges from the fields and the trees and the blue sky. I drive in on Main Street once again, and the town is every bit as quiet as it was when you and I arrived. I half expect to see a rolling tangle of tumbleweed blow past. I think about stopping at one of the churches, but I pass each one. The diner is still calling me.

Somehow, though, the air changes as I pull into the diner's parking lot. I don't know if it's because I'm alone or if the chilly air of my favorite season is reviving my spirits, but I feel a lightness there as I park. The sun glares bright off the glass, and when I get out of the car, I can smell the greasy fare of my teenage years: French fries cooking and hamburgers on the grill.

Inside, the counter is fifty percent occupied, and there's almost a busy hum to the place. I walk behind the stools and make my way to what I still think of as my booth. The sticky floor squeaks under my shoes, and the sound brings a smile to my face. This crazy old diner. So many memories.

Why am I here? I feel deep in my soul that I'm here for a reason. That this is precisely where I should be. But why?

The same waitress we had before comes to the booth, and she seems downright pleasant. I wonder if she has changed or if it's my mood that's changed the way I see her. I order a burger and fries and watch the door swing behind her as she goes back to the kitchen.

Seated at the counter are a few distinct groups: three old men hunch together and take turns talking, smiling at each other; two businessmen nod at each other's advice; at the far side of the diner sit the three men who were here when

Pearl and I first arrived. The bell above the door rings, and two women each wrangle a stroller through the swinging door. One of the businessmen gets up and holds the door. The two women find a booth right inside the door and place their respective children on the bench seat beside them. The children are small, maybe two or three years old, and they stand there staring out the glass, putting everything they can find in their mouths.

So there are children in Nysa.

The door swings open, and the waitress brings out my food. In that flash of a moment when the door is open, I can see into the kitchen. The shelves are full of supplies, and I think of Pearl's hypothetical. The witch queen of Nysa. A thousand stairs down.

I look up at the woman, and a flash of the old darkness passes over my eyes. I realize she's been talking to me.

"I'm sorry. Pardon me?"

"Is this everything?" She chews her gum, mouth wide open with each smack.

"Yes, yes, of course. Thank you."

She turns to go, but words erupt from me, unexpected words.

"Did you grow up here?" I ask.

She turns back toward me, suspicious. "My whole life."

"Did we know each other?" I ask, although I knew so few people in high school. And after I met Mary, I didn't care about meeting anyone else.

She sighs. I'm not going to give up, at least not easily, and I can tell by the look on her face that she's weighing her desire to keep her name to herself with the hassle that might ensue if she doesn't tell me. She gives in.

"Jenny Hudson."

I know that name. Don't I? "Did we know each other? I'm Paul Elias."

She can't possibly be more disinterested. "I don't know."

Again she turns to go, when a name emerges from my deepest subconscious.

"Gillian Hudson," I say. The girl who drowned at the beginning, when everything else started. Even though Jenny has taken a few steps away from me, she stops in her tracks. "Any relation?"

She turns around with a skeptical look on her face. And one a bit frightened as well. "You knew Gillian?"

"Not really. Only the name."

Tiredness descends on her face, and she puts one hand on her hip. "Then why are you asking about her?" But it isn't an accusation as much as a plea. She unties her apron and pulls it off in one smooth motion before poking her head in through the door that leads to the kitchen, shouting, "I'm taking a break."

A panicked voice shouts back, "Right now?" But she doesn't reply. She crouches down and slides into the booth beside me, leaning forward on both elbows. Everything about this situation startles me.

"I remember when she drowned," I say, picking up a French fry and putting it back down again. Her eyes are sad. It's a wonder to me how I can misread someone so much.

"That was a long time ago. Why bring it up now? Why come back?"

"I wanted to show my granddaughter where I grew up."

Jenny is the first person who isn't taken in. "Sure," she spits out. "Okay. Why else are you here?"

I weigh telling her everything. "My wife died here, in Nysa, many years ago. She had . . . mental challenges. She saw a woman who wasn't actually there, a woman with silver-white hair." I shrug. "Maybe you knew her? Mary? Her mom worked here."

Jenny nods. "I remember her."

"Now my granddaughter is seeing the same thing, the same person. I don't know if that's why I'm here. But it all feels connected."

Jenny's face is frozen. I can't tell if she is going to slap me, stand up and walk off, or go on staring for the next thousand years.

She doesn't do any of those. She leans back in the booth, rubs her temples, and shakes her head. "My friends and I saw her."

"Who, my wife?"

"No." She shakes her head again. "After my sister drowned, we were devastated. Not only my family. Everyone. All of my friends, all of Gillian's friends. We didn't know what to do with ourselves. We started going down to the lake a lot, like a pilgrimage. We all wanted to be close to the water. That sounds strange, I know. You'd think that with everything that happened, we'd want to be as far from there as possible." She pauses. "But something drew us there. We couldn't stay away."

I don't know what to say, so I sit there. I'm aware of my food growing cold, but I have no interest in it.

"Anyway, I was sitting there one night, oh, probably a few years later, on the banks of the lake, and out of nowhere there's this woman sitting beside me. It was dark, and I couldn't get a good look at her. All I could see was that she had this silvery-gray hair, almost white. Figured she had come out with our group of friends or was a parent coming out to pick up her kid. I don't know. There were so many of us."

She stands abruptly, and I think I've lost her, but she bustles to the coffee maker, pours herself a cup, and raises a flat hand to a few customers who call out "Ma'am!" after her.

"I'm on break!" she says.

She settles into the booth and looks up at me as if I was the one talking. When I don't say anything, she recovers.

"Right, right." She shakes her head once more. "Here's the thing. This woman, she tells me that when my sister died she took something of hers. This woman was missing something. She asked if I could help her find it. I didn't know what to tell her."

"Do you know what she was missing?" I ask.

Jenny shakes her head. "My sister never would have taken anything. She was a scared little wimp." She laughs. "Anyway, this woman got a little pushy, made me mad, so I told her to bug off."

"And that was that? You never heard from her again?"

"Not me. But when a few of my friends started acting weird, I managed to pry it out of them. She'd approached them too, asking for help to get this thing my sister supposedly stole."

"Do you think they'd share their story with me? I'm trying to help my granddaughter."

Jenny takes a deep breath. "My friends? No, I'm sorry. They disappeared soon after I saw that woman."

"Disappeared?"

"It happened one night while we were out there by the

lake. One minute they were there, the next they were gone. They were fun girls, not into any serious kind of trouble. They never would have run away."

"Where do you think they are?"

"Where are they?" She gave a cynical laugh, but there were tears in her eyes that she tried to blink furiously away. "I think they drowned, like my sister."

Heavy Things

I t is nearly dinnertime. After I got back from the diner, I fell asleep on the floor beside the couch, and now I'm waking up, yawning, looking around and feeling a bit disoriented. Tom turns on the reading lamp beside the armchair, and the rest of the house is so dark. Fall is here, and with it comes early dusk and cold breezes through the open windows.

Tom stands and walks over to the couch where you are cocooned in your blanket. "Could we have a little chat?" he asks.

You nod, your face placid.

"Why don't you sit up, Pearl?" I say.

With a sigh you bring yourself up to a sitting position and remove the blanket from your head, still keeping it close around the rest of your body. Tom comes over and sits in one of the padded, antique wooden chairs perpendicular to the couch. I walk away, across the room to his armchair, the one he had been perched on all day. Interestingly enough, I can see the lake from there, through the glass deck doors. I didn't know he could see the water from that spot.

"Now, Pearl," he begins, and there is something fundamentally different about him. I can't quite put my finger on it. The easy explanation is that it's his counselor persona, but I feel that it's something deeper. "I want to have a heart-to-heart with you."

You give a resigned sort of nod like you know what's coming, aren't looking forward to it, but see no reason to avoid it.

"Your grandfather says—"

"Grampy," you interrupt. "He's my Grampy."

"Of course," Tom says, smiling agreeably. "Of course. Your Grampy says that you've been talking with an older woman the last few days."

You nod, and your face is like calm water. "She's not older. At least I don't think she is. Not old like you and Grampy, even though she does have silver hair. I can't really see her face very clearly all the time. If I had to guess, I'd say she's in her late forties. But she's in very good shape."

Tom seems impressed with the detail you're providing, although I can't tell if that's part of his strategy or if it's genuine.

"Does she have a name?"

"Not that I know of."

"Hmmm. Doesn't that seem a little strange to you?"

"Not really," you answer. "There are plenty of people we don't call by name."

Tom raises his eyebrows in a question.

"You know, like a police officer. You call them 'Officer.' Or the lady who works in the crosswalk. I always call her 'ma'am,' but I don't know her name."

"That's a good point, Pearl. I understand. What should I call her, you know, when we're talking about her?"

You shrug as if this is the last thing in the world that matters to you. "'The woman,' I guess."

"When did you first see the woman?"

"I guess it was in art class, although I think I saw her around the city a couple of times, back when I used to go for walks."

When you used to run away, I want to interrupt, but I have a feeling Tom wouldn't be happy with me if I did. Probably something about invading the process or some such nonsense.

"In art class?"

"She helped me draw my map."

"It's a fascinating map."

"Thank you." Your face brightens at the compliment.

"For example, how did you know so much about this area without ever having been here?"

"She told me about it."

"Your Grampy?"

"No, the woman."

"Perhaps you overheard your Grampy talking about Nysa with someone else. That's possible, isn't it?"

When I speak up, I immediately feel like it's a mistake. "I've never talked about Nysa since I left. Not once. Not with anyone."

When Tom looks over the couch and finds my gaze in the corner, there's a flash of annoyance in his eyes. But he defuses it well.

"Were you afraid of her when you first met?" he asks you.

"You mean in the art room?"

Tom nods.

"No," you say thoughtfully. "There were lots of people around."

"Did anyone else see her?"

You shrug. "I don't know."

Tom pauses, his head cocking to one side. "So if you weren't afraid of her in the art room, are there ever times when you are afraid of her?"

You take a deep breath, and it comes out in a sigh. "Sometimes."

"What's one time you felt afraid?"

"I was afraid today, when I saw her under the water and she told me to follow her."

"She told you to follow her under the water?"

You nod.

"I can understand why that would be scary," Tom says, and the conversation dies.

I feel a wave of nausea coming, but I don't want to miss anything, so I sit there and fight it down. When it passes, I feel exhausted, and the knot is throbbing. The ache streaks down my neck, down my back, all the way to my knees, and I can't tell which direction the pain is going—up or down.

The pain is me, I think.

"Does this person remind you of anyone you know?" Tom asks.

I can tell by the setting of your shoulders that you don't want to answer.

"Pearl?" Tom asks quietly.

You reply, but neither Tom nor I hear your answer.

"What was that?"

"You." Your head ducks.

257

"Me?" Tom asks, jolted out of his counselor persona.

You nod.

"How does she remind you of me?"

"You're both good at keeping secrets."

Tom's face goes blank, white. The air in the room feels charged, and I grip the armrests of my chair. Darkness leaks in as the sun drops, and now the only light in the house is the lamp beside me. I watch you and Tom in the shadows.

Tom seems to be drifting away, losing himself. You, on the other hand, seem to be finding yourself. When you speak, your voice sounds clear, as though you and Tom have switched roles.

"Shirley saw the same woman," you say.

Tom nods, seemingly unable to talk.

"What did she tell you about her?" you ask.

Tom's voice comes out flat, like he's talking to no one. "She said she was kind, that she asked Shirley to go with her." He looks over you to me, and our eyes meet. "She said the woman was Death, but not someone to be afraid of. The woman said she needed Shirley to do her a favor."

Your voice is gentle now, and I feel pride rising in me. But that pride freezes after what you say next.

"Today, when she pulled me under, she said that you know what that feels like, putting someone below the water."

Tom stands. His limbs are rigid, his jaw clenched. "That's enough for now."

"Tom," you say, "secrets are heavy things. They'll drag you under if you don't let them go."

He turns and walks through the kitchen, through the darkness, disappearing in the direction of his bedroom.

I stand up and walk over to the couch, sit down beside

you, and don't say a thing. I have no idea what to say. I have no idea what it is that I just witnessed.

You turn to me with sadness in your eyes. "There are too many secrets in this house," you whisper. "Too many secrets."

She's Gone

I scrounge up some dinner for you and me from the kitchen. We eat without talking, and the house feels empty. After finishing, we walk together slowly back through the winding hall to your bedroom.

"Are you okay?" I ask as we push open the door.

You look up at me with weariness in your eyes, but you smile through it. "I'm okay."

Your eyes are hazy, and instinctively I feel your forehead. "You feel warm," I say. "Are you sick?"

You shrug and crawl into bed, pulling the covers under your chin and sighing. "Just tired."

You fall asleep in moments, and I'm upset with myself for letting Tom question you so soon after you nearly drowned. But I also smile slightly, thinking that he got much, much more in return. It wasn't fair, really, him going into that conversation with you—he had no way of knowing how you can turn a chat on its head, how you can know things you should never know. I guess I'm used to it by now, or as used to it as one might become. But Tom found it disarming, and understandably so.

I go to each of the tall windows and double-check the locks. I stack the three books neatly on the table. I sit in the chair and look out the window, but it's dark, and all I can see is a reflection of this room: me, the books, the bed, the small ridge in the blankets that is you, now asleep.

The longer I sit there, the more I think about what you said.

There are too many secrets in this house.

I remember the photographs in the book and the one I took back to my room. I would like to see those photos of Mary again, but I'm not sure I should leave you. I walk over to the bed and stare down at you, waiting for you to move, waiting for you to wake up, but you are so deep in sleep that your breathing seems like something being done to you, not something you are doing. I reach down and gently nudge your hair from your face, tuck it in behind your ear, and leave the room.

By some great act of chance, I find my way to the basement hallway without getting turned around, and I walk all the way to the end, to the door that leads into the storage room. The house is silent. I wait for the sound of a door slamming somewhere in the hallway, but it doesn't happen. I open the door and turn on the light. Before I even get to the shelf, I can tell that something is wrong.

Before, when I was in that room, the photo books were packed tightly in place, organized and arranged perfectly. But there is a small gap so that one of the books leans through the empty space. I don't have to check the notebooks on either side of the gap to know which album is missing. But I do anyway.

The album with those photos of Mary is gone. I place my

hand in the gap, and it feels like a missing space in my memory. The entire room tilts to one side, and I put both of my hands on the shelf, lean forward, gasp for air. What's going on? I turn toward the door, and the room spins. I have to close my eyes to keep my balance, but I still end up dropping to my knees. I can feel that ache of nausea forming deep inside of me and crawl for the door, but I don't make it—I throw up all over the cement floor. I feel like my body is revolting against itself, trying to get something out that is too deeply lodged.

I wipe my mouth on my sleeve, but unlike other times in my life when I've vomited, I don't feel any better than before. I lean against the wall and try to stand up, but it's difficult, and the room keeps tipping and spinning. I make it to the door, leaning hard against the frame, then feel my body twisting through midair. It takes ages to reach the ground, and by then everything has gone dark.

This coming up out of unconsciousness doesn't feel anything like waking up. When I wake from sleep, I open my eyes and see where I am, what time it is, and I do a quick self-inventory to see how tired or awake I'm feeling. But this is different. This is like rising out of deep water—I can see a pinprick of light at the end of the tunnel, and it's rushing at me. Objects come into focus, but I can't move. I'm a passive observer of the room I'm in.

It's the living room, and I'm lying on the couch you had been sitting on when Tom asked you questions. The kitchen light is on, but besides that, everything is dark. I can move now, and I lift my hand to check the knot, but it's so tender it starts to hurt before I even touch it. Something about it has moved into my jaw, or at least that's the sense I have, that my jaw movement is impeded somehow, especially on the side with the knot. And in my ear on that side of my head is a distant rushing, the kind I hear when I place a conch shell up to my ear. It's the sound of some faraway sea.

Someone is in the kitchen. I can hear a cupboard open, the whistling of a teapot, the sound of porcelain, the clinking of a spoon as it makes its rounds. Tom emerges, carrying a coffee mug and a plate of crackers. I try to sit up, but pain flashes through my head, and I decide to stay lying down.

He sits in the wooden chair beside the couch. "Tea and crackers. You okay?" he asks, placing them on the end table.

"Never better," I mumble, sighing.

I try to sit up again, and this time I make it, although my head is throbbing and my stomach feels like an empty pit. I take a cracker and let it dissolve in my mouth before swallowing it.

"How'd I end up here?" I ask, though I have hazy memories of coming up the steps, my arm draped over Tom's shoulders.

"I had to help you up the steps. You're not as light as you used to be."

"I'm sorry. I threw up in your storage room."

He waves it off with one hand. "It's okay. I took care of it."

I sigh, reach up, hold on to my forehead. I hate it that Tom had to help me. I don't want to be indebted to him for anything. It makes me feel weak and inferior.

"What happened, Tom?" I ask, staring at the floor.

"I don't know. I found you on the floor in the hall."

"Not that." I pause. "What happened to us? What happened to our friendship? What happened to you?"

"That's a lot of different questions."

"I know it is. But something's changed. Something's here between us that was never there before." Yet even as I'm saying it, I know it's not true, because I had felt this way once before—on the day Mary and I got married. I felt this emanating from Tom when we first broached the topic and during the whole ride to the mobile home chapel. It's here again, this sense that something is between us, something we can't find our way past.

He doesn't reply. I think of you.

"What time is it?" I ask.

He glances over his shoulder. "Around ten p.m."

"Pearl," I whisper. I make a move to stand, but the blood rushes to my head along with a streak of pain, and my stomach twists. I can't get up.

"Would you like me to check on her?"

I nod slowly, reach for the tea, and hold it in front of my face, the steam clearing my nasal passages. Tom vanishes into the dark shadows of the hall, and only then do I think of the ruined carpet rolled up in Shirley's old room, the scratches on the floor. I consider going after him, stopping him, coming up with some excuse that I should be the one to check on Pearl. But resignation sets in, and with it, some small relief.

I think through what it will be like for him to demand that we leave. Am I fit to drive? How many stops will we have to make on our way home? Who can come to the house and watch over you if I don't recover from this particular bout of sickness?

To be honest, I'm eager to leave, especially after hearing Jenny's story. I think of your teachers at school and wonder why I didn't consider asking any of them to take you in. I know it's a big ask, but they seem to care deeply for you. I rack my brain for other people we might know, but I live an isolated life, and the list is short. Actually, it's nonexistent.

I am running out of time—that much I know—and I've wasted a precious amount of time with this pointless trip to Nysa. And me with anytime to three months. I find it hard to imagine that, at this rate, I will last three more months.

I hear Tom before I see him, his light footsteps coming across the hardwood floors, the carpet in the living room. It is such an empty house, and I feel a surge of sadness for him, living in this expansive place on his own. I remember the rug, the rug in your room that you destroyed, and I expect anger or something like it, so the serious look on his face doesn't surprise me.

But the words that come out of his mouth do.

"She's gone."

Our Future Spelled Out

The four of us moved to the cabin the day we graduated from high school, and one thing that the years have obscured is exactly how my parents felt. I can't remember talking with them about it, or arguing, or pleading. I can't remember if they came out to see the place, or what they said when I told them Mary and I were married and she was pregnant. I guess some memories simply aren't able to make the passage through time with us. They're too heavy, forgotten, dragged to the bottom by their own weight.

A few things changed when we arrived at the cabin that second summer. Each couple took one of the bedrooms—that was different. Even though we were all of age by that point, we drove across the border and went to the same chapel, went through an identical ceremony for Tom and Shirley, the only difference being that I drove with Mary in the passenger seat while Tom and Shirley sat in the back.

Another thing that changed was our lifestyle. In one magical year we had somehow turned into adults. Shirley had taken a job as a clerk at a small supermarket about twenty minutes from the cabin. Tom worked on a construction site and spent Sundays filling out applications for colleges. Tom and I each had a car, but Tom's hours were early, so I drove Shirley to the supermarket before going to a local insurance office on Main Street in Nysa and typing up paperwork for them. I thought I would hate it, but there was something therapeutic about the sound of the striking keys, the winding of the return, the satisfaction of an error-free page.

Mary stayed home and played mother to all of us.

I guess some things remained the same—Tom and I spent much of the weekends fixing up the old place, painting and repairing. Most evenings we took the kayaks out onto the water, drifting into the late dusk, watching bats swoop down over the water, their wings scraping the thin skin that otherwise provided a perfect reflection of the gathering night. We'd sit out there on our small boats, paddles resting on our laps, listening to the sound of fish gently rustling the surface.

"Does it get better than this?" Tom asked as we watched the sun dip down in the west, dropping behind the trees, beyond the fire-orange water reflecting it.

No one answered for a long time, because we all knew the answer.

"You okay, Mary?" I asked, looking over my shoulder. I paddled back to her when I saw how far away I had drifted. I reached out my hand to her and she took it, pulled me and my kayak close. Our boats bumped together. Her stomach filled the opening.

"Only a few more weeks, Mary," Shirley said, something wistful and faraway in her voice.

I couldn't look at her without getting choked up, without

being bowled over in a wave of joy and uncertainty and fear and hope. A dad. I was going to be a dad.

"I sure hope that baby looks like you, Mary," Tom said.

"Hey!" I said, using my paddle to send some water his way. He shouted at me, laughing.

Even though we were far from shore, I could hear the crickets chirping. Early summer fireflies blinked in among the trees like a thousand lighthouses, each trying to guide us home.

"Aw," Mary said, smiling, staring up at the navy-blue sky where the stars had begun peeking through. "I hope he takes after Paul."

Shirley laughed her joyous laugh. "How do you know it's a boy, Mary? Better not get set on one or the other."

"I just know," Mary said so quietly it was almost a whisper.

"There's Orion," Tom said. "There's the Big Dipper. And there's Cassiopeia."

"Where'd you learn all this stuff, hon?" Shirley asked.

Tom didn't reply, and we all stared up into the sky, searching it, as if there in the combination of stars we would find our future spelled out to us, plain and simple.

"What do you want to do with your life, Paul?" Tom asked, his words coming smooth across the black water.

"Do with my life?" I repeated. It was something I didn't think too much about. I had Mary, a place to live. I made enough money for now. I wasn't sure what else there was to be thinking about.

"Yeah!" Tom continued. "What do you want to do? You're not going to spend the rest of your life on a typewriter, are you?"

Somehow it felt like a mean question now that he was pressing the point.

"I don't know, Tom," I said. "I figure it'll come to me."

Tom laughed, and there was something spiteful in his voice. Something derisive. "Oh, Paul," he said, and I felt like I was about six years old.

I started rowing back to the cabin. Eighteen years old and I could feel hot tears rising. Why couldn't Tom let me be? Why did I have to be so sensitive?

"Paul?" I heard Mary calling, and I hated to leave her out there without me, but I couldn't take Tom. I couldn't take the sound of his voice or the way he questioned my future, my motivation, my ambition. I paddled harder.

Twenty minutes later I was in bed, and all the lights in the cabin were out. The windows were open, the summer air leaking in at the perfect temperature. A slight breeze kicked up, and I could hear the trees hushing each other. Then I heard the kayaks bumping against each other, and I felt bad for a split second that Tom would have to pull all three of the boats up onto the dock, but that feeling passed quickly. I heard the girls whispering to each other, silence, and then Tom walking up the dock, his footsteps heavier, distinctive. The back door closed, and I heard the dead bolt.

Mary came into the room, nearly silent. I heard her clothes drop to the floor, felt the bed sway as she leaned in. She arranged her pillows the way she wanted and nestled up against me, as close as she could with her round stomach in between us.

"Paul?" she whispered.

I didn't answer, but I turned my head so she knew I was listening.

"You'll figure it out."

"I know," I whispered back.

Enough time passed that I thought she was asleep.

"Paul?" she whispered again, and her voice sounded almost drunk with sleepiness.

"Yeah?"

"Please don't ever leave me out on the water. I don't like being out there without you."

"I'm sorry."

The moment came when Mary had such terror in her eyes that the terror left her and filled me, until I felt like I was drowning in it.

"I can't do this," she whispered. "I can't do it."

She squeezed my hand as the next contraction came, and the endless moan that left her turned into a suppressed scream at the end. That sound, that moan turned scream, was like a slap across my face.

I leaned in close, and I could smell the sweat and the blood and the fear. "You *can* do this, Mary," I whispered fiercely. "You can."

When Mary pushed your father out, it was one of the most miraculous things I've ever seen. That a baby could appear all covered in that fine shimmering white—it took my breath away.

"Mary," I said into her ear, "you did it."

She nodded, her face wrinkling into a full-on cry.

"You did it."

She nodded again.

"It's a boy, Mary. A boy."

She took in a quick breath, and it caught in a sob on the way out.

"It's a boy," I repeated.

Her crying turned into a laugh, a joyous sound, a crying, sweating, sobbing laugh.

"Let's call him John," she said as the nurses placed your daddy on her chest. "Little Johnny."

Screams at the Cabin

Tom pushes the throttle forward, the boat charges ahead, and I am thankful for the nighttime spray of the lake— the cold mist wakes me up and helps chase away my splitting headache. When Tom first suggested we take the boat to look for you, I was hesitant, wondering if crashing over the water would make me feel sick again. But it hasn't, at least not so far. I feel more alive than I have for some time and settle into the seat, close my eyes.

Where have you gone?

When I mentioned your story about the cabin, Tom shook his head.

"I'm sure she didn't go that far," was all he said, and the conversation was over.

I didn't object. After all, it was nonsensical to think you could have hiked all that way, either through the woods or along that winding country road, especially considering the state you were in when you went to bed, feverish and still weak from your near drowning.

But Tom and I had spent the next twenty minutes searching through the house, the surrounding woods, and the edges of the lake, with no luck. If he noticed the state of the rug and the wood floor in your room (which he had to have seen), he hasn't said anything about it. I'll take this as a good sign, although he may be waiting until we find you before he kicks both of us out.

The night is chilly and the stars are bright. I can even see the haze of the Milky Way, that cloud of stars that boggles the mind. I hope you are looking up, seeing the same sky. I hope you haven't gone far.

The cabin comes into view as the boat turns toward the shore. When I say "into view," what I mostly mean is that there is some strange shape to the shadows, the darkness begins to align itself, and the form of the house somehow becomes present among the trees, even if I can barely see it. Tom cuts the engine as we approach the bank, and the dock also emerges from the shadows. It all seems to happen magically, these things coming into view where at first there is only darkness.

Without the roaring of the motor, our approach feels almost ghostly. We drift seamlessly through the water, soundlessly, and the overhanging branches of the large oaks and elms and sycamores reach for us, drawing us close. There is a soft scraping as the underbelly of the boat makes contact with the dock, and our approach shifts slightly. Tom grabs one of the large wooden supports that rises above the deck, slows the boat to a stop, and ties us up. He steps out first and looks over his shoulder. We make eye contact, but he doesn't say anything. Not with words. But his eyes say, *This is completely ridiculous. I can't believe we came all the way out here.*

Meanwhile, I feel completely rejuvenated. Maybe it was the stars or the breeze or the spray off the lake, but I feel alive again. I reach up to touch the knot, overcome with this sense that it is gone, that life has returned to normal. Relief spreads through me even as I raise my hand—if it's not there, you and I can go home. Our life can go on. I can almost taste the hope.

But the knot remains. It feels harder than before, almost brittle. And instead of it shifting when I touch it, I can feel where its roots have lodged into my skull. The sensation makes me shiver. I wish I wouldn't have touched it. I wish I wouldn't have checked on it.

Tom and I walk up the dock to the cabin. The recently fallen leaves swish and crackle under our feet, and rising from the ground is that smell of the woods before winter, that smell of dirt and decay racing to finish its work before the first freeze. We make no attempt at silence. We check the deck door and Tom rattles the handle loudly, proving to me that he kept it locked, that there is no way you could have gone inside, even if you possessed the miraculous ability to come all this way. The two of us turn and walk to the other side of the cabin, which seems much bigger now that we are standing under its nighttime shadow. There is, in my mind, nothing to be afraid of.

Until we turn the corner, because there before us is the front door, open.

Tom looks frustrated that this open door could even possibly go along with the idea of you being here, so he peeks his head inside and shouts your name. We listen. Nothing.

Where have you gone?

"Satisfied?" Tom asks.

I stand there in the silence as he takes out his keys and locks the door. I lean my head back and take in the trees. The stars are slowly vanishing, disintegrating into nothingness as clouds sift into the sky above us.

"We should go." Tom clears his throat and seems to be making an attempt at some sort of peace between us. "There's a storm coming. Maybe Pearl has already come home."

While I would stay out all night looking for you, storm or no storm, his words remind me that you do normally return home on your own, in your own time. I nod, and we make our way to the back of the cabin, the dock, the boat, and the lake.

"I really don't know what to do with her," I admit. It is my own peace offering, and he takes it.

"Children can be . . ." He glances at me, keeps walking. "Children can be hard to understand. Their minds don't work the way ours do. They don't have the same inhibitions, the same fears, the same concerns. The future, in the minds of many children, barely exists. All that is, is here, now."

We stop walking. I can hear the rain on the lake, far away. The wind picks up, and a curtain of leaves begins to fall around us.

"Pearl is different," I say. "I know what you're saying. I've seen these precocious children at her elementary school. But there is something different about Pearl."

He nods, but I know what he's thinking: *She's different because she's yours.*

"So many times, she knows things she couldn't possibly know. So many times, her fantastic stories somehow add up. I can't explain it."

We stare at each other in that darkening night, and the

first heavy raindrops plunge through the leaves, rustle their way into the undergrowth like miniature projectiles fired at us from some faraway castle.

"You witnessed it yourself not too many hours ago," I say, looking away.

"We should go," Tom insists.

That's when I hear you scream, a short burst.

I glance at Tom to verify that I actually heard something, that it isn't a figment of my imagination or the sound of some horrific night animal I am not familiar with. It seemed to come from far off, even under the ground.

Tom's face echoes my . . . what? Fear? Anxiety? Terror? We stop in our tracks, standing as still as deer interrupted.

It comes to us again, this time louder, more urgent, and closer. Definitely from the cabin, seemingly from the front door. I move in that direction. Tom calls after me, but I can't tell what he wants. I don't think he knows what he wants.

We move as quietly as possible through the brittle leaves, around the cabin to the side opposite the lake. There is a flickering of light on one of the small windows, as if the glass is reflecting some far-off approach. I turn quickly toward the driveway, expecting to see a car, but there's only darkness. I don't see a light. And by the time I turn back around, I realize the light is coming from inside the house.

There is a crashing sound. The light goes out. Another scream, this one stifled. There is a fumbling at the lock inside the door. The knob turns violently and the door explodes open.

You fall through the open space, your eyes wild. When you

see me, you scream, hold your arms out to shield yourself, then recognize my face and fall into my wide-open arms.

You are soaking wet.

"Pearl!" I say.

Tom races up to us. But you interrupt me.

"Run," you say. "We have to run."

So Close

I try to hold you close once we're in the boat, but you keep straining to look behind us at the house we are now speeding away from. The wind has whipped the lake into a frenzy, and miniature whitecaps bounce us up and down. A torrential rain soaks us in seconds.

"It won't take long to get home," Tom shouts through the sound of the motor and the rain and the wind. "Hang on."

He leads the boat into an even greater speed, and I'm afraid one of us will fly off the back, vanish beneath the wind and the waves. Above us, the stars are gone.

"Are you okay?" I ask, trying to protect you from the elements and failing badly. It is so, so cold. "Pearl," I begin again, wanting to ask what in the world you were doing there, how you got there, why you keep leaving me. But I don't say anything. I squeeze you tighter, and now that the cabin is out of view, you give in, crumple into my lap.

I can see the light of Tom's house. He waits until the last moment to slow down, then rams the motor in reverse so that we lurch. He hops lightly up onto the dock, ties up the boat, and reaches down for you. I'm reluctant to hand you

278

over, but I do—I can't possibly get out of the boat while carrying you.

Tom carries you to the house, and I try to keep up. I can't help glancing back over the lake, for what, I'm not sure. The fear I heard in your screams has settled into a deep place inside of me. I won't forget that sound for a long time.

Inside, the house is quiet, although I can hear the distant roar of the rain, which has picked up. Thunder and lightning roll over the water.

Tom doesn't stop in the living room—he keeps going all the way to your room, and I follow him through the twists and turns. Finally, we go through your door.

The small lamp on the table is turned on. Your map is there, held down by the same three books. The window is open and a strong breeze pulses through, along with the rain, which has puddled in a round, glassy shape on the floor.

Tom has somehow grabbed a towel with his free hand on the way through the hall. He hands it to me. "Spread it out. I'll lay her down. You can help her change into dry clothes."

I follow his instructions. He eases you down onto the towel. I can feel him standing over us as I dry you off. You're so sleepy, almost like you're drugged.

"Pearl," I whisper. "Help me get your clothes changed."

"I'll give you a minute. You want some coffee? Tea?" Tom asks. His voice is laden with concern.

"Tea, please."

"Pearl? Would you like anything?"

You shake your head, your eyes heavy.

Tom turns to go, looks over his shoulder at me, and there are things in his eyes I never would have expected to see: confusion, even uncertainty. Lightning flashes at the window, and he starts to say something, stops, and walks out into the dark hallway.

I finish drying you off, and then together we change you out of your wet clothes and into something comfortable and dry. Even though Tom closed the window, the room still smells like the outside—wet and fresh and full of autumn leaves. I tuck you into bed.

"Pearl, what happened? What were you doing out there?"

You give me a small smile—despite the circumstances, despite the near drowning earlier that day and the screams from the house, you are rather delighted.

"I was so close," you whisper. "So close."

"So close to what?"

But you shake your head.

"Pearl, I need to know what's going on."

For a moment I think you've fallen asleep. The lightning blinds me through the windows, but the sound of the rain has slowed, and it's not being driven against the glass anymore. I have never felt more ready for a sunrise, for the morning, for light to bring a sense of normal along with it. I consider leaving tomorrow, going back to our home and figuring things out there. I know you had your struggles there in the city, I know you vanished many times and concocted the wildest stories, but what's happening here feels extreme, even for you.

"Pearl, please."

That same light of adventure is in your eyes. "Grampy, it was amazing."

When You Arrive at the End, Keep Going

When she showed up outside my window, knocking on the glass, I rolled over, faced away from her, and tried to go back to sleep. I was so tired, and all I wanted to do was sleep. And I was angry at her for pulling me down into the water. But when she kept knocking, I thought, *I need to go over there and tell her off! I need to tell her that it isn't okay what she did, and that she shouldn't ever come back here again.*

So I crawled out of bed and walked slowly to the window. I took my time, because I didn't want her to think I was going to do whatever she wanted me to do, and I even stood by the window for a minute, glaring out at her. I gave her a scowl and finally opened the window.

All the light she used to carry seemed to be gone. The silver in her hair had dulled to gray. She was even more like a shadow than before, long and stretched, her face hidden. I asked her what she wanted.

She said it was time. She had waited long enough. If I

wanted to save you, Grampy, I needed to go down into the basement, through the door, and do what she wanted me to do. I asked her why I would ever do such a thing when she had nearly drowned me only a few hours ago! And even though I couldn't see her face in the shadows, I could tell she was staring straight at me. She said she was trying to help me. If I helped her, she could help me.

"Who are you?" I nearly shouted.

She paused. "Pearl," she said in a quiet voice, "I'm Death. I need your help."

I stood there for what felt like a very long time, Grampy. Her voice was sad, and when I thought of helping you, I knew I would do it. Whatever it was that she needed me to do, I would do it. For you.

"Why'd you try to drown me?" I asked her.

"I wasn't trying to drown you. I was helping you learn how to swim underwater."

"How do I know you won't try to do something like that again, something that might kill me?"

"I can't make any promises, Pearl. You might die. Everyone does, you know. But you're the only one who can help me now. The town is nearly empty."

So I climbed out the window.

Running through the woods that time felt more familiar, and I even kind of enjoyed it. She didn't forget about me, not once, and she set me down gently outside of Tom's cabin, right by the front door. She told me what she wanted me to do.

"Can't you at least come down the stairs with me? You came the last time," I said.

"You have to go someplace I can't go. I'd rather wait here."

"How will I know what you want me to get for you if you don't come with me?"

"You'll know."

"But how?"

"Trust me. You'll know."

"But—"

"Go!" Suddenly her voice was like the thunder.

I took two steps back from her. It hurt my feelings that she shouted at me like that. And I could tell that she wished she hadn't.

I turned and checked the door. It was unlocked. She handed me a flashlight. Then she melted into the shadows.

"Are you there?" I asked.

"I am always here."

Pure fear melted right through me. Grampy, I've never been so scared in all my life. Never.

"You can't tell me anything?" I begged.

"When you arrive at the end, keep going," she said.

I opened the door, walked through the part of the house we had walked through before, down the long hall, and finally came to the doorway at the top of the stairs. I opened it and started going down.

The walk down took me so long that at one point I thought maybe I had imagined the bottom, that the stairs went on and on forever. That old flashlight kept shining down farther and farther on rickety wooden steps, and I started to panic a little, thinking about what I would do if the batteries died. I even stopped and sat on the steps and almost cried. I doubted what I was doing and why I wasn't home in my warm bed.

I thought about what she had said: "When you arrive at the end, keep going."

I stood up, sighed, and kept going down. Eventually, I got there and stood in front of those three doors. I guess I didn't see it the first time I was there, but it was such a strange place, like an in-between place, like it didn't really exist except it was where the stairs ended and whatever was beyond the doors began. I took a deep breath, pointed the flashlight back up the stairs one more time, and went through the door all the way on the left.

As soon as I opened the door, I could tell something was different, Grampy. The air was humid, like on a cool summer day when a storm is coming. I stood there holding the door-knob, and it was slick in my hand, and smooth. I was staring down a dark hallway, but it was more like a narrow cave with a low ceiling—the passage was cut through rock, and hidden in the rough places were veins of something shiny. The floor was like smooth glass, but when I took a few steps forward I saw it wasn't glass. It was water.

I started walking, and the farther I went, the deeper the water got. It was very gradual, so at first I didn't feel it getting deeper, but it was. And the ceiling was getting lower. I walked all the way into that cold water until it was up to my waist. I started to get nervous that my flashlight would get wet, so by the time the water was up to my chest and the ceiling was down to my head, I found a kind of rocky shelf in the wall to place the flashlight.

Straight ahead and not that far in front of me, the ceiling came down low and met the water.

The only way forward was by going under.

I stood there for a while, so long that I started shivering.

When you arrive at the end, keep going.

Grampy, I was so scared. But I took a deep breath, and I went under.

It's True

Tom knocks lightly on the door and peeks his head in. "Everyone okay?" he asks.

You nod. You already seem so much more clear-eyed than at any other point today.

Tom eases into the room, carrying a mug in each hand. "For the lady," he murmurs, handing you a steaming mug of tea. "In case you've changed your mind. And for you, sir."

I breathe in the mint smell rising. "Thanks, Tom."

"I'm going to grab mine and come back. You don't mind, do you? I think I'd like some company tonight."

I can't tell if he's asking me or you, but I know what you'll say. Your face is so white, framed as it is by your dark hair. Your kind eyes smile.

"Sure," I say, trying not to let a lack of enthusiasm infiltrate my voice. "Join us."

He leaves, pulling the door closed behind him. I can't even bring myself to ask you what happened next in your story. Your skin is so pale it's almost blue, so I reach over and tuck the blanket tighter around you. You take a sip of tea.

Pearl, your imagination has clearly gotten the best of you.

I can't even begin to imagine where all of these things have come from, all of these . . . I can't call them lies, because you so clearly believe what you're telling me. Untruths? Misrepresentations? I don't know. Confusion? I feel a deep weariness setting in.

"Pearl," I finally say, shaking my head, my tired eyes blinking slow and heavy.

"Grampy," you whisper. "It's true. All of it."

The Other Side

When I went under, the very next moment I didn't feel cold anymore. I felt like I was one with the water, like I *was* water, and I grabbed the stone walls and pulled myself through the darkness. I kept my eyes open, and I've never seen water that was so clear. I could see the light from the flashlight laying a skin of glaring white on the top of the water, but that wasn't the only light—there was something in front of me, something farther along the tunnel that was lighting up the water.

I kept going, holding my breath. Every so often, a few bubbles would escape through my nose. I didn't get very far before I felt like I was going to burst.

That's when I saw it.

Just as I thought I was going to run out of air, when I thought I'd have to take in a big breath, lights started shooting past me, like those veins of light in the rock. It was like seeing shooting stars, but they were all around me. Up ahead it got even brighter. I thought I was going to make it. I pulled myself farther through the water and saw that it was about to open up above me—I was through the tunnel! I could see it! It wasn't night there, above the water. It was beautiful and bright, a new world waiting for me above the surface, the brightest greens and blues. And as I got closer, I had this feeling that it wasn't an ordinary place—it was someplace very special.

But as I started rising, I realized the surface was a lot farther away than I thought, and those lights started flashing past me again, and I knew I wasn't going to make it. I felt like I was running out of air, like I had to take in a deep breath.

Eventually, I couldn't hold my breath anymore. I gave in. I took in the deepest breath I've ever taken, and my lungs filled, and the lights went out. I thought I had died, Grampy. I thought that was it. I started floating down toward the bottom.

But then something pulled on my foot, dragging me back through the tunnel of water, back through the darkness. The person or whatever it was dragged me through until I burst up out of the water on the near side of the tunnel, back where I had started.

I was gasping for air, choking, and someone else was there too, coughing and spitting up water. I reached quickly for my flashlight and saw, Grampy. It was her.

"What are you doing?" I whispered. "I was almost there."

"You were dying. If you die, you can't come back here again. I had to bring you back. You're no good to me dead."

I stared at her. "I thought you couldn't go there. I thought only I could go get whatever it is I'm supposed to get."

"I can't. I shouldn't have gone as far as I did. Getting you out . . ." She paused, coughing long and hard. "I'd rather not talk about it."

I could tell she was weak and upset with herself.

"Thank you," I said, erupting into another coughing fit.

"You're not a very good swimmer, you know that?" Now she sounded angry.

I felt embarrassed. I told her I did the best I could, and I could tell she immediately felt bad for giving me a hard time. She might sound a little harsh at times, but she's actually quite considerate.

"You need to practice swimming under the water," she told me. "You don't have that much farther to go. You can do it."

We waded back through the water until it was shallow again, barely up to my ankles, and I saw the door appear at the end of my flashlight.

"Let's go back up," she said wearily. "We can try another time."

We began the long, long walk up the stairway, to the top. I was so tired, so worn out, that eventually she had to carry me again, all the way up that long stairway, and I fell asleep in her arms. When I woke up, she was gone, and I was sitting in the dark with no flashlight at the top of the stairs. It was like waking from a dream. I turned the knob and crept into the dark house, through the long hallway, and toward the front door.

That's when I felt a hand on my shoulder, a cold hand. It was a woman's hand, and the nails were long, and her skin almost glowed white. That's when I screamed. I tried to run but I fell, and I screamed again.

I crashed through the door, and you were waiting for me.

Reality

D o you still think this is harmless?" I ask Tom. We are sitting beside the small table at the far end of your room. The only light on is the lamp beside the table. The window is open a few inches, and the air has gone chilly, so I lean over and close it.

"I never said Pearl's behavior is harmless," Tom says in the same flat voice he had when we first crossed paths with him at the diner. There's something in me that wants to punch him, to tackle him from his chair and wrestle him to the floor. Would that bring the old Tom back? Would that inject life into his cold eyes?

"You don't seem to be taking her stories very seriously. Tom, she's seeing people who aren't there, going to places that don't exist, for goodness' sake!"

He glances over at you to see if my outburst has disturbed you. You have not moved.

"You know that's why she destroyed Shirley's rug, right? Why she cut squares into it, etched lines in the wood floor? She was searching for a door, Tom. A door! This person she sees told her there was a door under the carpet, and so she cut it to shreds. Can't you see how serious this is?"

I run my hands through my hair, and it's one of those moments where I completely forget about the knot until it's too late—one of my fingernails catches on the rough edge of it, pulling on it, and an electric line of pain streaks down the side of my neck. I wince, take in a sharp breath, but Tom is sitting to my right. I wonder why he hasn't said anything about the knot—his determination to pretend it's not there is starting to make me angry.

"I'll talk to her again tomorrow." Tom's eyes wander to the three books still on the table. He picks the smallest up and leafs through it. "You know, at the end, Shirley said some pretty strange stuff too."

Shirley. I wish she was here, with her quick smile and light touch. She would have loved you so much. The thought of Shirley wrapping you in a hug brings tears to my eyes, and I wipe them away quickly with the back of my hand. Why did she have to die? Why couldn't she take care of you after I'm gone?

"At the end?" I ask. "The end? Pearl isn't at the end, Tom."

I stare at him, but he refuses to return my gaze.

"We never did talk about the pictures," I nearly whisper.

"What's there to talk about, Paul? I took some photos of Mary. What else do you want to hear?"

I give a bitter laugh and shake my head. "Those weren't just any photographs."

"I don't know what you mean."

I see the uncertainty in his eyes, the wavering that I expected to find.

"Those were beautiful photos, Tom. You captured Mary in a way that none of Shirley's photos ever did."

He doesn't reply.

"You captured Mary the way I saw her." I pause. "The way a husband looks at his wife."

Tom doesn't reply, and this time he doesn't stand up and walk out.

I take a deep breath. I stand up, and the chair makes a grating sound on the bare wood. The distance from the table beside the window to your bed feels so far. I stop and look down at you, reach down and feel your forehead. Your hair is soft, and I smooth it behind your ear.

"She's exhausted," I say. "There's no reason for me to sleep in here tonight. I'll start keeping a close eye on her tomorrow."

"All the same," Tom replies, "I think I'll sleep in here, on the floor."

"Suit yourself."

Swimming Underwater

Nearly a week has passed since your last incident. The days all run together, with little to differentiate them. We wake up late, eat brunch, and go out on the lake after Tom comes back from town. He gives you a swim lesson, and I watch with apprehension. I sometimes go into town for lunch, but while Jenny and I have been polite, we do not revisit our last topic of conversation. You and I walk through the woods or go farther out on the lake or, if it's raining, find something to do in the house. Yesterday we worked on a jigsaw puzzle.

Now I'm sitting on the back ledge of Tom's boat, watching another swim lesson. I allow my eyes a moment's rest from you, take in the trees on the bank that seemed to have transformed overnight from an end-of-summer pale green to subtle hues of red and orange and yellow. In another month, maybe even a few weeks, they will all be brown.

"Good job, Pearl," Tom says, treading water beside you. His voice is steady, even in the exertion.

"Can we work on our underwater swimming again?" you ask.

I continue to be amazed at your commitment to this delusion. It concerns me more than I can explain.

"What about freestyle?" Tom suggests. "That's usually a good first stroke to learn."

You shake your head. "I'd really like to swim underwater."

"Okay," Tom says. "How do you feel about diving?"

He spends the next hour teaching you to dive off the back of the boat, even convincing me to get in the cold water so I can wait for you. After the first few times, mostly belly flops, you start to get the hang of it. You come up from the water right in front of me, gasping for air, smiling, blinking the lake out of your eyes. You wrap your arms around my neck and laugh, and I would do anything for you in those moments, forgive any misadventure.

"Go back farther," you say. "I want to see how far I can go under the water."

So I do, and after the hour is up, with a few tips from Tom, you are swimming so far underwater that I find myself holding my own breath, waiting for you to come up.

"Nice job!" I cry, laughing out loud when you come up far from the boat.

"One more time!" you say.

"One more, and then we have to get out. I'm freezing."

You jump from the boat again, slipping into the water like a sewing needle piercing cloth, and in those short moments when you are gone from me, I think of Mary.

Only the Deepest Pools Remain

We eat the quiet lunch of people exhausted after some worthy pursuit, slowly chewing our sandwiches and bananas and drinking hot tea to warm us up. You eat your apple down to the core, nibbling at the sweet fruit that remains around the stem. You keep looking up at Tom and me, smiling a melancholy, knowing smile.

"How about a nap?" I suggest, and you nod, your eyes heavy.

I leave you sleeping in your room and rest on the sofa in the living room. There is no sign of Tom, and the house feels empty, so I stand up, walk into the kitchen, and glance at the garage, but I can't tell if he's home or has gone into town.

I wander the house, not looking for anything in particular. There's a quiet room on the third floor with a small rocking chair in front of a picture window that stares out over the lake. I fall asleep there, warm and mellow.

The day passes slow and heavy, but it is fall, which means the sun is creeping down the western sky by late afternoon.

This house seems built for dusk, when the dim light gathers around the heavy curtains and cold, hard floors stretch out under my feet. Everything feels like a quiet daydream. I find my way back to the kitchen, where Tom is gathering a few things for dinner.

"Have you seen Pearl?" he asks.

"No. You?"

He shakes his head. I don't make eye contact with him. I know what he's thinking. You've run off again.

But when I arrive in your room, you are not missing. You're asleep in your bed. Light from the dusk comes in at a soft angle, and the books with golden lettering on their spines glow in the radiance of it. There isn't a cloud in the nearly night sky, and stars have begun peeking through.

I reach down to wake you and can feel a strange heat emanating from your body. "Pearl?" I cup my palm over your forehead, and it's like a fire has taken residence inside your skin. "Pearl."

You moan.

"I'll be right back," I whisper.

I leave you to go find Tom, but when I'm in the hall, the floor buckles under my feet, and when I reach out, the walls melt under my hands. A red curtain drops slowly over my vision. Everything goes black.

When I open my eyes, it takes me a moment to recognize where I am. The books give it away—I'm back in your room, lying on the floor beside your bed. A soft pillow is under my head, and I'm lying on one of those roll-out mats that can serve as a mattress when you're camping. I push my way out from under the warm blanket and sit up, looking over at you in your bed, where you're still sleeping. I reach over and touch your forehead. You don't feel quite as hot.

"I gave her some Tylenol."

Tom is sitting at the small table at the other end of the room. Behind him, through the window, I can see that night has fallen.

"Are you okay?" he asks.

I nod. "I don't know what happened."

He waits a second, as if giving me a chance to tell the truth. "I found you in the hall, passed out."

I take a deep breath. "Thanks."

"You're deteriorating quickly, Paul. Want to talk about it?"

I shake my head. I do not want to talk about it.

When he doesn't say anything more, I lie back down. My head is still reeling, aching, and there is a pulsing throb going from the area of the knot throughout my entire body. I cannot go on like this for much longer. Soon I will have to ask Tom to take me to the hospital. I will die there. I will have to ask him to watch over you. It's not that I like this new Tom or what Nysa has become. There are a thousand things I'd choose about who to give you to after I'm gone, and few of those things are here, in Tom or in this house, but the thing is, I don't have much choice.

I don't have long.

"If her fever is still this high in the morning, we should take her to the doctor," Tom suggests in his therapist's voice, so that it feels less like a suggestion and more like a diagnosis.

"I didn't think there was a doctor in Nysa."

"There's not. It's about an hour and a half drive."

I turn my face toward your bed. "Thanks, Tom," I say, wondering if now is the time I should tell him about my condition, if now is the time to ask him if he would consider taking you in. But I can't form the words. I close my eyes.

I wake up later, and the table lamp is out. Tom is gone. You are still sleeping. I stand up, legs shaking, and walk over to the window, look out into the bright night—the moon is out, spreading a silver skin on the lake, and the shadows move in a stiff breeze. I can feel the cold outside air pushing in around the edges of the glass.

I pick up *The Light Princess* from the small table and carry it over to your bed. It's too dark in the room to read the words, so I turn on the hall light, leave the door open a crack, and read from where you last marked your page.

For the princess kept her room, with the curtains drawn to shut out the dying lake, but she could not shut it out of her mind for a moment. It haunted her imagination so that she felt as if the lake were her soul, drying up within her, first to mud, then to madness and death. She thus brooded over the change, with all its dreadful accompaniments, till she was nearly distracted. As for the prince, she had forgotten him. However much she had enjoyed his company in the water, she did not care for him without it. But she seemed to have forgotten her father and mother too. The lake went on sinking. Small slimy spots began to appear, which glittered steadily amidst the changeful shine of the water. These grew to broad patches of mud, which widened and spread, with rocks here and there, and floundering fishes and crawling eels swarming. The people went everywhere catching these, and looking for anything that might have dropped from the royal boats.

At length the lake was all but gone, only a few of the deepest pools remaining unexhausted.

I fall asleep while I'm reading to you, leaning against the wall beside the door. My eyes are heavier, the evening heavier still. The door drifts closed, and shadows stretch through the room.

The Open Window

When I wake up, my back is killing me. At some point in the night, I must have slipped slowly down the wall, and instead of crawling over to the mat and curling up under the blanket, I simply slept on the hardwood floor. My shoulder aches, my neck is cramped, and I don't feel rested in the least. It's so cold in the room. I sit up. Filtered gray light comes in the windows. It is early in the morning on a rainy day.

I stand up and walk over to your bed, checking to see if your fever broke in the night. A bath might be a good idea, and some more of that hot tea Tom is constantly pushing on us. Thinking of Tom, I shake my head. I have to tell him. I have to ask him if you can stay here. No matter the circumstances, I know you could have a good life on these shores.

But when I check your bed, you're gone.

Of course you are.

That's why it's so chilly in the room—the window is open.

When I Knew

How empty the lake felt the day Mary left me, how wide the sky, how alone that point of rock. My kayak drifted over to where the rocky bottom of The Point met the water, and the sound of the boat scraping against the granite was the loneliest sound in the world.

I didn't know if your grandmother would come back, if we would find her, but I had a deep sense that she was gone forever. That I would not see her again. And in that despair, I wondered if I had the courage to climb The Point and jump headfirst down onto the rocks. Or perhaps sink down into the water and not come up again.

Only one thing kept me in the boat, caused me to lift my oar and paddle back to the cabin: your father, John. That tiny baby who I thought was probably crying back in the cabin, crying for milk, crying for his mother. That's why I chose to live that day.

During the next two or three days, the whole town flocked to the lake, and I didn't care if they did it out of curiosity or a morbid fascination with the idea of a missing person or because they genuinely wanted to help—the more people there, I figured, the better chance of finding Mary. But always there was this belief in me that she wouldn't be found.

On one of those nights, Tom and Shirley and I sat in the cabin waiting for news. All of our parents were there, and one of them was holding John. He kept crying, so I took him and walked down the dock and stared into the darkness. I didn't know how to tell him that his mom wasn't coming back. He was still just over a week old, after all.

The early fall air was heavy, and the water was so still. Out on the lake I could see flashlights sweeping back and forth, at least twenty of them, like tiny, lost lighthouses. I wanted to call to them all, tell them it wasn't any use. But as I stood there and watched, John stopped crying and started making these little cooing sounds. The stars wavered in the humid air, and that's when I heard it.

Someone was shouting, but not in anger. It sounded like a wounded animal—a very large, dangerous animal that everyone would want to steer clear of. The cabin door was open, and inside I could see Mary's father, barely able to stand up. He went from shouting to moaning like a woman in labor, and I knew the grief was too much for him. That's when I did something really foolish.

I placed John down on the dock, on his back, and when I was no longer holding him, he started crying again, that sort of naked bleating that newborns will do, shrill and inconsolable. I climbed into my kayak, took him from the dock, and held him on my lap, and with one hand I half-heartedly pushed us out into the water.

I guess Mary's father had heard John crying, because he came stumbling out onto the dock, followed by Mary's mother and Tom and Shirley and all of our parents, a whole crowd, and the dock groaned under the weight. Mary's father called out to me, and his voice was so confused I couldn't tell if he was angry and coming after me or desperately sad and wanting some kind of consolation. I paddled out farther.

A loud splash broke through the night, followed by a few more splashes. Mary's father had jumped in, completely clothed. I guess Tom had jumped in along with one of the other adults to haul Mary's father back out again. He was wailing and crying, and by the fading of it I could tell someone was guiding him back around to the front of the house.

It was out there in the dark that I knew for sure. Mary was gone. I held John close and drifted for a long time on that black sheet of water, and eventually I managed to paddle my way back to the dock.

That's when we packed, and the next day we left Nysa.

And I never came back, not until now.

This time, with you.

The Clouds Bear Down

I don't even take time to put on shoes. I run barefoot through the woods like some prehistoric human, not caring that the branches are scratching my face, the briars tearing at my clothes. I have to get to the cabin. I'm not telling Tom this time, and I'm not taking the boat. I want to go there the way you do. I want to figure out, somehow, what is drawing you back time and again, what is pulling you from the house.

Within a few minutes, my feet are freezing cold and my breath pants out in a fog, but I don't stop or go back. And there, among the poplars and the oaks with their changing leaves, the overgrown vines hanging like snakes, I find a trail I didn't know existed. Is this how you get there and back? Is this how you go to the cabin? And why is this trail here in the first place? Did Tom and Shirley return there more often than Tom has led me to believe?

Rain begins to fall, and I hear the drops stirring the leaves around me, tapping on the hard dirt of the path. Through random clearings in the trees off to my left, I can see the western sky, and what I thought was simply a curtain of gray bringing rain looks more sinister than that—the edges of the sky are nearly green, and the clouds boil back on themselves. I run faster, scanning the lake, the woods, wondering how long it will take me to run to the cabin, or if this is even the right path.

The morning grows darker as the storm approaches. I can't catch my breath, so I stumble to a slow jog, then a determined walk. I don't have the energy to be upset at you, not anymore. It's all been run out of me. All I feel is a deep sadness that this is how it has been, and perhaps this is how it will be until I die.

I don't know how long it takes me—maybe thirty minutes—but I finally arrive at the clearing surrounding the old cabin, and seeing it again like that, on a stormy morning, takes my breath away. It might be lonely, and Tom might be part of the last generation that keeps it from crumbling into disrepair, but it is still the place where I fell thoroughly in love with your grandmother. The darkening gray light casts every edge into sharp relief, and memories bombard my mind—Tom and me laughing while fixing the roof, and Mary and Shirley rigging up a pulley system to raise a thermos of cold water up to us; that early evening when we played a game of tag around the house, when Mary and I hid in the brush; that feeling of having nowhere to go and nothing to do but sit in the sun and look out over the water.

I stand at the edge of the clearing and put my hands on my knees, try to catch my breath. My heart beats so hard it feels like it might break one of my ribs. I move closer to the cabin. The memories draw me in; I am helpless. But I don't have time to think any longer about the old days, because as I come around the side of the cabin, I see something bobbing along the edge of the lake. At first I'm sure it's a pile of clothes one of those trespassing high school kids left behind. As the rain comes down harder, I stare at the spot, and I nearly go into the house looking for you, but something about it makes me stop. And that's when I realize it.

That floating pile of clothes is you.

You are facedown on the bank, but your body is a rag doll, dipping up and down with the small waves created by the wind of the approaching storm. I race through the clearing and slip through the mud and the wet leaves, fall down, get back up. Fortunately, at that particular spot the bank is shallow, so I reach down and gently scoop you up.

Your face is pale as death.

I start to cry. "No, no, no! No, Pearl, not you. Not you."

I hold you close, trying to convey all of my warmth into you. I would give it all to you if I could. I carry you back to the path, and the cursed branches pull at your hair and our clothes as we leave the cabin behind.

We don't go very far before I lay you down on the packed dirt. The rain is falling even heavier now, so I lean over you to try to keep you dry. I can't tell if you're breathing. Your skin is the color of white-gray clouds, your lips blue, your black hair somehow darker than black. I put my ear to your mouth.

Are you breathing?

I cradle you in my arms as if you're an infant, the same way I cradled John when I paddled out into the lake with one arm. I run, and this time I do not stop the whole way, even when my legs burn and my lungs can't catch up and my head swirls. I keep running, and I'm not thinking about any of these things—all I'm thinking about is the way your arm sways beside me, a pendulum, bumping against my hip, keeping the time.

I will never be able to remember the facts about that journey through the woods—it was endless and took no time at all, through bright light and the strange dim breaking of dawn brought on by the storm. I sense a groan from your tiny frame, and it is like someone has brought down a whip on my back. I find unknown energy and run even faster.

Tom is looking out through your bedroom window, and when I get there, I pass you through the window to him. I follow close behind and think of your stories of sweeping through the forest, riding on the shoulders of Death.

The clouds bear down on us, and lightning flashes. Soon it is raining so hard we can barely see out the window.

"Pearl," I whisper into your ear. I climb into the bed and hold you on my lap, my face pressed against yours.

"I'm calling a friend who might be able to help," Tom says, walking quickly out of the room.

I hear a sound that blends in with the gentle swishing of the rain. I hold still. The room is quiet. The sound fades, returns.

It's you. You are whispering. Each sentence comes out like a sigh, slow and light. You tell the story, but you never open your eyes.

The Far Green Country

had to do it, Grampy. She came back, and I had to do it for you.

She took me back to the cabin, and I walked down the endless stairs all the way to the bottom, all alone. I went through the door, walked into the water, and put my flashlight on the same ledge. I held my breath and went under, but this time I swam as hard as I could, not wasting any time. Tom's underwater swimming lessons are what did it, and the lights were shooting past me again, like tiny comets. I reached out and tried to touch them, and they went right through my hands.

I could feel my breath running out, so I swam harder. I pulled on the rock walls, pulled myself through, and there it was far above me, the surface. I kicked and swam and started to black out like I had before, but this time I kicked the way Tom taught me, and I pretended you were waiting for me there above the water.

I made it.

I burst up out of the water, and I didn't know if I would ever stop gasping for air—I didn't even care where I was, I was so thirsty for air. But soon I realized I was on my knees in a shallow ocean of warm water, stretching like glass all the way out into an endless sea, all the way to the horizon with no far bank. How had I gotten there? How had I come up through the water into this new place? I thought maybe the passage had led me to the lake and I had swum all the way to the surface, but the cabin was nowhere to be seen.

In front of me was a beach with white sand so fine it was like a powder, and when I stood up the sand stuck to my knees and hands. The sky above me was gray and low with rain clouds ready to burst, but they filled me with comfort. No sadness at all, not like storms often do. I only felt a kind of lightness, like I might float away.

The powdery sand was the softest thing I'd ever walked on. I drifted up out of the water onto the beach, and a warm breeze dried me. I still felt a little hazy from holding my breath for so long.

I kept walking. There was something about that sand—the warmth of it radiated up into my feet and made me feel alive! The beach led up to grass that felt like strands of silk, so soft I had to lie down on it. I stared up at that beautiful, low, gray sky, and Grampy, I wasn't sure if I wanted to come back to you. I'm so sorry I felt that way. That place filled me with such peace. I stayed there for a long time, stretched out on the grass, soaking in the gentle warmth, watching the clouds drift overhead.

I remembered the silver-haired woman and I remembered you, and it was mostly because I had promised her that I would bring back what she needed, and her promise to help you, that I was able to get up. I walked inland for a long time—it felt like days—until I came up over one hill, and there in front of me was a short stone wall. Beyond that, a bending path led down into a valley between two mountain ranges, and tucked away in the far corner of that green valley, alongside the path, was a white farmhouse with a small barn.

Here the grass was up to my knees and made whispering sounds as I walked through it. Everything smelled like spring, like life, like the first day of a vacation in the mountains. I approached the house down the path, and the closer I got, the quieter the house seemed. From a distance the house had looked completely white, but as I got closer I could see that the trim around the eaves was painted the lightest of blues, the same as the door and the shutters. There was a chimney, and smoke eased its way out and mixed with the low clouds that hid the tops of the mountains. Off in the distance, what I thought were boulders on the hillside were actually white sheep grazing. Everything about the scene was comforting—the green of the grass and the hills, the low clouds, the mountains disappearing into the sky, and the slow sheep.

When I got to the house, I peeked through one of the windows. Who lived here? Through that window I could see the kitchen, not fancy at all but clean and tidy and welcoming. And on the table, in the middle of the room, lay a small, leather-bound journal with a leather tie that wrapped around it and kept it closed.

That was it. Somehow I knew. That's what she wanted me to bring back.

Grampy, that's the first time I felt fear over there—the thought of going into the house and taking the book scared me. But I knew I had to do it if I wanted to save you. So I walked around the house until I found the door and opened it as quietly as I could. It still made a slight clicking noise, and

I stopped and held my breath. But the house stayed quiet. I stepped through the door and left it open behind me.

That's when I panicked. I was overwhelmed with this feeling that I had to get that book and get out of there as quickly as possible. So I shoved my way through the house in the direction of the kitchen, and there the book was, still on the table. I darted in, but as I put my hand on it, I heard someone else walk into the room behind me.

"Hello, Pearl."

I gasped, held my breath. My hand was still on the soft leather. I didn't want to turn around. I froze.

"Dear Pearl." The voice was so, so kind, and I had to turn and look just to see who it was.

Standing there was a beautiful woman. I could tell she used to have jet-black hair, but now there were glorious white and gray streaks through it, the kind that made me want to reach out and touch them. Those silver highlights reminded me of the lights in the underwater cave and of the silver-haired woman.

"Hi," I said, my voice barely working. "How do you know my name?"

I could see in her eyes that she was nearly crying but also happy.

"You can take it," she said, motioning toward the book with a nod. She sounded a little nervous, like she didn't want to scare me off. "If you need it, you can take it."

"I don't understand."

"I came here, like you, a long time ago, and I found this book. It's what she wanted. I refused to come and get the book for her, but I died anyway, and I couldn't go back." She paused. "No matter how much I loved Paul, I couldn't go back. I thought the woman would come for it someday. I thought she could take me back if she did, but it's been so long. I know I can't go back, not now. Not anymore."

"She can't come here. She's tried to send others, but they all died and couldn't go back."

"I know. I've seen them come and pass by. I've told them which way to go." She shrugged and gave me a sad smile. "Are you going to go back?"

I nodded. "I have to. I have to save my Grampy."

"Will you tell him I said hello? That I still love him?"

She was talking about you, Grampy. I nodded again, not knowing what to say.

Tears rose in her eyes. "You won't be the same, you know. You can't come this far in and stay this long and go back un-changed."

"I understand, but I have to go back. I can't leave Grampy there on his own."

I started to cry, and I didn't even know why, Grampy. I sobbed as I held that leather book to my chest. Before I knew it, she was there, putting her arms around me. The reason the valley and the hills and the sky, even though it was gray, felt so kind and warm was because of her. It was all her. It was all some beautiful extension of who she was.

My grandma. Mary.

"Do you want to know what's in the book?" she asked me.

I shook my head.

"It's a journal of the most beautiful moments you've ever read about. The woman with silver hair has a difficult job, and she kept this journal through the years, writing down all the beauty she's seen. Maybe as a reminder that even in death, beauty abounds."

"That's hard to believe," I said.

"It is." She sighed. "It is very hard to believe. Maybe that's why she needs this journal so badly. So that she can remember."

"How was there beauty in your death?" I asked her without even thinking. "You died so young, with a child. Where's the beauty in my dad losing his mom?"

I wept again.

"Pearl, look over here." She took my hand, and I followed her around a corner. "What do you see?" she asked, and I realized I was looking into a mirror.

"I see me."

"There is beauty even in death," she said again.

I think she was saying that if she hadn't died, you wouldn't have left, my parents wouldn't have met, and I would never have been.

"You should go," she said. "Any longer and you won't be able to go back at all."

I wiped my eyes on my clothes and sniffed. "Yeah. Of course."

I turned and walked to the door, and she came with me outside, even to where the path left the house and went back toward the stone wall. I didn't look back because I was scared I wouldn't be able to leave her—she felt so kind and wonderful, like everything that's good about being home. Everything inside of me wanted to stay there with her. I walked the path, and she was still coming along with me.

I shouted to her over my shoulder, "You'll still be here someday when I come back?"

"Always," she called back to me.

I crawled over the low stone wall and began walking to the

beach, clutching the book. Then I heard someone else, another kind voice, this one light like the air.

"Mary, I was walking up in the mountains, and did you know there are two new lambs?" Her voice stopped, and I knew she had reached the one she called Mary, and I knew without even turning around that they were both standing at the low stone wall, watching me walk away.

"Is that . . ." the new voice asked with astonishment.

"Tell him I'll be waiting here," Mary called to me. "Don't forget. Tell him I'll be waiting in the white house, beyond the shore."

I raised my arm to let her know I had heard, because I knew for sure if I turned and saw those two kind women standing there, I'd never be able to leave.

The walk from the beach that had seemed to take days took only moments going back. That could be the way of things. Maybe going in is always a long journey, but it's not as far away from us here as we think. And then there was the shore and the long stretch of glassy water.

I stopped and felt the life of the sand pulsing through me. How was me bringing back this journal going to help you?

Then I was back in, swimming out as far as I could, clutching the book. I went under, and it was so much harder to swim like that, with a book in my hand. Going down was so much harder.

I couldn't do it. I felt my lungs begin to let go, preparing for that deep breath in, but when I thought I was drowning, the silver-haired woman was there, pulling me back through the water.

This time, though, we came up in the lake. The water was icy cold, and she pulled me to the shore.

"Thank you, Pearl," she said, gasping, weary. I felt the book in my hands, and then it was gone. She took it, and she was gone.

I realized something, Grampy, but too late—the only way I could have helped you. It was the sand. I should have brought back some sand for you.

Gone

There are three days of doctor visits, expensive house calls that I know I can't afford, and we can't get rid of your fever. You are in and out of sleep or unconsciousness or something other than reality. You whisper things I can't quite hear, your eyelids alive and fluttering with visions or dreams. Tom is in and out of the room, bringing cold compresses and Tylenol and coffee. I do not leave your side.

On the third day, you are worse, which hardly seems possible. Your skin goes clammy and white, and your breathing is raspy and holds long pauses that leave me counting the seconds. Tom and I decide you need to go to the hospital, so we load up his car and head out the driveway on a cool autumn morning. I sit in the back with you resting against me, and I open the window a few inches so that the cool air rustles around us, promising better days.

Your eyes crack open as if the last weariness has come on you. You reach into your pocket, pull out your hand in a fist, and raise it up. The car leans as we go around a turn, and Tom accelerates onto the back roads. You open your fist, and in your palm is the thin shimmer of what looks like sand, but lighter, like a teaspoon of talcum powder. When you speak, your voice is so weak that I have to lean in closer. Each word is a quiet whisper.

"She brought this for me. As a thank-you." I can barely hear your voice, and I have to lean in closer. "I have no idea how she was able to go in and get it. But she promised, I guess."

Outside, lightning strikes.

You hold out your hand, offering the powder to me like a gift. I reach out to take it, but a gust of wind shoots through the windows, blowing the dust around us like starlight. I try to grab at it, but this precious stuff, whatever it was, is gone.

"No," you whisper.

You reach up and touch the knot on my head, tears forming. It is the only time you ever touch it. You close your eyes. Your breathing slows. I grab your wrist and cannot find your pulse.

"Faster, Tom," I say. "Faster."

The Fly

om?" I say hesitantly, walking into Tom's house at the end of that day, the longest of my life.

It has been a wearying stretch of tests and doctors. Tom left us at lunch because there was nothing to do, and I don't think he knows what to do when there is nothing to do. I stayed beside you until dark, but I needed to get our things, get my car, and they said you were stable. So I returned to Tom's house.

The sound of my voice dies quickly in the empty house. I can hear the taxi—probably the most expensive taxi ride of my life—make its way down the driveway. The sun is setting on this longest day of my life, and everything has that after-storm stillness, that quiet ache, that broken-down weariness.

I start to walk to your room, but I notice the deck door is wide open, so I cross the living room and look out into the dying light.

"Paul," Tom says, his voice sad and strange and wavering. If he hadn't said my name, I might have missed him.

I walk that long expanse of deck.

"Sit," he mumbles. "Sit."

So I do. I sit in the same chair I sat in on our first night here. The sun is setting, but all we can see from the deck, the eastern side of the house, is an easing into the darkest blues, a few strands of clouds, and a lake that fills me with sadness, because I know in that moment I will never come back to Nysa.

This is my final farewell.

"Paul," he starts again, taking a deep breath. Even from where I am, I can see his mouth trembling with emotion. "Pearl?"

"She's . . . stable but not well. The doctor is having problems diagnosing exactly what's wrong. He said he's not seen anything like it. Her breathing is the main problem, and the fever. They had to put her on a ventilator." My voice breaks. I swallow hard. "They'll try to wean her from it in a few days. But they don't expect . . ." The lake water rustles in the dark. My vision blurs.

"What? They don't expect what?"

"They say her chances of survival are small. She gets weaker by the hour."

"What does that mean?"

"I don't know."

Tom startles me when he swears and slams his hand against the armrest of his chair. There is a rustling sound in the sky to the west, and a large shadow skims the treetops, then heads north, over our heads. It's the largest bird I've ever seen.

"What was that?" I ask, awe in my voice.

"Some species of owl," Tom says absently. "I've never gotten a good enough look to identify it."

It disappears among the trees.

"I packed your things in a bag and put them in your car," he says. "The clothes are clean. With a few parting gifts for you and Pearl." His voice catches when he says your name. "I wish you would have called me to come and get you. You didn't have to get a cab."

I wave him off, not sure what to say. The air shifts, and a wave of leaves, loosened earlier that day by the storm, falls from the trees.

"I never could understand what she saw in you," Tom says, chuckling to himself.

I feel a coldness drop into my veins because I know he's talking about Mary. I can't tell what amuses him more—what she saw in me, or his inability to see what she saw.

"That first night, at the Halloween party, she was the one I had my eye on." His speaks reluctantly, as if walking out slowly on the ice, testing the thickness.

I am surprised at this. I never had any idea Tom had feelings for Mary. I always assumed he felt the same brotherly affection for her that I felt for Shirley. But the tone of his voice doesn't invite a reply, and I find myself growing rigid, bracing myself for a punch.

"But of course, Shirley was special too. And after that night in the field, after Shirley and I kissed, and after we came out of the field and found Mary clinging to you, I knew things were set. You and Mary. Me and Shirley. Sometimes these things can't be changed, you know? I knew it from that moment. The longer things went, the more solid the arrangement. Like setting concrete. One moment it's a liquid, and before you know it, firm."

The air grows cold. I rub my arms, wishing I had worn

a jacket. To be honest, all I want to do is leave—get out of this damp autumn air, avoid hearing whatever it is that Tom is going to tell me. But I can't do it. I can't leave. I'm too curious, and his voice is too commanding. I'm in it until the end.

"I don't know what happened to me after John was born," Tom says, his voice hollow and far away. "It was hard when you guys got married. I mean, you were so young. What were you thinking? But when John came along, everything I had felt for Mary when I first met her was resurrected out of nowhere. I couldn't stop thinking about her. Whenever I saw you holding John, a surge of jealousy coursed through me like electricity."

He stops, seems to be overcome by the force of his own emotion.

"I hated you, Paul. I didn't know what to do."

I try to take slow, deep breaths, but a trembling has begun in me.

He takes a long drink from a small glass I hadn't noticed before. Takes a deep breath. Shakes his head. I can tell that part of him is telling himself to shut up and the other part is forging ahead.

"That morning, when the three of us took out our kayaks—Shirley and Mary and me—and you stayed back with John, it wasn't supposed to be that way. I had invited Mary to go out. Just Mary. I was up early that morning, couldn't sleep because of how I felt for her, and she came down, radiant."

His voice trails off, then returns with regret in it.

"I never meant for that. For Shirley to come along. I couldn't find my oar, and I was pretty sure it was Shirley's fault, that she had borrowed it the night before. So I took the heavy wooden canoe oar with me. You know, the one we found in the woods? And I got upset at Shirley while we were paddling out. How was I supposed to tell Mary how I truly felt while Shirley was there? But really I was angry at the world, Paul. An ocean of anger. It kept building and building. And on top of everything, a fly."

He shakes his head and laughs, but it's a laugh completely devoid of any humor, the kind of laugh that chills to the bone. I feel myself tense, ready to run.

"This horsefly, Paul, you wouldn't believe it. This thing kept landing on me. And it bit me right when we got out to The Point. I crawled up onto the rock, and the girls were down in their kayaks, not sure what we were doing out there, why I was getting so worked up over a fly, but it was so much more than that."

"Why are you telling me all this, Tom?" I ask, but he waves me off.

"Even when I climbed up on those base rocks around The Point, the fly wouldn't leave me alone. In one instant I saw it clearly, hovering, and I raised that oar and swung it as hard as I could. I put every ounce of anger into that swing, Paul. How I felt about everything. All for a stupid fly."

There is sadness in his voice, and regret, but also the heaviness of guilt. My stomach drops.

"I missed."

Those two words empty me of everything.

"I don't know what I was thinking. And as the oar swung around, it struck the rock of The Point so hard that it stung my hands. I dropped the oar, Paul. That's how hard it hit." His voice trembles. "But when I turned to pick it up, I realized I hadn't hit the rocks. Paul. I hadn't hit the rocks."

I don't want him to say it. But I need him to say it.

"Tom." That's all I say. His name.

His face crumbles, and he holds it in his hands. His body shakes with sobs, but he doesn't make a sound. He gasps once for air.

"I hit Mary, Paul." He's shaking his head, as if I'm the one saying it and he's denying it. "Right above her ear."

I stare up at the sky, now almost completely dark, and I feel like I'm spinning higher, higher, higher. I reach up and touch the knot above my ear.

"I didn't even know she had gotten out of her boat, Paul. I guess she followed me up there to talk, to see what was wrong. Honest to God, it was an accident. After I hit her, she crumpled and sort of slid down over the edge of the rock, real gentle, and disappeared into the water."

Tears ache in my eyes, but I can't touch them. They'll burn me.

"Shirley was in complete and utter shock. She couldn't move. She sat there in her kayak, mouth open, like that guy in the painting. You know, *The Scream*? Even had her hands up on her cheeks. And I couldn't move either. I don't know why not. I should have jumped in right away, but I was frozen in place."

The crickets are singing now, chirping, and I wonder how late in the fall they go, how cold it has to get for this lake to fall into silence. I picture Mary slipping under, and I try to imagine the silence that greeted her there.

"I waited too long, Paul. By the time I jumped in, she was

gone. The water's deep at The Point, and the underwater currents are unpredictable."

"Shirley knew?" I ask, my voice trembling from the cold and the story.

"Shirley knew."

I try to rearrange things in my mind now that I know. I try to change my perspective on the last forty years, the nature of your grandmother's death, the years I spent away from here. I don't know how to think anymore. If I didn't know Tom and Shirley, did I even know Mary?

But I think of Pearl's vision, of the story she told me about going through the water and seeing Mary in the white farmhouse beyond the shore.

Waiting for me.

"A month later, after a storm, I found her." Tom's voice is so far away now that I can barely hear him. I can barely see him. "I did some research on it. They say storms can dislodge bodies that have sunk to the bottom of lakes and ponds. She was bobbing against the bank. I buried her where I found her, right here, where my house is now. And you were gone. No one knew where you went. So I didn't tell anyone that I found her. Not even Shirley."

I stand up, and I'm surprised that I'm not angry. The only thing I can think about instead of his words are the words Pearl shared with me, the message Mary told her to tell me.

"Tell him I'll be waiting here."

"Goodbye, Tom."

I walk back through the house. When I get to my car, I can see our packed bags in the back seat. The trees droop down low over the lane in the dark, and the headlights shine on the autumn leaves that coat the drive.

Driving through Nysa at night, I realize memories are heavy things, heavier still when we don't let them go. Everything feels like a dream, and all I can think about is you lying motionless in your hospital bed and the image I have of Mary with silver streaks in her hair, standing on some far green bank, looking out over a glassy sea.

The Nesting Doll

This particular hospital where you are staying is small, and the lady working at the front desk glances up when I walk through the doors, then waves me on. I'm carrying the bag I packed when we left home to go to Nysa, the bag Tom had filled with our things and put in the back of my car. It feels like decades since you and I made that drive from the city to Nysa, but it hasn't even been two weeks, apparently. Time is something I'm not entirely convinced I can trust at this point in my life.

"Oh, Mr. Elias?" the woman at the front desk calls after me in her singsong voice.

I turn around and raise my eyebrows but don't say anything.

"Your daughter is so beautiful. I'm so sorry."

"Thank you. She's my granddaughter."

"Well, she's clearly a very special girl. I hope things turn out well."

I nod and turn away, then walk seven or eight rooms down the hallway to your door. Somehow Tom's confession has washed over me and left me strangely at peace. His words, in some ways, give me that satisfactory feeling of the last puzzle piece fitting in place.

And there are still your words as well. The story you told me, the vision you had of Mary and Shirley and the house beyond the sea. I don't know what to think about it, besides sadness that I could not keep you from doing this thing.

I go into your room and set my bag down at the back, beside the window, before returning to the side of your bed. I can't help but cry a little as I stand there, your limp body completely still, tubes going in your nose, a machine breathing for you while other machines chart your journey with beeps and dashes and numbers I can't possibly understand.

I don't know how long I stand there, tracing the lines of your hair, the perfection of your nose and mouth, the gracefulness of your closed eyes. I turn and arrange the chair against the far wall so that I can see you and also lean my head against the wall while I drift off. I unzip my bag, searching for a warmer shirt, and I notice a few things.

Tom washed and folded my clothes. He is a very organized packer. Everything is arranged perfectly.

He has included items I was not expecting.

The first is the notebook of photos taken of Mary during that summer before John was born. I page through them, reminded again of your grandmother's beauty, how she moved, how she laughed. I set the notebook down beside me on the floor. I'm not sure I want to keep it—I'm not sure if I want to see her through his eyes. But we'll see. I sure wish I could have shown these to you.

Under the notebook, tucked in with my socks, is the Russian nesting doll I saw all those long days ago when we first went to the cabin. I pick it up and spin the top half of the first doll, and on a whim I take off the top and pull on the next doll. I place the open halves on a small side table, pop open the next doll, and pull out the smaller one. I arrange all the halves on the table and keep going until there is what seems to be the last doll that can be opened.

I pull it apart, fully expecting to find that one solid doll in the middle of everything, the root of the entire exercise, but that is not what I find. I sit there taking it in, almost unable to breathe.

I reach in and take out the twist-tie wedding ring I gave Mary when we got engaged.

In the middle of the night, I wake up in your room, stiff from sleeping on the small hideaway bed. I sit up, feeling completely different. The air seems easier to breathe, the light clearer. Hearing Tom's confession has cleared me of some deep anguish.

But that doesn't seem to be it. There's something else.

I don't feel any pain.

For the first time in months, there is no dull throbbing at my core.

Your machines begin to go crazy, beeping and buzzing. Alarms sound. A nurse comes in quickly, followed by your doctor, followed by more nurses. More people than I thought were even on shift that late at night in this small hospital. I see the earnest nature of their attempts, the speed with which they move around the room. No one even looks at me. No one says anything.

I stand up, not sure what to do, not sure where to stand.

I wonder if this is the end, and I reach up to touch the knot on my head.

It's gone. It's completely gone. I dig around the roots of my hair, check behind my ear, squeeze my skull. There is no pressure, no spreading ache.

No knot.

I bring my hand back down and stare it. My fingertips are coated in a fine white powder. The powder you took from your pocket when we were in the car, the powder that I thought had blown away.

The doctors, meanwhile, seem increasingly concerned.

I look at the nesting doll, pulled apart.

There is a long, steady beeping, as if the world has ended.

Two Months Later

I pull the car to a stop along the sidewalk in front of our house, and the sound of the gear stick dropping into park, the weightless sensation of my hands as they fall to my lap, the bright winter sunlight slanting through the window—all of it feels so much like the end that I lean forward and put my forehead on the top of the steering wheel. I take a deep breath. Another. I wipe my eyes, my nose, put my hands on the wheel as if I'm about to drive away, but I'm not. This is home. It feels good to be here.

It feels good to be here with you.

"Don't worry," I say to you. "I have to get your chair out of the trunk. Then I'll get you out."

I open the car door, and the air is cold, smells of snow. The sunlight glares off of everything—the windows of the row homes and the windshields of passing cars and the icy puddles that line the gutter. The trunk pops open, and I lift out your wheelchair, a parting gift from Tom, much nicer than the standard-issue chair from the hospital, the one my meager insurance would have paid for. I unfold the chair and wheel it over to your door.

He came to see you once. You should know that. Maybe you do. We didn't say much and he didn't stay long, but he was there, and that means something. I know he carries a heavy weight.

I hesitate, wishing you would open the door yourself, but I know you won't, so I pop it open and put a smile on my face.

"Hey, beautiful," I whisper, leaning in close and situating your arms just so, as I've grown accustomed to doing. I lift you out.

Your eyes are so bright, and one hand is up under your chin, a spot it tends to find naturally, a spot that makes it look like you're thinking. I know you are thinking. A deep, quiet, guttural sound comes from your throat, a kind of speaking that I somehow feel I understand.

"Welcome home, indeed," I say, standing up straight.

You are so light, as light as you were at four or five years old, so light I think you might float away from me, and I don't yet put you down in the chair—I stand there in the bright sun and the cold air and watch the traffic go by. Your dark hair blows in wisps around my face, like tiny promises, and I feel a sob rise in the back of my throat, but I keep it down by staring up at the sun, blinking hard, then turning away.

I nestle you into your chair and pull the soft blue blanket from the car, tuck it in around your thighs, your shoulders. You make a long, quiet moaning sound.

"I know, I know. It's cold. We'll get you inside."

I push you carefully along the sidewalk to our front steps, easing over the uneven cement. I should probably move, find a place with easier access, a one-story house without front steps. We'll see.

"What do you think, Pearl? Would you like to move?"

When we arrive at our front porch, I look up, and my body goes numb.

Your father is standing on the porch.

"John," I say.

But he has eyes only for you. At first he was rubbing his arms, trying to get or stay warm, but when he sees you, his face wrinkles up in confusion and sadness, and his head tilts to the side. His eyes squint as if he's trying to see something, see it clearer, see it from a different angle, because if he can do that, surely it will change what's in front of him.

"John," I say again, not knowing where to begin. His eyes are hollowed out, as they always are when he returns, his cheeks sunken in, his skin the color of old slate shingles. His hair has been cut by someone who didn't know what they were doing. But there is something clear about the air around him. His eyes are awake. I can tell he is sober. For now.

His movement down onto the step is part sitting, part falling. I reach out to catch him, but he's already there, crouching on the steps, searching your eyes for something.

"What happened, Dad?" he whispers.

"We went back to Nysa," I say, shaking my head. I can never tell him everything.

"Nysa?"

"We stayed with Tom. Pearl nearly drowned." I find it hard to believe the words coming out of my mouth. It feels like someone else is talking, and I want to tell that person to shut up, stop it, no one cares what you have to say, you with your lies and your made-up stories. But I'm the one who's talking, and it's all true.

"Same as Mom," he says.

Since it's not a question, I don't reply, though I think I might be nodding.

"We almost lost her. The doctors say she went quite a while without oxygen under the water. And the fever nearly did her in. But here we are. Here she is."

He reaches up to touch your cheek. His knuckles are swollen. His nails are chewed short and stained around the edges, but when he touches your skin, he is gentle, and that is a relief to me.

"How long have you been here waiting for us?"

"I came by a month ago and waited," he says. "You weren't here, so I left. I guess this time I've been here two or three days, back and forth between here and the shelter."

"You must be hungry."

He nods.

I walk over and unlock the door, push it open. He doesn't move from where he sits in front of you.

"I'll carry her in," I say. "You grab the chair. It folds in on itself. Or you can wheel it in, whatever. I think it will fit."

I move to pick you up, but he reaches out and grabs my wrist. It's a soft touch, as much a request as anything else.

"Can I do it, Dad?"

I hear his voice, but the words float past me.

"Can I carry her in?" he asks.

I shake my head, not because I'm telling him no, but because a flood of regret is moving through me. It does that a lot these days, when I think of all the things I should have done differently, ways I could have kept this all from happening. It should have been me—that's what I want to say. That knot on my head should have taken me, should have been the end of me. I keep shaking my head until the tears come again.

John stands up and stares at me, moving in slow, giving me space and time to reject his approach, before wrapping me in a bear hug.

I don't turn him away. I hug him hard, and his body is like a memory, something that fits into my arms the way it always did, and I weep on his shoulder.

"I'm so sorry, John," I try to say, but I don't know if either of us can tell what I'm saying.

You moan again, and I chuckle through the tears, pull myself away from your father.

"She's cold," I say with a small smile, wiping my face. "She doesn't like to be cold. Go ahead, you carry her. Careful, though. She's light as can be."

He picks you up and cradles you in his arms, and I remember those early weeks of your life after your own mother died, when he and I took turns getting up with you in the night. I entered the room, bringing a lukewarm bottle of formula, and I always found him there, swaying with you, singing some old lullaby. I would stand there and watch him holding you for a long time.

I watch the two of you go through the door. He turns sideways to keep your head from hitting the door frame. I feel a lightness rising inside of me, something I haven't felt for years. I fold up the wheelchair and follow you inside, into the house.

Floating Away

April came when we weren't looking, and it's been six months or so since our trip to Nysa. During the whole long month of March, we weren't sure if spring would ever come. All during this endless, dark winter, I wheeled you down to your elementary school on Tuesday and Thursday and parked you at the front corner of the class. The kids treat you like a princess, fawning over you, fighting over who can sit next to you at lunch. They remember what one of the teachers referred to as "the old Pearl," but I know there's nothing gone about it—you are still here with us, and for that I am so grateful.

But spring held off for a long time. We had no early glimpses of it in February, no unexpected warm days to give us hope. There was very little snow too—most mornings brought a hard frost, the days filled with the glaring of an icy sun. John would come home from his new job at the corner store, blustering and shivering and pounding his hands together. It is not where I would choose for him to work. It seems the sort of place that could pull him back under the water again, back to the depths he has so recently risen from. But it is a job, and it's close, and he comes home every night, kisses you on the forehead, and reads a book to you while we eat dinner together.

During the last few weeks of March, as an act of hope, I would bundle both of us up, you and me, and we would sit out on the porch in the cold sunshine and watch the traffic go by. Sometimes I talked to you about various things. Sometimes I told you the old stories. Sometimes we sat in silence. I wonder if you could see me staring at you, watching, waiting. I can sense a change in you, even though the doctors gave up hope long ago. They don't say that, of course, but I can see it in their eyes, a kind of moving on, a kind of gentle acquiescence to the way things are. But there is something deep going on inside of you. I can sense it, the way the birds can sense an earthquake coming and lift off from their perch moments before the tremor.

Now April has arrived.

The last few days have been beautiful. The grass has sprung suddenly green. The tips of the trees, only last week brittle and cold, have grown swollen buds. John arranged some hanging baskets of flowers on the front porch and planted tomatoes in pots along the back alley. I don't know that they'll get enough sun there, but I try to let him do this thing since he's come back. I don't want to discourage him. Planting tomatoes where they might not get enough sun seems a thing too small to object to, and what if they do grow? What if they thrive? It would be nice, in July or August, to be slicing juicy tomatoes or making salsa or pasta sauce. I should see if it's too late to plant onions.

All the time I was checking on those tomato plants out

back, debating on whether or not to tell John to try another spot, I kept reaching up, touching the side of my
head, feeling over and over again how the knot is still gone.
I had brought you out back with me, placed you gingerly
in one of the patio chairs we now have back there, and
propped you up with your arms comfortable, your head
leaning slightly back. When I looked over at you, I'm sure
you were smiling at me, at least with your eyes, deep in
your eyes, where I know your imagination is still making
up stories.

There is a depth to this world I have been so unaware of
throughout my entire life until now. When I look at a tree,
I don't only see the bark anymore—I can see the crevices
in the bark, each a Grand Canyon, life teeming all the way
in. The roots too—I can feel them spreading. I can almost
sense them under me, deep in the earth, doing their work.

I am this way now because of you. There is something
at work deep within you, and it's in watching you that I've
learned to watch the world in a new way.

It's a Tuesday. John doesn't work on Tuesdays, so all
three of us go down to the school. He's pushing you slowly,
as he always does, careful for pebbles or cracks in the
pavement that might stop your chair with a jerk. He has
a brighter countenance these days. I wake every morning
with an edge of dread in my gut, yet I don't dare go to
wake him up. I did that for the first few days last winter,
after we found him waiting for us on the porch, but the
anxiety I felt between turning his doorknob and finding
him perfectly fine, asleep in his bed, sent my heart near

to bursting. So I had to let that go, and now I wait for him to come down, but there's still something in the waiting for him that gnaws at me.

But never mind. Here we are. We walk along the parking lot where the bottom of the chain-link fence has been pushed out from years of snowplows shoving snow out to the edges of the lot.

"Watch yourself," I tell John, as I always do when we walk that stretch. "Don't cut yourself on that chain link. You'll need a tetanus shot for sure."

In the past, me warning him more than once about something would have sent him either into a rant about me being overprotective or down into a dark, simmering quiet from which he would not emerge all day. But now when I say things like this, he's able to brush them away gently.

"Got it, Dad," he says, and I feel myself blushing at my inability to stop warning him of the same old things. Like when he goes to work and I tell him to "make good choices."

We pass the old, abandoned building you hid in—was it only last fall? You show no signs of recognizing it. The next time we're walking this stretch without John, maybe I'll stop and turn you toward the old building, ask if you remember hiding in there last September, telling me about the map and the silver-haired woman. I could even carry you inside and we could sit together in that empty darkness. Would that bring you back to me?

"Come on in, you guys," Ms. Howard says in a kind voice. She always waits for us by the back door. She's not so bad.

The hallway through your school is one of my favorite

places now, almost like a second home. Teachers peek their heads out and wave, pat you on the head, or bend down level with you and ask how your day was. This is why we arrive early, to make sure we have enough time to navigate all the love that waits for you in the hall.

I see Ms. Pena up ahead, pretending to go back into her room. I know she'll come out as we're passing and pretend it's by chance. And she does.

"Why, hello, Pearl," she says. "How are you?"

I can feel you answering, though your body doesn't move besides the very occasional blinking of your eyes, the flutter of your pulse at the base of your neck, the uneven breaths that sometimes emerge with a gentle shudder.

"I guess I'll see you tonight," she says to Pearl, but she's also saying it to me.

She's been coming over a few nights each week, mostly to read to you. When John puts you to bed, Ms. Pena and I sit at the table and drink decaf coffee, talking about humdrum things like each of her students, and I tell her another story about my growing-up years or something trivial about your grandmother. One night last week she reached across the table and took my hand, and we sat there in a silence so still I could hear a cat rummaging through the trash in the alley outside.

I clear my throat, but words won't come, so I give her an uneven smile.

John laughs to himself and elbows me good-naturedly. "Say hi to your girlfriend, Dad."

I glare at him but can't help grinning.

We turn the corner and go into the small library. The children sit there waiting, chatting loudly, and the librarian, a rather large Ms. Battle, claps her hand three times and counts one-two-three-four-five. The children grow magically silent, and we park you at the front by the windows, where you can sit in the sunshine and hear the story.

Today we're starting a new book, one you know well. But I thought the schoolchildren might enjoy it. The chapters are short, and the main character is mischievous.

"This is *The Light Princess*," I say, choking up a bit because I could just as easily be talking about you, sitting there by the windows, bathed by the sun. "By George MacDonald."

I take a deep breath, and when I try to read, my voice wavers. I shake my head. Movement at the corner of my eye catches my attention. I look over, and Ms. Pena has settled into place at the door beside John. The look on my son's face is no different from the looks on the faces of so many of the children: eager, waiting, perhaps hopeful that this is the story that will change his life.

I start reading.

Once upon a time, so long ago that I have quite forgotten the date, there lived a king and queen who had no children.

And the king said to himself, "All the queens of my acquaintance have children, some three, some seven, and some as many as twelve; and my queen has not one. I feel ill-used." So he made up his mind to be cross with his wife about it. But she bore it all like a good patient queen as she was. Then the king grew very cross indeed. But the queen pretended to take it all as a joke, and a very good one too.

"Why don't you have any daughters, at least?" said he. "I don't say sons; that might be too much to expect."

"I am sure, dear king, I am very sorry," said the queen.

"So you ought to be," retorted the king; "you are not going to make a virtue of that, surely."

But he was not an ill-tempered king, and in any matter of less moment would have let the queen have her own way with all his heart. This, however, was an affair of State.

The queen smiled.

"You must have patience with a lady, you know, dear king," said she.

She was, indeed, a very nice queen, and heartily sorry that she could not oblige the king immediately.

The king tried to have patience, but he succeeded very badly. It was more than he deserved, therefore, when, at last, the queen gave him a daughter—as lovely a little princess as ever cried.

That's when it happens.

You laugh.

It's a gentle, joy-filled burst, and my breath catches in my throat, then escapes like a small hiccup or a sob. You are in the sunshine, your black hair brilliant and shining, and your face hasn't changed in the least. I wonder if I am losing my mind, if it was all in my imagination, so I look across the room at Ms. Pena standing in the doorway, at your father leaning against the door frame beside her. Their faces are illuminated like they've seen a visiting angel. John looks at me for a split second, then back at you, then crosses the room and kneels at your feet, holding your hands.

"Pearl?" he says, but there is nothing more.

The children in the room start clapping for you, quietly at first. Soon they are all laughing and shouting and high-fiving each other, up on their feet, a standing ovation, and

I have the strangest sensation. It starts in my fingers and toes, a kind of tingling, and I'm not sure what it is at first, this strange feeling. But I lock onto your smiling eyes and take in the rustling of your dark hair. The librarian tries to simultaneously shush the children and open a window to let in the spring air.

And then I realize what this sensation is.

I feel like I might float away.

LOVED THIS BOOK?

**Turn the page to read the first chapter of
another mesmerizing story from Shawn Smucker.**

AVAILABLE NOW

Revell
a division of Baker Publishing Group
www.RevellBooks.com

Available wherever books and ebooks are sold.

Prologue

A Confession

We move in a loose group, winding through the trees. We are more people than you can even imagine, yet there is hardly a word spoken. We smell like exhaustion, like miles piled on top of miles, like time when it has already run out. Yet somehow we also sound like hope, like fresh water washing through the reeds. We discreetly share food with each other, nearly all of us strangers, nodding politely, and in spite of our condition, we cannot keep the inexplicable hope from showing in our eyes.

This is our first day out from under the shadow of the mountain. Which sounds exactly like something he would have said in that deep, rich voice of his, if he was here with us. And he would have smiled—how happy he would have been, saying those words!

Then he would have laughed, and the thought of him laughing is too much for me right now. It brings up an ache that makes it hard to breathe. I shake my head and try to laugh it off, but my grin falters, and any kind of sound I might make lodges somewhere in my throat.

It's my fault he's not with us. There's no way around it.

How could I let him go back on his own?

It's more an accusation than a question, and now the aching wells up behind my eyes. I squeeze them shut. I stop walking and think about turning around. It's the guilt that threatens to consume me.

The path goes up and up and up, and everyone is so tired, but the old fears are fresh enough to keep us walking, to keep us moving through this heavy weariness. I reluctantly rejoin the movement up the mountain. Nearly everyone stares at the ground in front of their feet. Maybe that's all that matters right now. One step after the other. Moving farther up. Moving farther in, away from her. Hoping she won't find us, won't convince us to go back.

Up ahead and to the left, I notice that the trees clear along the edge of the cliff, and I find myself walking faster, faster, stumbling over my own feet, pushing between this person and that person, mumbling my apologies, my voice strange in the voiceless woods. I get to the clearing and it is what I hoped it would be: an overlook. A cold wind blows up from the valley, rushes through that open space, agitating the leaves behind me into the wild rustling sound of secrets. I climb a kind of stone platform, and the rock is gritty under my fingers. There's no snow up here, but the rock is cold. Everything feels present and real.

Have you ever, for a flash of time, understood the significance of being? The miracle of existing? That's what I feel now, climbing up onto the ledge: the particular roughness of the rocks under my knees, the chill of the wind on my face. The unique expression of my existence, here, as I stand.

I look out over that huge expanse of miles that all of us walked through, and I scan the valley. I hold one hand up, shield my eyes from the glare of those bright clouds, and hope to see nothing out there except empty plains.

At first I'm relieved and my shoulders relax because all I see is the undulating ground stretching to the west, as far as the horizon. The wind continues to whip up around me, and I draw my arms closer to my chest, duck my chin down, and try to find warmth in my body. It is there somewhere inside of me, that warmth, that fire. I can sense the rustling of all the people hiking, moving up the mountain behind me. I can feel them glancing at my back as they pass, taking in my silhouette on the overlook, probably wondering why I would stop, why I would look back. This makes me angry. I want to turn and answer them, answer all of their unasked questions.

I knew him.

I loved him.

Do you have any idea what our freedom cost?

But I keep looking out over the plains, and finally I see something like two ants wandering along a dusty pile. I sigh. All the way down there in the valley, where we began the climb up this mountain, through the trees, those two small specks walk away, walk west. Their progress is barely visible, but there is nothing to stop them, not as far as the eye can see. We will soon be separated by this great chasm.

Everything has fallen into a stark, dazzling white, the light glaring off endless miles of glittering frost. I can smell snow, but none is falling.

He is going with her.

I hoped that he might be among the last of the crowd, that he could possibly be tagging along at the back, that he would come up and surprise me. We would hug and I would laugh out loud—my first real laugh in a long time—and he would explain how he got out of going back and that all the wrong I had done was magically undone.

But he couldn't do it. He couldn't reverse my mistakes, couldn't easily untie my deceptions, and the only option was for someone to go back. He is doing it. I strain my eyes toward the horizon, but even from that height, I can't see the mountain we came from, the one whose shadow we have finally escaped. I don't think I'd want to see it, but I search that far-off horizon anyway.

"Do you see him?" she asks, walking up behind me. Not long ago, she would have wrapped her arms around my body, moved in close and held me. I would have felt her warmth against my back. But not now. Not after everything that has happened.

I close my eyes, imagining. I shiver and nod. "I can't believe he has to go back." Unspoken are the words, *It's my fault.*

We stand there in those words, the wind whipping them around us, catching on them, sailing away with them. She doesn't offer any kind of consolation.

"It was here all along," she says, a lining of amazement in her voice. "This mountain was here, waiting for us."

"Are you . . ." I begin, then start over. My voice is hoarse, and I clear it against the dry, cold air. "Do you . . . remember?"

"Everything. It's all coming back to me."

"Even before?"

"Even before."

"Me too," I whisper.

How is it that a mind can contain so many memories? Where does it all fit? Into what nooks and crannies do we place these recollections of love and sadness, horror and joy? Into what tiny space of our minds do we put a person we met long ago, or a disappointment, or a lie? And where do memories go when we forget, and how is it that they can come rushing back, unbidden?

I am embarrassed by what I did, the choices I made. There are things I would rather forget, but because I can think of nothing else to say, a confession emerges: "I'm such a liar. You know that by now, right? How many things I said that weren't true?"

She is still as a fence post. It almost seems like she's holding her breath.

"You know, I would lie for the fun of it," I whisper, "even when there was nothing in it. Just because. I don't even know why. What's wrong with a person who lies for no reason?"

I don't realize she is crying until I hear her try to stifle a sob, like a hiccup. She moves closer but we're still not touching, and we remain there for a time, watching the two people down on the plain. We cry together. She sighs a trembling sigh, and when she speaks I can tell she is trying to lift our spirits.

"The rumor coming back from the front is that the higher you go, the warmer it gets."

"Then we should keep walking," I say, but I don't move. A great silence falls on us as the last people pass by behind us. He is not among them. I knew he wouldn't be, was positive of this after seeing the two far-off figures walking away, but I had still allowed myself to hope.

"There they go." She steps away, as if she can't stay too close or she'll give in to old impulses like hugging me or pulling me close. "He saved all of us," she says, and I can hear the tears in her voice. "And now he's going back."

I nod again, the tears flowing. I wipe them away hastily with the back of my hand. They're embarrassing, those tears. They make me feel small.

"Dan," she says. "It's time. He'll find her, and he'll follow us over."

I look over at her for the first time since she came up behind me. "Will he? Will he find her? Will he find us?"

She doesn't answer.

"Will he find me?" I ask, my voice tiny and quivering.

Wordlessly, we climb down the rock and turn toward the top of this new mountain, this fresh start, this beginning. We can see the tail end of the procession of people moving up the trail. We will soon be back among them, or maybe we'll stay back a bit, find our own pace.

"I wonder," I say quietly.

"Wonder?" she asks, falling into step beside me. I want to take her hand again, but those days are long gone. "Wonder what?"

My response is a whisper. I can't imagine she even hears me. "Can he really cross from there to us? Or is he lost? Forever?"

The breeze snatches my words and throws them out

into the void, but she hears them. And she smiles. "He'll find us."

So childlike. So trusting. I want to question her. I want to raise my flag of doubt, but before I can, she says it again.

"He'll find us."

Acknowledgments

I'm incredibly thankful to God for this unexpected writing journey. It wouldn't be possible without those of you who faithfully read my blog in the early years or those of you who continue reading these books that stumble into the world. Thanks so much to all of you readers out there for hanging with me.

Ruth, you came along and believed in me at just the right time.

Kelsey, your unwavering support, belief, and enthusiasm changed the trajectory of my writing life, which would be unrecognizable without your confident encouragement.

Revell team, especially Michele, Karen, Jessica, and Nathan, your hard work, your kindness, and your willingness to stand with me at conferences and hand out ARCs to total strangers has meant the world to me. You have been tireless champions of my writing. Thank you.

Rachelle, thanks for taking me on, and for whatever else might be around the bend.

Mom and Dad, I know you didn't have a lot of money, but you bought me books, and that changed everything for me.

To the Kindred Collective, my Kentucky crew, for the love and space you've given Mai and me. It's nearly impossible to put into words what each of you means to me, or how you continually remind me that writing is about more than publishing. You help me circle back around to who I am.

To Dinner Club, for the laughs, the tears, and the life, for the stories and the late nights. We still need a hashtag.

Bryan, your friendship has made me a better person, despite your faulty adoration of Wheat Chex. This book is for Parker.

To Cade, Lucy, Abra, Sam, Leo, and Poppy, for being exactly who you are.

To Maile, my love. Let's keep writing.

Shawn Smucker is the award-winning author of *Light from Distant Stars* and *These Nameless Things*, the young adult novels *The Day the Angels Fell* and *The Edge of Over There*, and the memoir *Once We Were Strangers*. He lives with his wife and six children in Lancaster, Pennsylvania. You can find him online at www.shawnsmucker.com.

Cohen Marah is the primary suspect in his father's death . . . *But did he do it?*

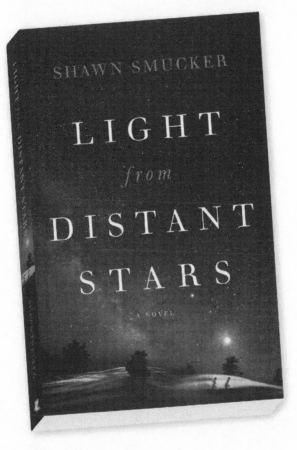

When Cohen Marah steps over the body of his dead father on a cold spring morning, he steps into a labyrinth of memory. In the week that follows, he must confront his traumatic past, a violent present, and the most frightening question of all—is he responsible for his father's death?

Revell
a division of Baker Publishing Group
www.RevellBooks.com

Available wherever books and ebooks are sold.

Could it be possible that
DEATH IS A GIFT?

When tragedy shakes young Samuel Chambers's family, his search for answers entangles him in the midst of an ancient conflict and leads him on an unexpected journey to find the Tree of Life.

R Revell
a division of Baker Publishing Group
www.RevellBooks.com

Available wherever books and ebooks are sold.

THE CAPTIVATING SEQUEL TO

The Day the Angels Fell

When Abra Miller goes to Saint Louis Cemetery No. 1 in
New Orleans to search for the Tree of Life, she discovers a
city teetering on the edge of chaos, people desperate for a way
out, and an enemy intent on enslaving the human race.

Revell
a division of Baker Publishing Group
www.RevellBooks.com

Available wherever books and ebooks are sold.

"A glimpse into the bridge-building, fear-silencing, life-affirming gift of cross-cultural friendship. This is an important and timely message."

—PETER GREER,
president and CEO, HOPE International; coauthor of *Rooting for Rivals*

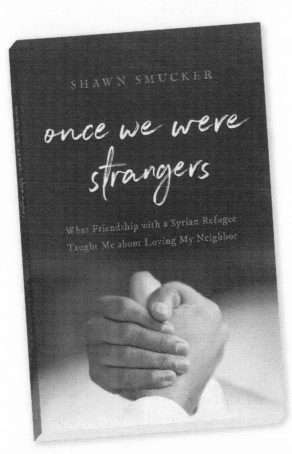

The compelling true story of how an American man became friends with a Syrian refugee and his family and what that relationship taught him about grace, compassion, and finding our shared humanity across cultural, religious, and political divides.

ℝ Revell
a division of Baker Publishing Group
www.RevellBooks.com

Available wherever books and ebooks are sold.

CONNECT WITH SHAWN

SHAWNSMUCKER.COM

f SHAWN SMUCKER, WRITER 🐦 @SHAWNSMUCKER

Catch an episode of *The Stories Between Us* podcast, hosted by Shawn and his wife, Maile, on Spotify, Apple Music, or wherever you find your podcasts.

Be the First to Hear about New Books from Revell!

Sign up for announcements about new and upcoming titles at

RevellBooks.com/SignUp

@RevellBooks

Don't miss out on our great reads!

Revell
a division of Baker Publishing Group
www.RevellBooks.com

LET'S
TALK
ABOUT
BOOKS

- Share or mention the book on your social media platforms. Use the hashtag **#TheWeightofMemory**.

- Write a book review on your blog or on a retailer site.

- Pick up a copy for friends, family, or anyone who you think would enjoy and be challenged by its message!

- Share this message on Twitter, Facebook, or Instagram: **I loved #TheWeightofMemory by @ShawnSmucker // @RevellBooks**

- Recommend this book for your church, workplace, book club, or small group.

- Follow Revell on social media and tell us what you like.

RevellBooks

RevellBooks

RevellBooks

pinterest.com/RevellBooks